JUDE AVERY

THE ANDROGYNOUS LOVE TALE

IS VIC VICTOR OR VICTORIA?

First Edition: March 2020

Cover artwork by www.goodcoverdesign.co.uk

ISBN 978-0-6488156-1-7 (paperback)
ISBN 978-0-6488156-0-0 (ebook)

www.judeavery.com

CONTENTS

1
The Lion of Masculinity

My name is Vic. Am I a man or a woman? It does not matter. I am a poor example of both. At least, it had not mattered until Devlin Knightsbridge happened. Devlin, the paragon. Devlin, the lion of masculinity. How I hated that man.

Like some dark thread on my pathetic soul, I felt him enter our bland, whitewashed office. The whole air charged and heated, and the office darkened into some kind of salacious jungle. *Ugh.* Two hundred years ago women would have swooned in his mere presence. Then again, two hundred years ago his presence would have been announced before he entered any room.

'Ah Sally, you look especially radiant today,' he said smoothly to our ancient receptionist in his deep, manly voice. It rumbled through the office like a faint suggestion from a dark hypnotist. 'Must you keep breaking my heart each day by refusing to marry me.'

Arse.

I forbade myself to look up from the newspaper I was reading. It was hard. My fingers crumpled its pages. There was something important in those pages... something about the Australian drought, which would impact the wheat price if it continued for another two weeks. But all I saw in my mind's eye was Devlin's dazzling, white-toothed smile, melting the poor woman's shrivelled and bitter insides.

Our indomitable, never-smiling receptionist giggled. 'Oh, Devlin, be off with you and your nonsense. Mr Ruttman wants to see you as soon as you arrive.'

He sighed. 'I live in hope you will take pity on my heart one day, my fair Sally.'

He sauntered through our cosy office of grey cubicles. I could feel his masculinity precede him, sucking the air out of the room. Oh hell. Once again, he took the path that would lead him past my desk.

Don't look up, don't look up. My treacherous eyes lifted up from the newspaper I was blindly staring at to watch him approach Paul Ellis' desk.

Devlin Knightsbridge was fairytale handsome; strong jaw, black hair, icy- blue eyes, and hot gaze. He oozed masculinity into our small office space, and took up more room than any human should be allowed to take, not only with his size, but with that prowl of his. How does a city man develop a walk like that? I imagined him practising in front of a mirror, and almost laughed. Almost. I did not like to laugh. Not unless I had imbibed enough alcohol to not care if my laugh came out like a confused bark. I had an ugly laugh.

'Hey Devlin, great game last night, hey? Seems you were right to bet against the reds.' That was little Paul Ellis trying to be chummy with the lion himself. Poor, misguided sod. If he was a dog, his tongue would be lolling, his tail wagging. *He'll chew you up and spit you out, you poor fool.*

Devlin had that effect. Either men made fools of themselves seeking his approval, or hid in their cubicles from his notice.

Devlin smiled at him, dashing and charming, with damned dimples in his cheeks. 'It sure was, Paul. Next time perhaps we could watch it together at the *River and Dead Trout*.'

'Well, if you want to watch it with us, I might be able to get some extra tickets from my brother,' Paul panted, and I thought he would swoon. 'That is, if you want to come with us to the next game.' Was he pleading now?

'I'd love that, Paul. I'd love that.' Devlin winked at him, then patted him on the back and strolled onwards... towards our cubicle.

Don't look at him, don't look at him, I shouted inside my mind. But his ridiculous feline prowl hypnotised my gaze. It was magnetic, enhanced by his perfectly tailored suit, with its crisp lines and a metallic sheen in the grey fabric. His shining black boots were tipped with gold. What else, of course? It was probably real gold too. *Ugh. For pity's sake.*

Look away now! A small voice inside me screamed and waved its hands to catch my attention. Too late. He caught me staring and winked.

I dropped my eyes, back to the article I was reading. Oh, yes, there it was... drought in Australia, rivers running dry, crops failing, a plague of locusts... and fires... hot burning fires... three shark attacks, five lethal snake bites... oh, and flooding, washing away homes in the tropical north of the country, where wheat did not grow. I mentally crossed off Australia as a refuge to run to if I was ever pursued by the law.

A shadow fell on me, blocking out the fluorescent light that brightened my office days, come winter or summer, night or day. Devlin was tall. Taller than any man I had ever met. He was of that ridiculously awkward height where if he sat in a normal human chair, his knees would be higher than his stomach.

He leant his hip on my desk.

I refused to look up

'Victor-Victoria,' he said suavely.

I recalled the first time I had met him, a week ago, when Mr Ruttman had introduced us. 'Here is our new promising wheat trader Vic Rash.'

Devlin had looked me up and down, and his smile spread slowly on his face. 'Vic? And would that be Victor or Victoria?'

My face had heated. I don't know why. It was an old joke I had suffered since school. It had never bothered me before.

'Just Vic,' I had mumbled in reply, trying not to trip over my own tongue.

I wondered whether he knew which one it was. I flattered myself by thinking he knew and was tormenting me, rather than being baffled like the rest of them. Men like him knew. They knew women from men. He could probably sniff us out with that perfect nose of his. It had just enough freckles to suggest he spent many days outdoors, no doubt in some manly pursuits.

'It's just Vic,' I mumbled now. I wanted to shrink away, but he would probably just laugh, and revel in that sense of power that men like him get when others cower before them.

'Sure you are,' he said smoothly. His smile was knowing. 'Did you watch the game last night?'

'No. Didn't watch it. Go away. Ahem. I mean, I have work to do.'

He did not go away. He nodded at my screen with its pitiful chart of flatline trading conditions. The wheat price was like that. It just stayed there for days and days. 'So, how's the wheat portfolio growing, Victoria?'

Very funny, arse.

'Heard there is drought in the new country,' he continued. 'Price is likely to go up in a few weeks if the Russian winter is as cold as they are predicting. And watch out for the Chinese Agriculture Minister's announcement tomorrow morning at half nine. Likely you will get a nice juicy price spike with it.'

'Thanks for the tip,' I said, feeling anything but grateful. He thought he knew everything there was about trading. He was probably right to think so, too.

'Sure. You settling in alright, Victor? Our office is not too snug for you?'

'It's been a week since I started. I'm settled. Thanks for asking. Now I'd best get back to work.'

'You do that, hey Victoria. Heard you got another client yesterday. Keep up the good work.' He winked again, and moved onwards through the jungle of grey cubicles, deliberately crossing paths with Lucy Valentine.

She was the lioness to his lion. She was everything female. Her dress was flowery, her figure curving, her breasts a generous handful, her hair long, and golden, her nails perfectly manicured and painted pale pink. Hell, she was even startlingly beautiful. She was everything Mr John Ruttman, my rather outdated boss, expected a woman to be. I avoided her as much as I could. Her talk was about fashion and gossip. I wondered how she had managed to land a lucrative copper trading job, especially since she had started at the firm as a secretary.

She was looking down at the stack of papers she was carrying from the printer room.

Devlin moved to block her path. 'So sorry, Lucy, m'dear.' He grabbed her elbow with one hand and steadied the papers she nearly dropped with his other. 'Did not watch where I was going.'

Liar.

'It's alright, neither was I,' she said lightly, and laughed in that pretty, feminine way that set my teeth on edge but made Devlin grin like a fool. 'I am a bit distracted after the game last night,' she continued, beaming at him. 'I bet against the reds, and made a small fortune.'

'Ah yes, you saw it too?'

'I would never miss a game,' she said with slight affront.

His gaze flicked back to me, as if to say, 'See, even she watches it'. I turned pink. Everyone in the office watched 'the game'. I was not into sports. They bored me into stupidity.

'Smooth as a snake,' Fred whispered behind me. 'I reckon they watched it together last night... in his bed, if you know what I mean.'

'Who?' I asked, pretending I was not watching the handsome Devlin and beautiful Lucy in their daily flirtations.

Fred occupied the other desk of our tiny cubicle, and as he leaned back to whisper, our chairs collided. 'The lion of masculinity, of course.' He jerked his head towards Lucy and Devlin. 'Reckon there's something between them.'

Fred Mason was one of those shy, slight men whom most people overlooked. There were days when I did not even notice him come in and take the seat behind me, until he spoke, startling me. The man should wear a bell. He was probably better suited to espionage than market trading.

Then again, I might have been overlooked as well, but for the conundrum that my appearance presented. Many could not decide whether I was a man or a woman. Some thought I was transgender, but going from what to what? Like some optical illusions, I could be either, depending on the light, their mood, whether they preferred slightly butch women or effeminate men. Some even squinted when they looked at me, as if trying to blur my edges. Fred was one of those who did not. I suspected he was one of the few who knew for certain, or at least guessed correctly. It was fifty-fifty after all.

'Most likely,' I said with a pang of irritation. 'He is handsome. She is beautiful. Man. Woman. So yes, they probably shag in the bathroom every lunch.'

He chuckled. 'You reckon? You know, you have a way with words... when you choose to, that is.'

It was not a choice. I would get locked up, and words would either be a jumbled mess or locked away completely. It was a wonder I had survived my job interview with Mr Ruttman two weeks ago. I was awkward, stuttering in my replies, my hand was clammy when he shook it. In spite of all that, he gave me a job, telling me I reminded him of his son when he was a young lad. All shy and awkward.

Alcohol untied my tongue. Once, after four failed job interviews, I downed a shot of whisky before yet another one with a major trading firm. I simply wanted to be able to speak fluently, confidently. I wanted to come across as eloquent, which I knew I could be, once my irrational fear of strangers passed. Their first question had been, 'Do you always drink before nine in the morning?' It had been the briefest interview of my life.

Fred leant back to watch the lion and the lioness sniff and circle each other. 'It's a modern world. 'Man, woman', means little these days where sneak shags are concerned, hey Vic?'

Oh hell, there he went again, probing. It was the next question people always wondered about me, once they had decided on my gender. Which way did I swing in bed? Lacking both sufficient traditional masculinity and femininity, did I prefer one or the other, or did I seek a gender neutral like myself? I had pondered those questions myself as an adolescent. I had talked them to death with my best friend Li. Then decided it did not matter. I liked what I liked when I saw it.

'If you say so,' I said, not meeting his eyes as they regarded me with speculation. I was used to being thought a freak. It rarely stung anymore. Fred was alright, otherwise. If I had to name a friend in the office, Fred would be the one I'd name.

'Devlin, my boy!' Mr Ruttman stuck his head through his door. 'Did Sally not pass on my message? I want a word, if you don't mind.'

'I was just on my way to see you, Mr Ruttman,' Devlin replied.

Liar. You were just looking down Lucy's cleavage. Well, he might have been, if Lucy had actually had some showing. At the moment, it was hidden behind her pink cardigan.

'I want your take on the unexpected gold spike we had this morning,' Mr Ruttman said. 'And Sarah Bern from *Spot Market Analyst* wants another interview.'

Devlin was Mr Ruttman's golden boy in every way. He traded gold, whilst I traded grass. His markets encompassed political and economic spheres, wars and conflict. He had to sieve through countless pieces of information and news each day to combine them into a likely price trend in gold futures, whilst I merely had to keep an eye on global weather. And he was excellent at what he did. Before him, *Ruttman and Son* had been on the verge of ruin, making losses after losses. Devlin had single-handedly changed all that with his unnatural Midas touch. All his predictions came uncannily true. He handled the largest account in the firm, with over a thousand clients. Each of whom he knew by name. He even appeared as the expert on gold trends on national TV in the popular *Spot Market Analyst* show.

Devlin put his arm around the portly man's shoulders. 'I am at your disposal, Sir.' And together they disappeared into Mr Ruttman's office, which overlooked the city park across the main road, and the sky-risers beyond the sprawling green.

Fred shook his head. 'It'll be a good day when someone teaches Dev humility. Nothing gets that guy down. Someone should take him down a peg or two. The way he gets chummy with everyone is sickening.'

Suddenly, my world found a way to right itself. Of course, why had I not thought of it before? Since our first meeting, Devlin had been the bane of my existence, with his teasing and winking, and those bloody smiles that set my nerves on edge. His very nearness made me feel slightly nauseous. Even at night, he invaded my thoughts. *Ugh.* I needed to purge Devlin out of my pores, and one way to do that was to get rid of those smiles of his; then I would not lie in bed awake, restless and annoyed, thinking of them.

I glanced at Lucy, who was back in her own corner. There was one way to bring down any man. Love. Love taught humility. I should know. The lack of it in my life had taught me plenty of humility and self-doubts.

Devlin flirted shamelessly with Lucy. Then again, he flirted with everything he came across: man, woman, or coffee machine. Lucy, however, received more of his attention than anyone else. The man fancied her, that much was clear. What did she think of him? Did they really shag in the bathroom at lunchtime? I'd never heard of it, nor witnessed it, but in my head, I saw it clearly. Her skirts hiked up, his trousers undone, him pummelling her on the sink, his hands and mouth fixed on her spectacular, naked breasts. Him moaning her name into her ear. 'Oh, Lucy, Oh, Lucy. You are perfect, just like me.' Well, something like that. The image irked me far more than it should have. But then, only Devlin Knightsbridge was ever able to raise my ire to bloodlust... or at least to the modern, less deadly version of it.

Fred was right. Someone should teach the lion humility. Had any woman ever said no to him? Well, one was about to, and I would make sure of it. Lucy was going to forget Devlin's name.

2

The Question of Masculinity

I did not have a clear plan. It was a misshapen creature of vengeance. I sat there watching the tiny fluctuations of the overriding flatline chart on my screen. Beside me, my phone remained indifferently silent. No one wanted to enquire about opening a grass trading portfolio. It was gold, oil and silver, and for a few fetishists, chocolate. Honestly, how was one to trade in a market which had less volatility than weekly fuel prices? No one traded in wheat, except perhaps the wheat farmers.

My attention wandered to Devlin lounging in Mr Ruttman's sofa. Relaxed, his arms spread wide, as if it was his own office. Mr Ruttman was nodding eagerly to whatever timeless wisdom came out of golden boy's mouth. My gaze shifted to beautiful, golden Lucy, the paragon of womanhood and femininity. I did not hate her. Not at all. She was alright, in her own way. Lucy was nice. Were someone to ask me what Lucy was like, I'd say 'nice'. Perhaps she was not the brightest light in the office, and a bit dull for my liking with her fascination in all things fashion, and celebrity news, and latest episodes of *How I Got Away With Cold-Blooded Murder*. But she was friendly enough.

My plan was simple. Make her fall in love with me, break Devlin's heart, and make him realise that not everyone swoons at his feet. Devlin learns humility and then... well, it did not matter what happened after that. He would become a better person. The world would thank me. And I could get on with my life having accomplished that one good deed for the rest of humanity. And never think of Devlin again. I thought it rather clever.

I just had to be careful not to take this too far. I did not need to bed Lucy, only turn her attention from Devlin to me, to make him jealous, and make him feel like he had to work to earn something.

So, onwards to part one of my plan. Make the gorgeous Lucy Valentine fall in love with me. Damn. How does one make someone fall in love? I have never been in love... well, not the crushing type of love which turns people into brooding zombies. I have seen Li succumb to it once. But after a week of lying in bed crying her eyes out, she got on with her life and was all the happier for it — once she decided that death was not the answer, after all.

My dilemma deepened. How does one compete with someone like Devlin? I was not an ugly person. Some called me handsome, others called me pretty. My hair was cropped to hang above my shoulders. I simply brushed it back with some gel to keep it out of my eyes during the day.

At school, after being mercilessly teased and shunned as a freak, I decided to put a real effort into appearing gender neutral, mostly out of spite. I knew it freaked the other kids out. It gave me a measure of power over what they thought of me, and it stung less to actually *be* the freak they thought me to be. If they thought me an 'it' then I would give them a reason to think so. They began to call me Victor-Victoria. So I decided to take it further, and dress and act masculine one day, demanding to be called Victor, and feminine the next, when I would tell them to call me Victoria. The kids began to be a little afraid of me. The verbal abuse increased. A few tried to push me around. I pushed them back. I stopped being an 'it' and became a 'mad, bad geno'. Then, when some gained some respect for me, I became 'mad, bad Vic'.

Even the teachers grew disturbed by my behaviour. They offered me counselling sessions, which tried to address my gender confusion. I enjoyed them greatly. I lied to the concerned councillors outrageously. I pretended I had two personalities, one called Victor, the other Victoria. I would talk as one, then the other. It was hilarious... until they sent me to a psychiatry clinic for drug treatments. I quickly quit all pretence and told them I was simply having a laugh. I sat in detention for six months.

The trouble was, in spite of my birth gender, I never really felt masculine or feminine. Perhaps it was because of my features, or the way the kids always made me an outsider when they formed their boy groups and girl groups. I hung out with the other rejects. Mostly, though, I hung out with Li.

When I left school and fell in with the Wild Riders gang, I dropped the Victor-Victoria charade. I was simply Vic. In official forms, I usually 'forgot' to tick the gender box. Somehow it always felt like lying. No one ever pursued me for clarification. Outside the official forms, no one had ever asked me about my gender. I suspected they would rather throw themselves off the bridge head-first onto speeding traffic.

This now led me to my first problem. What did Lucy think me to be? I was certain she fancied men. If she thought me a woman, then the plan could not work. As Fred pointed out, one could never tell. I thought about it and realised that Lucy never actually flirted with men unless they flirted with her first. I had not heard of her being in a relationship. She might like women... hell, it did not matter. A feminine woman like her was dressing to impress masculinity, be it in a man or woman.

'Time for coffee, Vic,' Fred said from behind me.

I glanced at the clock on my screen. Ten already? 'Sure,' I said, and followed him into the staff kitchen.

Mr Ruttman was not a generous boss, as bosses went. My pay was lousy. The office space was small, the computers were three years out of date. I was not going to complain. It was hard to get a job when my tongue tripped over itself each time I grew palm-sweatingly nervous. My job interviews were always a disaster.

When Mr Ruttman offered me the job, he explained the great opportunity he was offering me with the minimum wage contract. I was being given an excellent and rare opportunity to earn my unimaginable riches by trading my way to the top on a commission-based system.

'As my father and his father before him always said,' he had told me, 'the harder you work, the more you will earn.'

He sighted Devlin Knightsbridge as an example of what a man could achieve when he put his mind to it. Except that wheat was not the way to riches, as most farmers knew. Gold was. Two weeks into my job, and the commission I had earned was worth less than a pint.

Here at least, in the narrow galley kitchen, Mr Ruttman spared no expense. We had the best coffee machine money could buy. It could take men to space and win wars. It had rows and rows of flashing buttons and four filling stations. It offered every type of coffee known to man, and some that were known only to governments. It had a screen to tell you how to place your cup, and how to fill it. It showed a clock in five different time zones, and the latest spot prices in all the key commodities in futures markets, so you did not accidentally miss a trading opportunity. Evidently, wheat was not one of the key commodities.

The coffee machine greeted me in a lovely, feminine voice. 'Hello Vic, would you like your usual; black with one sugar?'

'Hello coffee machine...'

'Please reply using the following commands, 'Yes' or 'No',' the coffee machine advised me patiently.

'Oh, yes. Sorry, I meant...'

'Let's start again. Hello Vic, would you like your usual; black with one sugar?' I could swear there was a hint of exasperation in her voice.

'I was about to tell you...'

'Please reply using the following commands, 'Yes' or 'No'.'

'Yes, damn it. Yes!'

'There is no need to use inappropriate language,' the coffee machine chided patiently.

Fred chuckled. 'Come now, you two, no need to argue again.'

'Please place your cup in station four,' the machine advised me.

'It's already there,' I replied dully.

'No, you have to place it only after she requests it?' Fred corrected me.

'How stupid is this thing? It has enough controls to fly an aeroplane. It can talk and recognise my face. But it can't detect a cup on its station?'

Fred cleared his throat. 'I think it's best if you just do what she says.'

'Please place your cup in station four,' the machine repeated. 'Or say, 'I don't want any coffee today."

'Alright, damn you,' I snapped. I lifted my cup and pointedly slapped it back down. 'Happy now?'

'There is no need to use inappropriate language,' the machine reminded me coolly, and filled my cup with a perfectly measured teaspoon of sugar and black coffee of the quality known only to gods. 'Have a good day, Vic.' I swear there was sarcasm in her voice. 'Hello Fred. Would you like your usual; white with two sugars?'

He cleared his throat. 'My usual is black with one. You know that, machine.'

I had discovered soon after I had started my job here that Fred had exactly the same taste in coffee with me. He also had the same taste in books, music and shampoo brands.

'Oh, sure it is,' the machine said sarcastically, then asked politely. 'And how has your morning been?'

'Why is she never this nice to me?' I grumbled under my breath.

'Probably because you swear at her,' Fred replied to me from the corner of his mouth. Then more clearly, 'Very good, machine. Now, about that coffee.'

'Please place your cup in station two,' the machine said.

'It is the same coffee as mine!' I objected. 'Why does he get station two? How do you decide anyway?'

Fred was much more amenable. He simply placed his cup where he was told to. The machine filled his cup.

'Station one is reserved only for Devlin,' Fred explained. 'Station two is for people she likes. Station three is for those she dislikes.'

'So what's station four?' I asked.

He shrugged. 'I don't know. She's never asked anyone to place a cup there before you turned up. At the moment, it seems to be reserved just for you. Usually, it's where she washes her dirty components at the end of the week with industrial-strength detergents.'

My mouth hovered on the rim of my cup. I sniffed my coffee. Then sniffed again. 'Does this smell odd to you?'

He bent over and sniffed. 'Nope. Seems fine to me. Although my nose has never been the same since my chemistry experiment accident at school.'

'I hope you have a lovely day, Fred,' the machine said with no hint of sarcasm.

'I think she fancies you,' I said, and he choked on his coffee. 'The coffee is good, though.' I closed my eyes for that first sip of purity and truth. I was high in the sky, where gods feasted.

The first sip of coffee, I long ago decided, was better than sex. Not that I had much luck in that area recently. Not since I left the Wild Riders gang three years ago. It was surprisingly hard to get dates when half the people weren't sure whether I was a man or a woman, or maybe a man who was once a woman, or a woman who was once a man. The other half simply weren't sure whether I was straight or gay. To be honest, I was rarely fussy. It's just how it was in the Wild Riders.

'You can thank Devlin for this lovely lady here,' Fred patted the coffee machine. 'He said bad coffee in the morning threw off his trading, and Mr Ruttman promised him the best coffee machine that money could buy.'

'Why thank you, Fred,' the machine said, and her lights flashed in a pretty multicoloured display.

Show off.

'I would sooner be run over by a bus than be grateful to Devlin for anything,' I replied sullenly.

'Grateful to me for what?' Devlin asked, striding into the kitchen.

'Nothing. I am grateful to you for nothing,' I said.

'Why hello, darling. Have you a coffee for me today?'

I choked. 'What...?'

'I was talking to the machine, Victoria,' he said with a wicked glint in his eyes.

'Why hello, Devlin,' the coffee machine purred. 'I was hoping you would come by today and ask me for coffee.' Her voice became sultry.

'I think we should leave the two of you alone,' I said.

Fred laughed into his cup, but stopped abruptly when Devlin simply looked at him.

Oh, for goodness sake, Fred. How can a raised eyebrow terrify you?

'No need, Victor. I do not mind an audience.' Wink.

Yuk. I turned red.

'And what would you like me to do for you today, Devlin? Which buttons will you press today?' she said in a low sultry voice.

'Now, now, princess, we have company here, remember?' he chided gently and placed a cup in station one.'

The machine filled his cup with cappuccino and sprinkled chocolate powder in the pattern of a heart on top.

The man must have been weaned on a golden tit. Even the damned coffee machine swooned at his feet. What the hell was wrong with the world? Life had definitely been too easy for him. I grew more determined than ever to show him that he, too, was human, like the rest of us imperfect mortals.

'Thanks, darling. What would I do without you?' And unbelievably he winked at the machine.

The man was impossible!

'Oh, Devlin, you devil,' the machine giggled.

'Who the hell programmed it to giggle?' I asked in outrage. And before the machine could correct me, I snapped, 'Yes, I know. There is no need to use inappropriate language.'

'There is no need to use inappropriate language,' the machine said icily. 'And please note we may be running out of black coffee until next week.'

'Bitch!'

Devlin chuckled. He then toasted me and Fred with his heart covered coffee and strode off to his desk.

Fred and I drank our coffee in silence.

I watched Lucy at her desk. She looked oddly serious, thoughtful almost. Then her cubicle partner said something to her over his shoulder, and she giggled, all silly again, and tapped his arm with her hand playfully. Fools.

Fred cleared his throat, and I realised he was watching me watch Lucy.

'So,' he began painfully awkwardly, holding his mug in both hands. 'Seeing anyone at the moment?'

'No,' I said, and sipped my coffee. *Oh, hell, definitely better than sex.* Each warm mouthful was lifting me into the clouds.

Unlike most, Fred never took offence at my curt replies. I never meant to be rude, I just run out of things to say. If I tried too hard, I got all tongue tangled.

'Neither am I,' he said, sipping his own cup. He nodded to Lucy. 'Didn't think she'd be your type,' he observed casually.

'She looks like everyone's type,' I mused aloud.

'Not mine,' he said.

I suddenly felt awkward. I could feel him watching me. I blushed. He blushed. We both looked away. 'Too blonde for my liking,' he added quickly.

I glanced at Lucy again. She certainly had the silly girl facade, but when she thought no one was looking her expression looked intelligent. Maybe I was kidding myself. Either way, I was about to find out what lay beneath her surface. More determined than ever now, I was going to make Lucy want me.

As if feeling my gaze on her, Lucy looked my way, and not in the 'what the hell are you' sort of way. More like casual interest, a curiosity perhaps. She gave me a small smile. I turned away abruptly. How the hell was I going to do this, if I could not even smile back at the girl?

I thought about it and decided it was the question of masculinity. I had to be masculine to attract the feminine. I had to be more Victor than Victoria for Lucy. I had learned that from Li. Feminine was drawn to masculine... and vice versa.

'Vic, there you are.' Mr Ruttman's voice came from the other doorway of the galley. I choked on my coffee.

A firm hand patted my back. A warm, solid, heavy hand belonging to no other than the bane of my office existence. Devlin. An awful tingling ran over my skin, tightening my gut, my lower regions.

'Get off, I'm fine.' I stepped away from him.

'Just came to wash my cup.' He lifted his empty mug. 'Don't mind me.'

I ignored him. 'Mr Ruttman, you startled me.'

'Oh, well, sorry about that. I was just looking for you,' he said awkwardly, his gaze roaming my face disconcertedly.

When he had hired me, he was certain he was hiring a man. He even told me I reminded him of his son. I do not know what made him doubt himself, but in the last week, he had been staring at me wonderingly.

Like everyone else, he would rather hang himself by his tie than ask whether I was a man or a woman. So Mr Ruttman stared, and squinted, and turned his head this way and that for a better angle. He looked at my jaw for evidence of shaving. It was hard to tell and inconclusive. My jaw was strong for a woman, weak for a man, and smooth. Then he stared at my neck. I sighed inside. The Adam's apple test. I wore my collar up. Not to confuse anyone, but to hide an ugly scar from surgery that gave me a rather husky voice. Too deep to be a woman's, while not deep or resonant enough to be a man's. Besides, I had known women with bigger Adam's apple than some men.

'What can I do for you, Mr Ruttman?' I prompted.

His eyes flew back up to my face. 'Ahem, yes. Devlin and I were just talking about expanding your trading portfolio into coffee. Wheat is rather... ahem. Flat. Our clients are not really interested in it. Coffee is the modern buzz word, and Devlin tells me you are somewhat of an expert in coffee markets.'

'Ha!' That came from the coffee machine.

I choked on another sip. This time Fred patted me on the back. How the hell would Devlin know that about me, and why would he discuss it with Mr Ruttman? I did have a secret interest in coffee markets, and I did like to peruse coffee bean shops in my free time. I was fascinated by the effects of the soil, weather and bean variety on final coffee flavour, and ultimately coffee price.

Mr Ruttman stared at the coffee machine. 'Did it just...?'

'If by expert, he means that I know the difference between good coffee and bad, then I'm sure he is right.'

Devlin gave me his half-cocked grin. 'Oh, don't be shy, Vic. I know you know much more than you think you know.'

I frowned. Was that an insult? Devlin was the devil himself. It was hard to know his mind.

Mr Ruttman's eyes dropped to my chest. Ah, and here comes the tit test. At least he did not grope to check, as some men had done in the past. My loose shirt gave nothing away. His eyes, having committed themselves to the path of no return, dropped towards my groin in the alarmed sort of way. It was embarrassing for us both. I had to pretend not to notice. He had to pretend he was looking at something on the floor.

Of course, he got no answers there either. What did he expect? I wore standard office trousers. Loose enough to hide a rugby ball.

The poor man was a traditionalist. He thought men had their place, and women theirs. He liked men to be men, and women to be women. He was portly, and each day, I saw him take his heart medication. I suspected if I ever wanted to kill my poor boss, I need only wear a dress into work, no matter how ridiculous I looked in it.

'So, then.' Mr Ruttman lifted his eyes, having finished perusing me for answers he did not find, while Fred, Devlin and I made a point of looking elsewhere in the kitchen.

I do not think we fooled him. He turned bright pink to the top of his bald scalp. 'Well then, you can take over Rick's coffee account. Since Rick left, it's been neglected. I'd give it to Lucy, but she is snowed under with copper futures, or so Devlin tells me. I should go and speak with her. She has always been one of my most promising traders, in spite of being a young lady. But modern women are so much more capable. Would you not say, Devlin, my boy?' Mr Ruttman strained his head to look behind us to where Lucy sat, engrossed in her charts.

'Most certainly,' Devlin agreed.

Mr Ruttman pushed past us and left in a hurry.

Devlin cocked his eyebrow at me. 'Shame on you, Victor, teasing an old man like that. I think you frightened him.'

'I did not tease him,' I said.

'Sure you did, Victoria. You deliberately confuse the poor man. Just like you tease everyone you come across. It must amuse you to confound everyone.'

Damn, the man saw too much. It sent a chilly shiver through my body.

'So, do I frighten you too, Devlin? Do I threaten your masculinity? Would you like me to be more feminine around you and flutter my eye lashes at you.' I did just that to demonstrate, adding a coy, feminine smile. 'Or would you like me to be more of a man,' I said in a deeper voice, and reclined against the counter in a very masculine way I had seen Devlin do many times.

Fred burst out laughing. 'Brilliant, Vic. Great talent for acting.'

Devlin glared at me. Tut, tut, Victor-Victoria. You are the last person on earth to threaten my masculinity. You'd need to find yours first.' And with that, he strode off.

What the hell did he mean by that? Was he saying he believed me to be a woman, or some neutered male?

It was definitely time someone did threaten his masculinity. And nothing made a man question his masculinity and self-worth than the scorn of a woman. It would sting him doubly if it was I who shook the foundation of his manhood. Slowly, my plan formed. It was juvenile. I did not care. I would chew up his masculinity and spit it out.

'Why are you smiling like that, Vic?' Fred asked somewhat nervously. 'The lion just insulted you.'

'Yes, he did, didn't he. Let's get back to work.'

Insult I knew how to deal with. And now that blood had been drawn, I had a perfect excuse for retaliation.

3
Victor

The next day I rolled out of bed and staggered to the mirror. I went out last night to my usual hide out, the *Lonely Lizard,* got drunk, hooked up and snogged a woman. I did it to practice my rusty, outdated skills, before I plunged into the crystal waters of Lucy Valentine. I was certain it would take every bit of refined skill to make her fall at my feet.

Over the years, I found that women were naturally drawn to me. To them, I seemed safe. Half the time I spent in their company, however, I did not know whether they thought me a man or a woman. I did not think they did either.

Men were far more uncertain around me. Some, like Fred, liked me. Others fancied me and made themselves known. The lions of masculinity were the ones who did not like me. They were threatened by me. I suspected they saw their own insecurities when they looked at me. The better of them ignored me. The worst confronted me. I had been hit once outside the bar by a bloke who was desperate to find out if I was a woman. He tried to grope me. I shoved him away. He threw a punch. He was drunk and unsteady, and did nothing more than slightly bruise my jaw. Most men were not like that, so I took care to avoid the confrontational types.

I stared at my reflection. Handsome. Man or woman, I was handsome. Not in a stunning sort of way, like Lucy or Devlin. The scar on my throat was my worst feature. I was young when I had the surgery. And as I grew, so did the scar. It was an ugly scar. It made me look like I've been in a knife fight. I did not need any more insecurities when dealing with people. So I hid it behind collars and chokers.

I wet my hands with cold water and run them over my face. I looked like I had been drinking last night. It was not a good look. My hair hung limply around my face, softening it somewhat. Not a good look for someone who had to appear masculine today.

I tried to look at my face through another's eyes. I had seen ugly people with a striking quality to them. There was something in the way their features were set, something adventurous in their eyes; qualities that were desired above classical beauty. I was handsome enough, yet plain. Dull even. What was missing? It was not just Devlin's looks that made people turn to him. There was an energy about him. It flowed out of him, energising all who laid eyes on him.

I was most definitely not the gem of femininity, like hip-swaying, hair flicking Lucy Valentine, or the lion of masculinity, Devlin Knightsbridge. I was just Vic, the invisible, hide-in-the-corner, quiet Vic. Today, I had to change all that. No more hiding in a corner. To catch Lucy's eye, I had to emerge from the shadows. I had to be impossible to miss. I had to transform into someone the beautiful Lucy Valentine might want. Today, I had to be Victor, and not just Victor the confident bloke, easy in his ways, but Victor the charmer.

Determination flowed through me. Like a strong cup of coffee, it awoke my senses. To start with, appearances were everything. Seduction began with appearance. I had never thought of it like that. Then again, the stakes had never been higher. Before, I had simply wanted someone to see me for what I was, and care for the pathetic me I had become. Now, it was not about me, but Devlin. Someone had to teach him a lesson that life was not always rosy and easy.

I stripped and stepped into the hot shower.

I thought of Devlin. What was it about him that made men and women, and even coffee machines, want to be noticed by him? Promises. He was like a well-displayed home. People did not shop for a house to buy, but an illusion of a lifestyle. That was what Devlin promised. He was what men wanted to be and women wanted to date. Image was everything.

I shaved, scrubbed myself clean, left the shower, and rubbed myself down with a towel.

I tried to recall all Lucy had ever said in my hearing range. It turns out that I was actually listening when I thought I was not. She believed fashion was power, and power was sexy. She liked power. Very well. What was the image of power? Devlin came to mind, then a soldier, a police officer, a fireman, a doctor, a lawyer — no not a lawyer, creepy bastards — a pilot, a barista, a captain of a ship, a biker, a rock star... a biker! Yes, of course. Leather. Man or woman, leather was sex.

I flung open my tiny wardrobe. It was stuffed with a handful of hanging shirts and jackets, and trousers neatly folded on the upper shelf.

Green. I had green eyes. My mother's eyes. When I was ten, she died of breast cancer. My father died three years later in a construction accident. He had never been the same since Mother's death. I had always wondered whether he had willed the accident to happen.

I pulled out a dark green shirt. There was a fashionable silver sheen to it. Next, I pulled on black trousers. In the back of my wardrobe, I saw my silver-decorated black boots, with a respectable heel for extra height. They were my favourite pair in the biking days of my disreputable youth. It was time I brought mad, bad Victor back. I simply combed my dark hair back and gelled it into place. It was of the right length to avoid needing to be fussed over.

I reset my features into Victor's. There was a way that men walked and talked. It was in their expressions and body language. I learned those ways long ago by practising in front of the mirror. They were no more natural to me than the ways of a woman. But I had learned both ways for a lark.

Next, I took out the black leather jacket. I had never thought to wear it again. I had kept it as a cautionary reminder of my misspent teenage years of parties, sex, drinks and mild drugs. They were sordid, ugly years. I thought I had been enjoying myself. I was simply existing in the only way I knew how. Until one day, not unusual in itself, I had woken up in a pile of naked bodies. They breathed, and had heartbeats, and would soon wake up and crawl from the bed to find some leftover food. But inside, they were dead. I felt dead.

The bed was a mattress on the dirty carpet floor, one of three. Sheets hung on windows. Wall paper was either peeling or torn off in places. The house stank of smoke, stale alcohol, old sweat and sex.

Beer, cheap wine and vodka bottles were scattered everywhere. Some had spilled their remnants onto the carpet. Even the ceiling was stained. I felt dirty. What was I doing? Why was I here? I thought of my life and imagined waking up again here tomorrow. It made me want to weep.

The gang would sleep on until after midday. There were eight of us, five men and three women. Some of us grew up together in our foster home, others joined later. Lock, our leader, had convinced us we were family and had to look out for one another. I thought of the family I once had as a child. I thought of my mother and all her hopes for me. Cutting shame filled me. I suddenly wanted to go home to my mother and father. They were dead. I had no home to go to. This was all I had.

I could do better, I decided then and there. I could make myself a better home. First, I had to become a better person. I did not believe in heaven or god. Dead was dead. Yet, if by some chance, Mother could see me from another plane of some afterlife, I did not want to give her cause to weep over what I had become. It would crush her soul. I gathered my clothes and left before the gang woke up. I never saw the Wild Riders again.

Now, after all these years, I put on my jacket, feeling strangely afraid, as if it was some magic key that would propel me back into my old life and into Lock's clutches. Instead, it only sucked me back into the memories of the past I no longer wanted to face. I fought off those assailing memories.

At the bottom of my wardrobe lay my black helmet. I retrieved it, and tucking it under my arm, left my flat.

My landlord, Mr Gruleman, ambushed me on the staircase outside his flat.

'Vic. Where is my rent? You are late by a week. We agreed you will pay two weeks ahead.'

'Mr Gruleman. I told you, I will get my pay on Friday, and I will pay you two weeks ahead then.'

'It's Tuesday now. Friday's too long to wait. I want my money tomorrow.'

I put on Victor's charming smile. 'Look, I'm paid up this week. I will pay for the next two on Friday. I have a new job now. A good one, in the city. I won't be late again. You'll see.'

'Fine. But just this once. Next time you are out.' He slammed shut the door to his apartment.

Outside, it was cold and raining. I caught a cab to China town.

I knocked on a tall, bright red door of a mansion. A woman in bright red silks opened it. She looked me up and down. 'So, playing at being Victor today? I don't know which one I find more disturbing, him or Victoria.'

'Good to see you too, Li,' I said.

She opened the door wider. 'Come in, but I must warn you, I am spent. Busy night with Mark last night.'

'Mark the eighty-five-year-old?'

'He is only sixty-five, and a darling. Coffee?'

'Sure.'

She led me into her kitchen. It was a long walk past sitting rooms and a small ballroom. Her kitchen was larger than my whole flat.

Li was beautiful, and a gymnast once upon a time in school. She chose her clients, and they paid her lavishly. She could have done worse for herself.

She must have read my thoughts. She was uncanny like that. 'I told you before, Vic. You can make a good living doing this. You can come in as my partner if you want. Remember Rick? He was leaving that day you came to visit me. He owns an airline. Or is it a computing firm? Well, never mind which. He's been asking after you. And he is not creepy or fussy. Just straight forward pants down, give him a hole and he will be happy as a swine in mud.' She poured me coffee from her small, silent coffee maker, that did not talk back.

'Pig,' I corrected absently.

She spun around. 'What did you call me?'

'Pig in mud, not swine.'

'Oh, what does it matter? Pig, swine, it is the same. You tell me, do you want him. Rick has a cock the size of a ...'

'No, but thanks, Li,' I interrupted her before she gave me any more details.

She put the coffee in front of me, and sat across the table with her own cup. 'Your kind is in demand, you know. There are some tastes, that run into... let us say, indeterminate gender individuals. It's become popular to take on escorts of uncertain gender. And the more uncertain the better. You'd be an instant hit. Thousands, Vic! Think on it. You get to choose your sponsor, have regular sex, and no work to get up for.

It's not that different to picking up strangers in the bar and taking them to bed. Just more profitable.'

'Tempting how that might be, I just can't do it. Being reliant on another for my support.' I shook my head. 'I'll likely end up with someone like Jim.'

She looked away, flinching. I was the one who nursed her for two weeks, while she recovered in bed after one of her 'clients' took an exception to sharing her favours with other men. She never claimed it was exclusive. He had simply assumed, and she did not correct him. Jim the Skull Breaker, as he was known, was a professional boxer. She was lucky he did not kill her. As it was, the doctors thought the damage to her stomach was such that she may never have children. Li wept at the loss, even though she had told me many times before that she never wanted children.

After that, she became far more selective with her clients, and had them sign terms and conditions of their arrangement in front of her lawyers before she took them on. It was all very professional and proper.

She waved my reminder away. 'Jim's in the past. He can barely talk or walk now, since his last opponent ended up breaking his skull. Now that's a fitting end for the Skull Breaker.'

I was suspicious about that 'skull breaking' incident. One of the doctors had told the press that it wasn't the head damage from the fight that had crippled Jim, though he was at a loss to explain what else it could have been. And Li had a scary way of getting revenge on people who had wronged her. She never boasted of doing... things. But once, when we were kids, I had seen her take revenge on a boy at school with one of her needles. Since then, I had seen far too many unfortunate incidents befall people who had upset Li in some way or another.

She sipped her coffee. 'So, what brings you here so late in the day?'

'It's morning,' I said, glancing outside, as if to confirm I had not made some mistake. 'I'm on my way to work.'

'Well, it's late for me. I've just finished. How's that new fancy job of yours going? Have you made your millions yet?'

'I am late on my rent, that's how it's going. If I don't start making the commission I was promised my dedication would bring, I will be moving into a homeless shelter. I don't think there are flats cheaper and rattier than my own. I think someone was murdered there before I moved in. There are faint blood stains on the walls and carpet. Mr Gruleman denies it, of course.'

She snorted. 'I told you, if something seems too good to be accurate...'

'True. Something too good to be true.'

'Well, the same stands.' She waved her hand.

'I actually came to pick up my old Harley,' I said.

Her eyes narrowed. 'You going back to the Wild Riders? I thought you were done with all that. Better just take Rick's offer.'

'I am not going back to the Wild Riders. Honestly. I *am* done with all that. I just need to impress a girl. I thought a bike would do it.'

'Special girl?'

'It's not like that.'

'Ah, then special boy?'

Li was far too perceptive. It used to freak me out when we were kids at school. Half the time I thought she could read people's minds.

'I'll tell you everything the next time I come over, I promise. I am already late for work.' I downed my coffee. 'Good cup,' I said and stood up.

'Where are you going to store your bike? Can't keep coming here twice a day, I might be busy, or out.'

'Mr Gruleman has a lockup shed he offered me for storage when I first moved in. For an outrageous fee, of course.'

'Naturally, you agreed,' she said with a shake of her head.

'Don't worry, Mr Ruttman gave me the coffee portfolio. It's like a promotion. I'll be rich in no time. You'll see.'

'Well, come along then to the garage. I don't know if it will start after all these years.'

She had stored my bike under a white sheet. When I took it off, the bike was as beautiful as I remembered, shiny, black, polished to a glow. Hell, I'd missed it. I ran my hand over the leather seats. I had worked afterschool in the kitchens, washing dishes, sweeping floors, and cleaning tables. I had saved every penny for five years. When I left school, I had enough for a second-hand Harley.

I straddled the seat and felt at home. I turned the key. It started the first time, as if we had never been parted. I had kept it in perfect nick. I had always repaired and fixed it myself. I had dismantled and reassembled it countless times. I knew its every bolt and wire.

I put on my helmet and we were off. Only another biker can ever understand what it's like to straddle such raw power between your legs. I flew through the traffic, weaving between cars, feeling free, agile and unstoppable. I felt the force of the wind on my body. My bike and I pushed against it, laughing in its face. *Why did I ever give you up? You were not the Wild Rider. I was.*

I knew a moment where I simply wanted to keep going, to leave everything behind. I'd always dreamed of travelling the world on my bike, with just a rucksack on my back. One day, perhaps, I would own that dream. Maybe once I had made my fortune in Mr Ruttman's firm.

I parked my bike in the underground car park of our office building, one we shared with the building next door. I was late arriving. Quarter past nine. I felt a pang of anxiety, then shook it off. Victor was not afraid of being late. He answered to no one but himself.

I took off my helmet and saw Devlin's gold-plated sports car pull into his personal bay, two cars from where I'd found an empty parking space. He was always the last to get in. Probably sleeping in with one of his women after a long night of sordid sex.

Have you ever known anything but sordid sex yourself, Vic? Victor mocked.

Oh shut up, Victor.

Devlin got out, looking polished and pristine. The car locked itself behind him. He noticed me, began to turn away, then his gaze snapped back.

I winked at him and flicked my leg over the bike to get down.

He looked stunned.

Ha! Let the battle begin. *Not so masculine now, hey Devlin Knightsbridge, with your little toy car. What's the matter, could not afford the backseats?*

There was a sudden hard set to his mouth I had never seen before. His eyes drifted from me to my bike.

I smiled cockily. 'You like it?'

He stared at the bike, and something raw and angry crossed his features. 'I fucking hate it.' And with that he turned and walked away, his pace hurried, angry.

I gaped mutely after him, stunned by his fierce retort, and feeling strangely wounded. I had never seen him angry. It was unsettling. He was a different man when angry. I watched his back and noticed there was something wrong with his gait. He had a slight limp. Was he wounded? A twisted ankle?

He did not look back as he took the elevator to our office. When he was gone, I found all my confidence had drained away. I sat on the bike feeling dejected. Then I grew angry. This was exactly why someone should bring him down a peg. If I was Paul Ellis, he would no doubt have oohed and ahhed over my bike, telling me what a great piece of gear I had, and he'd love to go for a spin on it. But no, Vic deserved only his scorn and mockery.

I straightened my shoulders, trying to find my earlier confidence and the mad, bad Victor I had lost to Devlin's anger. I went to the lift, and up to the office. I mustered every acting skill I had amassed over the years. Confidence. *Smile, Victor. Lucy must fall in love with you.* I suddenly felt sick at the thought. I could not do it. Did not want to do it. I would have to talk to her, flirt with her. She had to notice me, see me above all others, above Devlin. It was impossible.

I took a deep breath as the lift doors opened. I stepped out, and walked forward with Victor's longer strides, as if I was the master here.

'Good morning, Sally,' I said in my deepest, sexiest voice. It came out awkward and strained. My false voice irritated my throat, and I coughed.

Sally lifted her wrinkled, grey face up to me. She passed bored eyes over my clothes. 'Have you just come back from a party? You are late.'

I was not a minute behind Devlin, who always came in fifteen minutes after nine.

Embarrassment flooded me. I felt as if I was standing naked before her, being scolded for forgoing to get dressed that morning. 'Um, yes... no... after work... a party after work,' I lied and rushed past her into the office.

Devlin was chatting to Paul Ellis. When he saw me come in, he fixed his icy gaze on me. I ignored him, going to my desk. I felt his eyes follow me. I began to have doubts about my sanity. This was stupid. I had done many stupid things in my life, some as a dare, others on the whims of youth. They never turned out well. This felt like that. Like I was challenging myself to walk through fire. What was I thinking of? Lucy would laugh at me. Then she and Devlin would laugh at me together. Ah hell, it's not like I'd never been laughed at before. Besides, Victor was not afraid of being laughed at. He laughed right back at the fools.

I glanced at Lucy. She was not paying me any attention. She was rather industrious for a... a feminine woman. I shook my head at myself. Mr Ruttman was rubbing off on me. If I was ever going to win her over to my side, I had to like her, respect her. *Just be suave, Vic. Make her feel appreciated.* Hell, I knew only too well what it was like to be seen as the sum of my surface features.

Again, I glanced at Lucy. She was not paying me any attention. Did she even see me come in? She was biting the tip of her pen whilst watching the copper price chart.

Be visible, be more visible than Devlin. I had to start by simply talking with her. Confidence. Women loved confidence. Time for Victor. I pushed back my shoulders, raised my head, and strode through the office towards my cubicle with a crooked smile. I greeted Pips the spotty oil trader. I coughed and made my voice deeper than it naturally was, and greeted Tim, the quiet, bespectacled silver trader. I spoke loud enough for my voice to carry to Lucy. She still ignored me. Tim and Pips, and even Jenny our accountant, who I was certain still did not know my name, looked at me as if I had lost my mind. Freak. Weirdo. The old names came back to taunt me. I was there again, crying in the school playground as other children jeered and called me 'it'. It was all I could do not to shrink away and slip unnoticed into my cubicle.

I dropped my helmet on my desk and took off my leather jacket. Not once did Lucy look my way. It was a rather poor start for Victor. Beneath the leather jacket, I was dressed in my best green shirt. I had bought it two years ago in the half-price sales and felt the tight pinch on my wallet. I could not help myself. It was a fancy-looking shirt, and I've never owned something so pretty before. I thought it made me look fashionable and well-off.

My eyes drifted to Devlin. I wondered what it was that annoyed him in the car park downstairs. Perhaps he was simply threatened by Victor. *Ha! Did not expect that, hey Devlin. Now who needs to find his masculinity?* Was he still angry? Did he realise his days of rule were over? Maybe. Or perhaps I had just made the biggest fool of myself yet.

He was now leaning on the grey cubicle wall, his arms crossed, listening to Pips showing him something on the trend line of his oil price. Devlin shook his head and said something back. When our eyes briefly met, his lips quirked upwards and he winked, as if he had not just growled at me in the car park.

Arse.

'You look good today, Vic,' Fred said cheerfully. 'What's the occasion?'

'Must there be one to look good?' I countered mulishly.

'For you, yes.'

I looked at him.

'That is, I am not saying... not that you don't always look good... I meant... it's just that you are not usually dressed up.'

'Fred?' I said quietly.

'Yes?'

'Shut up.'

'Sure.' He turned to his screen and pretended to study the charts of chocolate's daily price trends. The tips of his pointy ears turned pink. Fred had cute pointy ears that would have been adorable on a mischievous elf. They matched his face, with its pointy, upturned nose. Fred was a slight man, and in another time, another world, he might have been an elf prancing through the forest. The thought amused me.

I settled in to watching wheat gain momentum in going nowhere but straight ahead. Victor was bored. Victor did not wait for things to happen. He made them happen. Hell, why not, I was Victor today. Let's be reckless. A storm was brewing in the Indian Ocean. It just needed to defy all forecasts and change direction to the west coast of Australia, saving the wheat crops and flooding the market with unwanted excess. I set a number, nice and conservative, medium risk, medium exposure... then added another zero on the end. My hand hesitated. Vic was done with reckless. *No, I am Victor! Lucy will love me. SELL*. I hit the key and watched most of my clients' hard-earned money disappear into the fathomless trading void. Somewhere in the distance, an alarm rang out. It came from Mr Ruttman's office.

Oh, look, the wheat price moved... up... and up... and up again. What? Was this some universal joke on me? My eyes flew to the big, ominous red figure with a dreaded minus sign in front of it. The red figure grew and grew as the chart marched up. Was it waiting for me to make some kind of trading decision just so it could do the opposite of what I needed? The alarm in the distance grew shriller.

The door to Mr Ruttman's office flew open, and the alarm blasted through our modern-day office aether of clicking keyboards, ringing phones, and muted conversations. 'Viiiiic!' he yelled.

The office stilled. Silence hit us like a freak wave. Had the ground just shook?

'Viiiiiic! In my office!'

I fought the urge to crawl under my desk.

'What did you do?' Fred whispered behind me. 'He sounds pretty pissed.'

'Erm. I just opened some positions on the wheat futures.'

'Oh, good. You must have bought them just before the half nine announcement.'

'What announcement?' I whispered back with panic.

'The one where China said it would buy the entire world stockpile of wheat for the next five years.'

I looked at the screen and the evil chart climbed and climbed, and my losses had just added another zero. Oh, hell. Devlin had told me about this yesterday. He had told me it would spike up. It was a tip, and I missed it. Hell, I completely ignored it. I'd be damned if I owed any favours to Devlin.

The big red number grew bigger and redder before my horrified eyes.

'You can't hide from me, Vic!' Mr Ruttman yelled.

I stood up, reminded myself I was Victor today — who was now hiding in some deep corner of my psyche — and, holding my head up high, marched to the glass door leading into the office that I had only ever been in once.

It looked much the same in my interview. Cold, clean, white with great views of the park and the distant business district of the city. Mr Ruttman did not believe in high rents, and neither had the old Mr Ruttman before him, or the one before that. So they kept their tiny building from a hundred years ago on the edges of the city, while the sky-high office towers rose around them.

The firm started off as a bank. Made bad promises and worse investments, with the money which could never be returned to their customers. After a brief stint in prison for the current Mr Ruttman's grandfather, they reopened as an investment firm.

I sat down on the edge of the chair before his desk. He slammed the door behind me. The alarm was still sounding on his computer, growing shriller and more urgent as my losses compounded.

Mr Ruttman grabbed a packet of pills, took out three with shaking hands and swallowed them. Oh, hell, Victor almost killed my boss. The purple colour of his face lessened to red. I waited silently for him to compose himself.

'Why in the hell did you sell all the wheat? Tell me there is a reason to your madness. Tell me Devlin put you up to this because once again he knows something the rest of the world does not.'

'Erm...' I had to think quickly. But my mind froze. I forgot about the blasted announcement by the Chinese minister. I was too busy thinking of Lucy and Devlin and my plan. Victor was bored. He always led me into recklessness.

'Well!' Mr Ruttman demanded, and pulled on his collar.

'There is a storm, you see... in the ocean... the wheat needs rain, and the excess from the storm...'

My thoughts, which were clear and eloquent in my mind, came out as a vomit of words.

'What?' He blinked, then shouted, 'What are you talking about? Are you drunk? I noticed you came in late today. Are you taking drugs? What the hell does a storm in the ocean to do with wheat prices and the announcement by the Chinese Agriculture Minister today?'

The angrier he grew, the harder it became for me to talk. 'The storm is for Australia... wheat farmers are suffering the drought... so if... I mean *when* it hits, the wheat will be plentiful, and the markets saturated.' *There. That sounded clearer.*

'But China is buying up all excess stock for the next five years!'

I cleared my throat. 'It's a temporary spike. They won't buy high.'

Please let it be so, else I have just bankrupted my entire client list, and maybe even the firm.

His face cooled from red to pink. 'You'd better be right about this, Rash, else you will not last another week here! And by the way. I will not tolerate tardiness in my office. Nine o'clock start, Vic.'

I became indignant. I must have arrived a minute after Devlin, and he always came in at nine fifteen. 'But Devlin always comes in late.' And now I sounded like a petulant child.

'Devlin? I've never known him to be late. Now be off with you, and you'd better hope those losses do not keep going up.'

I turned to flee.

'Oh. And, as of now, I am taking you off the coffee portfolio, until you demonstrate some trading sense. Lucy will handle it.'

That stung. I left his office.

Silence.

I looked around. Suddenly, all the keyboards began to click again. Damn. They heard it all. The glass wall did not stand up well to Mr Ruttman's booming voice.

I went back to my desk and pretended to work until I saw Lucy get up and head for the kitchen. Without a word, hoping Fred did not notice, I slipped from my chair and sneaked away from my desk. I knew Fred would be wounded. He had commandeered my coffee breaks from my first day, and I never saw any reason to change the routine. Until now. Now I wanted Lucy by herself. I had to talk to her. Make myself visible to her, make her forget about the handsome, perfect Devlin Knightsbridge.

She was by the coffee machine, placing her cup in station two.

My palms began to sweat. I had always been terrible at beginning conversations with people I had not spoken to before. I was certain to be laughed at. My awkwardness and stammering would become a point of embarrassment. Hell, what was I thinking? Lucy was beautiful. I was not. Did she think I was a man or a woman? How would I even find that out? And how could I hope to compete with Devlin... unless Lucy fancied women, and thought me a woman... then why was I posing as Victor. I should have come in as Victoria. Victoria would never have opened such a disastrous trading position. Victoria thought before acting. She considered all possible consequences before plunging into any decision. Victoria was the sensible one, and Victoria did not swear... as much. Victor did not like goody-two-shoes Victoria.

Lucy picked up her dainty, pretty cup freshly filled with Chai, thanking the coffee machine for the wonderful tea.

'You are always welcome, Lucy,' the coffee machine said cheerfully.

'Hey Lucy,' I said, as I placed my cup in station four.

The machine remained silent.

'Hey, Vic,' Lucy replied, smiling. 'You look good today. Green's your colour, you know. Brings out your eyes.' She leaned into my face, and I could smell cherry lipstick on her mouth. Yum. I loved cherries. She leant in closer. 'In fact, I never noticed before how green they are.'

My jaw slackened in surprise. Well, this was a perfect start... too perfect. Did someone put her up to this? I glanced behind me to make sure Tim Potters was not there. He was the office prankster, though so far he had not done anything to me.

'Erm. Yes... green. I was born with them.' *Oh, what the hell am I saying? Confidence. Eloquence. Confidence. Eloquence.* Think of something clever to say... no, flatter her back... flirt. *Help me out here, Victor.*

Victor smiled crookedly. I had practised that particular smile in the mirror long ago, when I thought to charm a particular boy with my best smile.

It did not work. He laughed at me, called me an 'it', and flung mud at me. Later, I discovered the smile worked better on women.

'My eyes are yours if you want them,' I said to Lucy in a deep, husky voice.

Now, her jaw hung open. Her cat-like eyes widened.

'Go ahead, laugh,' I said feeling like a hundred types of idiot.

She smiled wide, then laughed. 'Vic, you are a darling. No one had ever said such an outrageous and charming thing to me in my life.'

'And what charming thing would that be?' A deep voice rumbled through me. My smile faded. My heart sank. And it was going so well. I almost had her. Now Devlin was here, overshadowing everything with his presence.

'Oh hello, Devlin. Vic was just flattering me,' Lucy said. 'We were just talking about fashion and all that. I know it's not really your cup of coffee.'

I pressed a few random flashing buttons on the machine. 'Hey, you. Machine. Where is my coffee? Black with sugar. Station four, right?'

A stream of black coffee flowed into the tray of station three. I snatched my mug and put it under the nozzle. The flow stopped immediately. Then sugar came out of station four. *Of for the love of... all that is lovable.*

'Looks like you broke it,' Devlin said smoothly and came to stand close behind me, his head bent over my shoulder looking at the machine. 'Which buttons did you press?' His soft warm breath brushed my ear, and

I forgot to breathe. For a frightening moment, I almost leant back into his heat.

'All of them,' I replied stepping sideways, away from his closeness. 'The machine refused to give me coffee. So I thought to try a manual setting.'

'How can she refuse, Vic? It's just a machine,' he chided gently. He placed his cup in station one.

'Hello, Devlin.' The sultry voice was back. 'Would you like your usual?'

'Sure thing, babe. When you are ready.'

He received a perfect cup of cappuccino, with a rose-shaped sprinkling of chocolate powder on top.

He turned to me, lifted his cup and drank. 'Seems to be working again.'

I smacked down my cup in station four again. 'Right. *Babe*. How about you do what your programming tells you to do and give me some bloody coffee.'

Steaming hot water poured into my cup. Followed by sugar.

'Please note that we no longer stock blood as an additive to coffee. As such your request cannot be fulfilled,' the machine said. 'Please refer to the trouble shooting manual for solutions.'

'You know that I can I pull a plug on you and rip out the cord,' I snapped.

'Now, now, Victor — that is who you are today, is it not?' Devlin chuckled softly. 'There is no need to be angry with the poor darling. Try being nice, hey? It's not like she can defend herself against mindless cruelty.'

I stared at him. Victor. He knew I was posing as Victor today. I hated that knowing glint in his eyes, as if he could see right through my clothes and through my skin, into my very guts.

Lucy giggled. 'Oh, Vic. You have quite an unexpected temper.'

Devlin sipped his tea. 'Please, Lucy, don't stop your discussion with Victor on my account. Just pretend I'm not here.' He leant on the counter as if he was the lord in his manor.

'That would be like pretending an elephant is not in the room,' I muttered. 'You take up far too much space.'

He smiled and I felt far too pleased with myself for amusing him. I was supposed to bring him down a peg not feed his overinflated sense of self-worth.

Lucy spoke to me. 'So, are you coming to the office party tomorrow?'

I completely forgot about that. It was Mr Ruttman's birthday, and Fred had told me that each year he hosted a champagne and cake party at the end of the day. 'It would be hard to avoid it, since its after work. I guess I could always try to sneak out and see if anyone notices.'

Lucy laughed and tapped my arm. 'Oh, Vic, you are a laugh. Fred was right about you. Said you weren't as shy as you appear.'

Why was Fred talking about me to Lucy? And speaking of the devil...

'Hey, Vic. Did not realise it was coffee time already.' Fred's voice was quite unabashedly accusing. 'Did not hear you get up.'

Lucy exchanged a look with Devlin. I hated those private, knowing looks people exchanged in your presence. Well, this was no time for stepping back and surrendering ground to Devlin.

'Oh, erm. I went to the bathroom and thought I'd grab a cupper on the way back to the desk, but the damn machine is broken.'

'What's wrong with her?' Fred shoved past me as if racing to his wounded child. I overplayed his contact and bumped into Lucy, drawing her attention from Devlin to me. I added a firm touch on her arm as if steadying her.

'Watch it, Fred, you almost knocked poor Lucy off her feet.' It was a long stretch, but it made me appear masculine and chivalrous. Victor tried to be chivalrous when he could.

Fred did not hear me. 'Machine talk to me Are you alright?' He tried to shake it, but it did not budge.

'I am well, Fred. Thank you for your concern,' the machine said happily.

'Oh, thank god for that.'

'Black and sugar today again, Fred? Or would you like the cup you might actually enjoy?'

'Ahem. Black, of course. You know me too well.' He placed his cup on station two and received a perfect, thick steaming cup of sugared coffee.' He turned to me looking relieved. 'Seems to be working fine.'

When I looked up, Devlin was watching me again. 'So, what's the occasion today, Victor?'

'It's Vic. Just Vic.'

'Is it?' He smiled mockingly. 'You look like Victor to me today. Thought maybe you had a date?'

Fred's head snapped up from his coffee. 'You have a date? I thought you weren't seeing anyone.' He sounded indignant.

'I was not... am not... not yet.'

'Yet?' Devlin raised his black, masculine eyebrows; thick and furry, they looked like they could hunt down a deer and tear it to pieces.

Lucy, too, was looking at me quizzically. The room suddenly felt crowded and stuffy. I checked my two exits either side of the galley. Devlin blocked one, Fred the other.

'It's nothing... just an acquaintance,' I blurted out.

Stop it, stop it! Don't do it!

Victor deepened the hole with his smooth lies. 'We are at the getting to know each other phase.'

Noooooo! Retreat. Take it back. Lucy will never want you now.

'So, in effect... a *date*,' Devlin pressed, his face unreadable.

'Who with?' Fred asked accusingly, looking oddly distressed.

I felt as if I had just kicked a small elf. Why the hell was he so upset about it? Maybe he hated to be the second to know. Some people were like that.

They were all looking at me, waiting for the answer. There was no way they could possibly know who I might be dating .. I sighed inside. Of course. They were not asking who but whom. Man or woman?

Lucy was looking at me with intent curiosity.

I wanted to throw myself under the bus I took to and from work each day, and then beg for it to reverse over me. 'No one you'd know,' I said evasively.

There was a collective release of breath, and disappointment. Followed by an awkward silence.

'I'd best get back to work,' I said, pouring the sugary water in my cup into the sink. 'The grass does not sell itself, you know.'

The awkward silence deepened. I guess they had all heard about my earlier trading blunder. They had all heard the alarm in Mr Ruttman's office, getting shriller as my losses reached new highs.

'Look at the time,' Devlin said. 'I've got a call with Sarah Bern from *Spot Market Analyst* in five.' He dashed out, unblocking my exit.

'Oh, yes, I'd best get back to work, too.' Lucy dashed after him.

Great. Now Lucy thought that I was dating someone else. I had almost killed my boss and probably lost the savings of all my clients. The coffee machine was sulking with me for reasons I could not understand — nor could I fathom why anyone would program a kitchen appliance to sulk — and Fred was looking at me as if I had just kicked him. Oh yes, Victor was back.

4
The Party

'So let me get this straight.' Li sat back in her lavish silk dressing gown, red wine glass in hand, watching me in that way of hers that made me feel like a fool. 'You are trying to pry the princess of your office from the prince of your office by dressing up as a... a rather camp looking knight.'

That was Li, no holding back, no soft words of comfort. She said it as she saw it.

'Women like sensitive men,' I said defensively. 'Victor had his share of interest from them.'

'What makes you think she would not prefer Victoria? Does she know which one you truly are? And don't tell me it should not matter. Men and women know what they like to bed. And it's not personality, sensitivity or your brilliant mind. It's what's between your legs. And you are most definitely not androgynous down there. Nobody likes surprises, Vic, as you well know.'

'You are right. I know you are. It's just... sometimes I hate it that they can't tell what I am. Am I supposed to announce to everyone I meet what's between my legs? One bloke in the coffee shop across the street from me calls me sir, while his co-worker calls me miss. I think they've been arguing about it for months. If I dress like Victor or Victoria it does not matter. Others then think I am transgender, and still stumble awkwardly when calling me sir or miss.'

Li waved her hand. 'You complain, but I know you enjoy being mysterious far too much.' She reclined like a queen on her velvet settee, sparkling in gems. Li only took rich, generous clients who enjoyed dressing and decorating their mistresses.

Li was from a poor migrant Chinese family. Her parents worked hard in their own restaurant, and when she grew old enough to be forced to help out, she swore she would never work as long as she lived. When I had asked her how she would manage that, she replied that she would become a mistress to the rich. Not a whore, she corrected me, but a kept woman. No different to a wife really, just richer, and with men doting on her. Mistresses, she informed me, were always treated better than wives. Why would you be a wife then?

Her logic seemed sound enough, but I had doubted she was serious. After all, at the time, I wanted to be a rock star and knew my chances of that were as slim as me suddenly discovering I was next in line to a royal title.

On her sixteenth birthday, however, Li sold her virginity to a rich businessman from Japan for the price of a flash city apartment in a building that once housed dukes. I was incredibly jealous. We snuck away from school so that she could show me around her new apartment. It was fully furnished and luxurious enough for a princess. Her parents did not know, of course. And still did not know.

Breathlessly, I had taken in the gilded architecture. 'You got all this for your virginity?' I could not believe it. 'Who the hell pays this much for virginity? Girls are giving it away in school for free.'

She snorted. 'Girls in school are fools. They do not know the market for such things.'

'How did you even find this guy?'

She shrugged. There are websites. I placed an advert. Told them the date of my sixteenth birthday, and what I wanted in return, with contracts drawn up and signed before I gave anything away. I'm too young to own property, so I put it in trust.'

I whistled. 'Bloody hell, Li. How do you know this stuff? It's a bit... erm, ugly, shagging for profit, isn't it?'

'Would you rather I gave it away for free to the first bloke who pulled down my pants?' She looked at me meaningfully.

I suddenly could not meet her eyes. 'I guess. Still, not sure if I'd be happy selling myself to some bloke I did not know. You might have been murdered, or worse.'

'Don't be silly. I had guards with me. You can hire bouncers for a few hours, you know.'

'You had sex for the first time in front of the guards?' I had asked her in amazement.

She had shrugged one shoulder. 'And two lawyers, his and my own, to make sure no one was cheated in the arrangement. Besides, it's not like they have not seen or done it before.'

I had gained a whole new respect for Li after that. She had always been mercenary, and smart to go with it. I also grew a little afraid for her. She did not know what men could be capable off when they had someone at their mercy. I did. I had told her about Lock, but it seemed she had not taken that warning to heart.

She swirled her wine now, looking thoughtful. 'Why does this guy chafe you so much, anyway, that you would go to such lengths to piss him off? Can't see it myself from all you've told me of him. No crime in being handsome, rich and well-liked.'

'I said he was arrogant, full of himself and smarmy with everyone he comes across...including the damned coffee machine!'

Li smiled. 'He really gets your hackles up, doesn't he? Maybe you should just bed him, and get him out of your system that way.'

The idea was outrageous. The image of it, however, invaded my mind. My stomach lurched sickeningly at the thought. 'No! I hate him. Why on earth would I bed him? Besides, did you not listen when I told you he fancies Lucy?'

She sighed and drank her wine. 'If you say so, Vic. Well, I'd best go to bed. Mark is taking me on his yacht later today for some function he is hosting at sea. I am to be his escort for three days. He is a sweetheart, he is.'

Yuk. 'He is sixty-five,' I reminded her, rising to my feet.

'They are the most generous, dear. Heading towards the end of their lives, they discard money like clothing. Mark told me he did not what to die rich. But he's got so many businesses and investments, it would take a lifetime to sell them all.' Her hand twiddled a ruby necklace at her throat. 'He brings me new jewellery whenever he comes to visit.'

'You are rich, Li. Why not retire? Why keep doing this?'

'Honey, I live and walk amongst the richest. Why would I retire? Who will I socialise with then? I met a prince once, you know ' She walked me to the door. 'It's a grand life where I am, Vic.'

I waved as she closed the door behind me, got on my bike, and was in work before anyone else turned up, including Mr Ruttman.

Someone must have stayed behind last night and decorated the office with tinsels and 'Happy Birthday!' signs. Oh yes, the party. My chance to flatter and impress Lucy.

But first... I raced to my desk to check my wheat account, hoping that overnight some of the losses had been reversed. With dread, I opened my trading platform. The big, ugly red number had grown bigger and uglier overnight. The wheat had continued to climb, breaking through the first resistance point, a six month high, and was happily climbing towards the next one, laughing at me all the way. *See how high I can go. If you'd only listened to Devlin's tip. That frightening figure could have been your profit. Just think of all the commission you missed out on. Now you'll have to work for years to gain back the losses and return your account to positive. You will die shrivelled and poor.*

I wondered whether it was possible for wheat to cost more than gold by next week, trading in ounces rather than tonnes.

'Hey, Vic.'

I jumped in my seat. 'Bloody hell, Fred. Can't you walk a little louder? Kick a bin or something as you enter.'

Fred was sullen. 'So, how was your date?' he asked mulishly and sat at his desk.

Hell and damnation. I forgot about my imaginary date. Only one of Victor's lies could get me out of this without making me look like an idiot. Pretending it went badly would make me look like a loser. Pretending it went well would make me look like a cad if I pursued Lucy.

'Alright, I suppose,' I hedged.

'Hmm,' he hedged in reply.

'You sound like you are in a mood today. Bad night or something?'

He huffed. I thought he was about to say something when Lucy came in. She was taking off her pink coat when she saw me watching her. I quickly looked away, then remembered I was supposed to be Victor. I looked back up and smiled crookedly. 'Morning, Lucy,' I said in a deeper voice. Today, once again, I had taken extra care to look good for her.

Fred stared at me. 'What's wrong with your voice?'

Lucy strode over. 'Hey, Vic.' She smiled sweetly. 'How was your date last night?'

I shrugged. 'Not my type. We did not click. So we parted amicably as friends.'

'Oh,' she said, while Fred stared daggers at me. 'Well, I'm sure you will find someone you like.'

Here is my chance. Don't lose it. Don't muck it up. I gave her a knowing grin. 'You know, darling, I think I just might.'

She blushed, then smiled and tucked her hair behind her ear. 'Well, I'll speak with you later, Vic.'

She retreated to her desk with a backward smile at me.

'What are you doing, Vic?' Fred hissed next to me. 'Lucy can't possibly be your type.'

Here we go again. People see one thing and think I like another thing, before they realise I am another thing who likes something completely different. 'And what type would that be, Fred?'

'You know...' The poor fool actually blushed. 'Well... not a woman, for a start. You can't fool me with your...' He waved his hand in the general direction of my body.

'Yes?' I raised my eyebrows now, wondering how he would get himself out of this pit.

'Dressing as if you might like women while ogling Devlin.'

My jaw dropped. 'I am not ogling him. I hate him!'

'Well, you were ogling my arse the first day you started.'

I heated. This was getting worse and worse. It was true, I did ogle Fred's arse. Men had rather nice arses. It was a weakness of mine, I admit. But then, women had nice breasts, and sometimes, like with Lucy's, I did tend to perhaps... umm... ogle. But then again I stared at car crashes too. It did not mean I wanted to be involved with one.

'I did not,' I lied. I was not going to admit to checking out his arse, not under any type of pain. 'I was only wondering who your tailor was.'

'I don't have a tailor! That's Devlin you are thinking of again.' Fred was growing unreasonably angry. 'We shop in the same store, remember!'

When I had told him where I shopped, it was another thing we apparently had in common.

'Look, Fred,' I said, trying to calm the angry elf. 'I don't ogle Devlin, and if I did ogle your arse, I've forgotten about it. So it couldn't have been that memorable, now could it? How about we grab some coffee, hey buddy?'

'What do you mean it was unmemorable? What's wrong with my arse?'

'Nothing... I am not getting into this with you, Fred. Now, about that coffee...'

'Oh, very well. But don't tell me you fancy Lucy.' He was adorable when he pouted, for his mouth was a little too wide for his face.

I was torn between reassuring him and having to explain why I was acting as if I did fancy Lucy. No, best to keep it to myself. Somehow, rather bizarrely, Lucy was interested in me... male me or female me, I had no idea. Either way, Devlin was likely to notice soon that Lucy was paying me more attention than she was to him. Yesterday, when I spoke to Lucy at lunch, he was watching us through Mr Ruttman's glass door. My crazy plan might actually be working. Devlin was going to learn what it was like to be unmanned.

After another spat with the coffee machine, Fred ended up sharing his coffee with me. I drank out of his cup, feeling miserable. My losses were increasing hourly. By tomorrow I might have busted my account, been sacked, and forced to sell my body to anyone who offered. Worst of all, I might not have enough time to stitch Devlin. He and Lucy would laugh and flirt and probably date as soon as I left... if they weren't doing so already.

How often does someone like Devlin have sex anyway? Probably twice a day, maybe even with the same woman... or man... no, I was certain Devlin lifted skirt. Lucy's skirt. I flushed the image out of my head with some toilet paper made from prickly jealousy. *Stop thinking about his cock in Lucy! Stop thinking about his cock! Damn Li for planting those thoughts in my head.*

'Want my cock, Vic?'

'What?' My head shot up to look at Fred.

'I said, do you want my cup?' He was holding out his cup of coffee to me again. I stared at it as if it was about to bite me. 'What's wrong with you today? Still thinking about your date last night? Or perhaps you are coming down with something?' He put a hand on my head.

I brushed it off. 'I'm fine, just lots on my mind.'

'Ah yes, the disastrous wheat spike. Who would have thought it could rise so much in one day. Well, at least there's a party to cheer you up later.' He downed the rest of his coffee. 'Want to share another cup?'

I twiddled my empty cup in my hand, thinking about my next move with Lucy. 'Maybe later.'

Later came the party. At five past five, Mr Ruttman came out of his office, wearing a cone party hat and carrying two bottles of champagne. One was suspiciously half empty. 'Where are the glasses?' he slurred loudly.

'He is drunk,' I whispered to Fred.

'Poor man gets drunk on one pint. Something to do with his heart medication being at odds with alcohol.'

'Erm. Mr Ruttman,' Paul Ellis said. 'I don't think we have glasses here. I have a coffee mug though. Would that do, Sir?'

Someone released a party popper.

'I said glasses. Sally!'

Sally came in with a tray of nibbles, small rolls of pastry, sandwiches, and mini pies. 'Yes, Mr Ruttman?'

'Where did you put the glasses for my champagne?' He raised one of the bottles.

'We never bought any. You told me that in your time people were happy enough to drink out of mugs by the roadside. And flutes were a needless extravagance.'

'Oh, right. I did say that, didn't I? Mugs it is. Well, come on then, get your drinks.' People approached him, cups in hand. 'Vic, put on some music for us.'

'Sure thing, Mr Ruttman,' I replied.

I always prided myself on my great music collection. So I turned the speakers up on my computer and found my music list. Ah yes, no one can possibly dislike hits by *Vampires Suck* rock band. Just the thing the party needs.

I turned up the volume and let it rip.

Fred looked at me in horror. *No! Turn it off*, he mimed waving his hands across his throat. There was no accounting for some tastes.

'These are great!' I mimed back over the music, and turned to the rest of the room. Everyone was looking at me as if I had just pissed on their cake. Mr Ruttman was weeping on Devlin's shoulder.

Oh, for pity's sake.' What is wrong with these people?

Lucy ran over to me, looking like a pink and white fairy darting through the forest of grey cubicles. She grabbed the computer mouse and turned off the music. She looked at me apologetically. 'Sorry Vic, but Mr Ruttman is very sensitive about *Vampires Suck*.'

I could now hear Mr Ruttman's wailing on Devlin's shoulder. 'What am I to do, Devlin, my boy. Here I am, sixty-seven this year, and my son cares nothing for me or our one-hundred-year-old firm. Four proud generations of Ruttman in the *Ruttman and Son*, and now what do I have.'

Devlin was patting him on the back. 'There, there, Mr Ruttman, I am sure your son will come about.'

'No. I only have you now.'

I looked at Fred. 'What's wrong with him?'

Fred gave me the what-were-you-thinking shake of his head. 'Not your fault, Vic, I guess you are new here. The drummer of the *Vampires Suck* band is Mr Ruttman's errant son. His only son. Poor Mr Ruttman still keeps the 'son' part of the firm name in the hope that Tom Ruttman might come back and take over the business, like he was trained to do from birth. But the boy has a face tattoo now, and a tongue stud.'

Lucy leant in to add in a whisper, 'And Tom is... ahem... rather modern in his partner tastes for Mr Ruttman's peace of mind.'

'The whole band is gay,' I said.

'Shhh!' Both Lucy and Fred shushed me urgently, looking around in case anyone overheard me. 'Don't let Mr Ruttman hear you say that. The last person to mention his son was gay was sacked the same day. The poor man is still broody for grandchildren that will never be.'

'Take me out of here, Devlin,' Mr Ruttman wailed.

'Sure thing, Sir. How about we go to the *Goat and Frog* for a nice pint of ale.'

'Oh. yes, my boy. You always know how to cheer me up.' Mr Ruttman wiped his eyes. 'Right ho! Party at the Goat everyone.'

Fred shook his head. 'Someone has to stop that man drinking and taking medications at the same time.'

We trudged outside in the sleeting rain and wind to walk a block to the pub. It was on the corner of one of the least fashionable streets in the city. The street stank of piss. The pub was warm and cosy, though. Old wooden tables and benches lined the walls.

Devlin took out his wallet and gave the barman his card. 'I'll take care of the bill.' He turned to the rest of us and winked. 'Drinks are on me today.'

Everyone cheered.

Sly bastard. Only the poor, like me, still held on to the hope that love couldn't be bought.

Mr Ruttman was back to being his cheerful drunk self again. He was sitting at the head of the long table happily telling Pips what it was like in his day, when they did not have computers, and how he had to draw his own charts each day using pencil and paper, so he could predict long-term market trends. Paul was nodding eagerly to everything he said. Tim adjusted his glasses, looking bored. Devlin returned after placing an order for drinks. He looked like he was about to come and sit next to me and Fred at the farthest end of the table from Mr Ruttman when the man waved him over.

'Come and sit next to me, my boy.' He patted the small space next to him, and everyone shuffled towards me.

Lucy sidled up to me at the end of the table. She was drinking a Rosé, her fingernails pink and perfectly shaped. I dropped my hands into my lap. My nails were mostly chewed. Fred squeezed himself into the space on the other side of me, his ale in hand. It appeared we liked the same dark ales as well, as he had been only too happy to point out while we waited for our beer to be poured at the bar.

More drinks arrived. Devlin was happily engaged in talking with Mr Ruttman. Paul Ellis was nodding to every word out of Devlin's mouth.

Two hours later, twenty pint glasses and six wine glasses sat in front of us. 'Someone should really take these away,' I slurred slightly at no one in particular.

Lucy next to me giggled. She must have been on her seventh glass of wine. 'Oh Vic, you are a funny one.' She tapped my arm for the hundredth time that evening.

'I think Lucy's had too much,' Fred slurred beside me, also patting my arm.

They definitely did not stand up to alcohol as well as I did, I thought drunkenly.

'You know, Vic,' Lucy said, as her head hit my shoulder. 'I like you.'

Yes!... No! She's drunk, you idiot. She likes everyone in sight right now.

'Sure you do, Lucy. I think it may be home time for you, my girl,' I said.

'Am I really your girl?' she asked looking up at me and fluttering her eyelashes rather prettily. Wow, she was good. That had to be a practised skill. No one can flutter like that on demand. 'Will you take me home, Vic?

Oh, hell. This was not good. If I say yes, I will seem a cad. If I say no, I will seem a cad. 'Erm, how about I catch you a cab.'

Mr Ruttman stood up and swayed. 'How shplendid, every one.' He hiccupped. 'You youngshter's...' *Hiccup, burp.* '...shtay here and party on. But an owld man like me musht get to bed.' He took a step and swayed some more.

Devlin was there, putting his arm around the old man. 'How about I get you a cab, Mr Ruttman?' Devlin sounded suspiciously sober. Had he been nursing the same pint all night?

The shhneeky shneek.

'Oh yesh, my boy. You are the son I always — *hiccup* — wanted.'

And off they went, out into the rain.

'I'd better go too,' Lucy said and stood up, unsteadily. She wrestled with her coat as she put it on, then fell into my lap when she tried to scoop up her handbag.

She giggled and wriggled.

I sighed. Right, drunk as a fish, as Li would say.

I gently pushed Lucy up to her feet. 'Come on, princess, up you go.'

She giggled. 'You think I'm your princess?'

Best make sure she gets a cab safe. 'Sure you are, why not?'

I led her out. There was no sign of Devlin or Mr Ruttman.

Lucy staggered and I gave her my arm to hook hers through. I walked to the curb and watched for passing taxis. I waved one empty cab. It ignored me. I waved another, and another. I must be hard to spot right under this bloody street lamp.

'You are so chivalrous, Vic,' Lucy slurred into my ear. 'I think I will make you some cookies.'

'Just making sure you get the cab safe, that's all.' I was suddenly uncomfortable. *What was that about cookies?*

Fear crept up my spine. Odd. Why was I suddenly afraid? My plan was working... too well. Yet something felt very wrong here. My urge to flee grew into its own small being, pulling on my sleeve, telling me urgently with its small muted mouth and hand signals something I could not quite understand. My sense of danger was never wrong. *Think. Think.* Lucy wanted me to take her home. Lucy did not strike me as the type of girl who would take you to her home for one night. My fear slowly matured into panic. She struck me as the homemaking type... *Yikes! Homemaker!* Why had I not realised it sooner?

I stared at Lucy in horror as she smiled drunkenly up at me. I did not realise until then how petite she was, a perfect doll... *who made cookies!*

I was taller than many women, about the height of an average man, so I was looking down at her. I could push the pixy away quite easily if I tried. But she looked so sweet and vulnerable. Victor would never do it. Victoria in one of her snotty moods might. But Victor actually liked Lucy, and did not want to be unkind. I began to gently untangle my arm from her, hoping not to alert her to my retreat.

'I think you might be very shy, Vic.' She swayed and gripped my imprisoned arm harder. 'It is rather shweet you know. You looking at me, when you think I'm not looking.'

'Erm, I am not sure that's...'

She let go of my arm, and threw her arms around my neck. 'Kish me, Vic.'

'Erm... I don't think that's a good idea, Lucy.' I tried to untangle her hands. But they were in a vice-like grip. Bloody hell, she was strong.

She stood on her tiptoes and pressed her lips against mine, falling forward against me as she did so, crushing her soft breasts against me. I staggered back, and my arms flew around her waist to steady her. She sighed into my mouth and began to work in earnest on my lips, which were currently frozen in surprise.

There is an odd physiological reaction to someone's mouth chewing on yours. It's the urge to chew back. I could not help myself. Honestly!

I tasted her cherry lipstick. *Yum, my favourite flavour.* I loved cherry in all its natural and unnatural forms, like smeared on the lips of a woman trying to kiss me. My tongue flicked out to taste the cherry. Her mouth opened and my tongue shot past her lips and into it.

Oh, hell. I tried to retrieve my errant tongue, but she came chasing after it with her own. *This is going to look bad tomorrow morning.* But Victor seemed to be enjoying himself far too much to pay that thought any attention.

Homemaker, Victor. Commitment. Cookies!
He startled. *Yikes!*

I tried to simultaneously push her away with my tongue, and rip my mouth from hers. Her grip on my neck grew deadlier. She was frighteningly strong for a small pixie. I pushed her harder by her shoulders, ripping her off me.

'Lucy, I think you've had way too much. I'm not certain you want this with me.'

She opened her eyes and sighed. Then giggled and leaned in to me to slur into my face. 'You are so chivalrous, Vic. I love that about you.'

This was beginning to feel more and more like a disaster of proportions that got men killed. *Looks like Victor landed himself a ladylove.* Suddenly, my plan seemed ridiculous. I did not want to date Lucy. I most certainly did not want to kiss her. And I did not want cookies!

'All right, Victor, let the lady go.'

I jumped at Devlin's hard voice behind me.

I felt a flood of relief, almost wept with it. It was quickly followed by indignation. Where the hell did he come from? And how much did he see? Oh no... I meant, oh yes! Please let him have seen our kiss. That should rile him.

Come on, Victor, don't let me down now.

I looked up at Devlin with a cocky grin. 'Do you mind, the lady and I are having a private... conversation.'

That made him scowl. He looked at me as if I had stolen a kiss from his mother; a mix of disbelief, disgust and betrayal.

Ha! Take that, Mr Perfect Devlin Knightsbridge, the lion of masculinity. Not feeling so masculine now, seeing your princess kissing me?

'Oh, Devlin, you are a darling, coming to my rescue.' Lucy tapped him on the arm. 'But there is no need, Vic is taking me home.'

Again he scowled at me. 'I think I'd better take you home, Lucy. I don't think we can trust *Victor* with a drunk lady.'

'Hey, why should she trust you?' I demanded, snatching Lucy's arm from him. 'You might take advantage of her with your... licentiousness.'

He quirked an eyebrow at me. 'Licentiousness? Where the hell did you get that about me, Vic?'

I crossed my arms and looked him up and down slowly. 'Oh, please. Look at you. No. Don't. You probably spend far too much time in front of the mirror. You hardly hide your dissolute, wanton proclivities. There you stand, oozing lust and shameless lasciviousness.'

He raised an eyebrow. 'You've been thinking about my proclivities, Victor-Victoria?' Then he smiled and crossed his arms. 'And what was I doing in my dissolute wantonness, and lusty lasciviousness... and with whom?' He smiled devilishly.

'Everyone!' I exclaimed. 'You flirt with everything that pays you the least amount of attention. Including the blasted coffee machine.'

'Are you jealous of the coffee machine, Victoria?'

'No! And don't change the subject. We are talking about your libertine ways and lecherous intentions towards poor, unguarded Lucy.'

Lucy fell forward and put her head on my shoulder, her eyes closed. 'Oh, Vic. You are so warm and tasty,' she murmured.

Devlin grabbed her arm and pulled her towards himself. 'Last I saw, it was you who was making lickerish advances towards Lucy.'

She was now happily sleeping on his shoulder, still standing up.

'Ha! I knew it. You are jealous, and now you want to get Lucy alone with you, so you can use your debauched tricks to try to make her forget that she prefers me to you. Admit it. And drunk as you are, you have no self-control over your insatiable randiness. You are probably hard as a bull now.'

Oh hell, did I say that out loud?

'I can't believe you just said that out loud, Victor,' he said with a pitying shake of his head. 'As it happens,' he continued, his voice suddenly low and angry. 'I am the only one who is sober amongst you clowns. I had only a pint all night. Now, how about you leave Lucy alone from your drunken attentions, Victor, and I will make sure she gets home safe and unmolested.'

He lifted his arm without looking away from me, and a taxi pulled up with a screech behind him, as the Universe aligned the stars to bring his every whim and want on demand. He manoeuvred Lucy into the back seat, where she curled up to sleep against the window, and got in after her, slamming the door behind him.

Then I watched them drive away, standing alone in the street, as cold rain plastered my hair to my head and seeped through every item of clothing I wore.

Thanks for offering me a lift, Arse.

I did not even have enough money for a bus fare.

I lifted up my collar and hunched my shoulders against the cold. I turned, kicked an empty bottle from under my foot, and made my way home. As I walked the cold, lonely streets, I imagined Lucy throwing herself at Devlin as soon as he got her to her door. I imagined them ripping each other's clothing and falling into bed. It was a long and miserable walk back home.

5

Victoria

I awoke drooling on my pillow. My mouth tasted like stale ale, rum... and cherry. My head, thankfully, did not hurt... as long as I did not move.

I was still wearing my clothes from last night, and they were still sodden from the rain. I rolled over. On my bedside cabinet, the rum bottle was only half empty. *Thank the stars for small mercies, I did not drink it all.*

My clock told me it was nine. Hell. I had slept through my alarm. Hopefully, Mr Ruttman was still sleeping off his own hangover and would not witness my late arrival. No, the Universe would never be that kind to me. It was too busy looking after its golden boy. I wondered if he'd spent the night with Lucy, and felt sick. Of course the randy libertine spent the night with her.

I ran to the toilet and threw up rum and half-digested dinner. *Yuk.*

After a hot shower, with plenty of scrubbing and shaving away the unwanted hairs on my body, I examined myself in the mirror. I did not look too bad considering how terrible I felt. From the pain, I had expected my head to have been cracked in two and bleeding. I scrubbed my teeth. Threw out the toothbrush, and scrubbed them again with a new one.

I went to the wardrobe and stood there for some moments thinking. Something moved in the back of my mind, some recollection trying to break through the wall of hangover fog. I remembered startling awake last night from some nightmare, covered in sweat. I rarely had nightmares. I had drunk some more rum and went back to sleep. Now what was the nightmare about? Oh yes, cookies. *Oh hell, cookies!*

'What mess did you get me into now, Victor?'

That's it. The game was finished. Either I have proven to Devlin that Lucy fancies me over him, or they had sex last night and I've lost. Either way, it was time to get rid of Victor. Hopefully, Lucy had forgotten all about those cookies she wanted to bake for me. And hopefully, she had forgotten all about our kiss last night.

It was time to bury Victor. *Sorry, buddy.*

Don't do this to me again, Vic. I can be good, I promise.

You say that every time.

I only did what you wanted me to do! He wailed pitifully as I shoved him into the dark recesses of my mind.

I sighed. Back to being the plain old hide-in-the-corner Vic again. I reached in to take a pale blue shirt...

But what if Lucy didn't forget? What if she woke up and imagined it was *I* who had kissed *her*? She'd think I'd made advances towards her. A girl like Lucy would have expectations...

Victoria! I needed Victoria. She always tidied up Victor's messes. If Lucy liked Victor, she could not possibly want Victoria. Lucy would meet Victoria, and simply realise that she had made a drunken mistake in pursuing me, laugh it off, and we would all go off into our separate office spaces.

I pulled out a lilac shirt with frills on the front and pale grey trousers with a feminine cut to them.

'Hello, Victoria,' I mumbled.

Once or twice I had worn a dress, mostly to frighten the other children at school with Victoria. I looked ridiculous. I was tempted to do it again for a lark. Then I thought of Mr Ruttman, and simply could not bring myself to kill the poor geezer from the stress this would no doubt cause him. No, best keep Victoria subtle. I only needed to put Lucy off, and make her realise that last night meant nothing between us. I was probably kidding myself, anyway. After her night with Devlin, she'd probably forgotten my name.

So I dressed in the frilly shirt, and instead of gelling my hair back, I allowed it to hang loose around my face. It had the effect of softening the harsher lines of my features. The natural curl in the tips gave me a feminine look.

Victor did not wear jewellery. Victoria loved it. I put on a few rings and a simple silver bracelet, which I sometimes liked to wear as plain old Vic. For good measure, I added rose flower cufflinks. Finally, I hung a silver chain around my neck with a compass pendant. It was a gift from Li for my sixteenth birthday. She told me it would help me find my way in life. I treasured it too much to wear it every day.

I plucked a couple of eyebrows, softened my expression, and smiled coyly. And there was Victoria. At school, Victoria wore makeup. Today, I added only a subtle touch of lipstick that I kept in my secret makeup case. I did not want Victoria to be too obvious.

I was late, so it was too late to hurry. Late was late. Fifteen minutes or one hour made no difference in my experience. The crime and censure were the same. So I decided to make myself some coffee and ease into my role as Victoria.

The kitchen was two steps along the hall from my bedroom. It was icy this morning. The type of damp cold that infuses deep into your bones and does not leave until the summer. It was mid-March, and I hankered for spring to finally arrive. I made myself some instant black coffee and sipped it slowly, looking out of the tall, leaky window. Snowflakes drifted past, turning to slush as soon as they landed.

My one-bedroom apartment might be too small to swing a hamster, as Li would say, and the noise of the main road was only overshadowed by passing trains, but it had a nice view of the old city, with its crooked buildings and enormous beams made from ancient trees. I loved the little alley shops, with their quirky little businesses, like the old-fashioned laundrette, snug ale houses and hidden, rustic restaurants. There was a rough, timeless character to this part of town. Here, I could see the ghosts of horse-drawn carriages, women with baskets of pies to sell, and pick-pocketing orphans darting through the crowds. A quaint, old world I sometimes wished was here still.

I finished my coffee and looked in my fridge. It was mostly bare. I grabbed half a sandwich left over from the day before, and while chewing it, emptied my tin jar of the last of my savings. Outside, I caught a bus into work. My bike was still at the office. Long ago, after a near-miss with a train, I made a rule to never drink drive.

On the bus, as we rolled through the business district, I stared out at the grey-suited men and women rushing to their respectable office jobs. The dizzying unreality of becoming one of them at last still struck me each morning. I was finally here, dressed respectfully, going into a fine, proper office job. And not just any job, but one where I could earn a small fortune in market trading. I was one of the elite. Maybe one day I, too, would have a gilded car, like Devlin. Except in my case, it would be a gilded bike. I smiled to myself. Ma and Pa would be proud of me now.

As we neared my stop, I reminded myself that today I was Victoria. Her voice was higher. She was coy at times, maybe a little flirtatious. She put one foot in front of the other when she walked. I had to remember to do that. Her steps were shallower and lighter. She walked slower than Victor, as if each step was a conscious choice. And most of all, she did not swear. She was the sensible one. She was also the snotty one.

As a teenager, I spent hours practising Victor and Victoria. I wanted the difference between them to be more than just the obvious dress and voice and hair. I did not want to turn myself into some type of drag queen. I did not want to pose as man or woman but *become* one. It had to be in the movement. Men moved with a certain firmness of form, a rigidity to their motion. Women were more fluid, their motions more elegant. Victor stood with his legs further apart, and his hands would rest in his pockets. Victoria's hands moved when she spoke, often drifting up to touch her necklace.

There were also subtle differences in the way their eyes roamed over the world. In their facial expressions and smiles. Victor was bold and prone to staring. Victoria watched the word from the corner of her eyes, never confrontationally. They reacted differently to the same situation. It was one of the things that freaked the other kids out the most, including Li, who knew me best of all. I practised those reactions, for they were different to my own, to Vic's. When Li had once asked me whether I was happier in the role of Victor or Victoria, I told her I was happier as simply Vic.

It was a game, a prank I played on the other kids. It freaked them out. It made them question their own sexuality. And it made them hate me even more. Some, like Li, thought it hilarious. She was always good for a laugh. I was also friends with a few boys, who admired my weirdness. Though most of them were nerds, who also found themselves on the edges of the norm, as defined by adolescents.

In those days, I had learned to hate all that was normal and decided to be as outrageous as I could. I would be different, I had decided, like every other teenager in the world. Of course, like all of them, I simply fell into a different group of sheep, where norms were merely rebranded.

Lock showed me how different I could really be. I could be one of the elite of his group, the Wild Riders. Abandoned by everyone, we answered to no one. Rules and laws did not apply to us, for as orphaned children we were cast out of society. We could do what we wanted, when we wanted it. If there was no society chastising you, there were no consequences, no guilt, no shame. Lock made us all believe that trash since we were kids. He fed and predated on it. I saw it clearly now with an adult's eyes. At the time, I worshipped him. We all did. He was our rock, someone who would never abandon us, someone who would protect us.

I regretted those days. Yet here I was, back to my old tricks. A sense of trepidation warned me this would not end well. Such masquerades never did. Just this once, I told myself, just until Lucy realised I was not really her type.

It was after ten when I arrived at the office. Sally gave me a dark look she reserved just for me and the latecomers. Mr Ruttman was in the office, watching me walk to my desk.

I dared a glance at Lucy. She was busy at her charts. Did she remember kissing me? Did Devlin make her forget? My eyes found him immediately. He was bending down to look over some figures Paul was showing him. He raised his gaze to me. Slowly, his eyes unashamedly and lewdly perused me head to foot, stripping me naked with that icy gaze of his. I heated and grew angry. Does his erection never go away? Or was he simply trying to rattle me? *Evil bastard.* His lips quirked in amusement, and he turned away to give Paul his undivided attention. I could breathe again.

'You are late today,' Fred said as soon as he saw me. 'Sleep in, did you? Heard Devlin took Lucy home last night.' He sounded far too cheerful about that.

'Was anyone else late today?' I asked, glancing at Mr Ruttman's office.

'Nope, just you. No one else would dare.'

Bloody perfect. No. Victoria would not swear.

I sat down graciously on my chair, like a woman of good breeding might, rather than plonking down like I usually do. Victoria was from a well-to-do family, with good manners.

My chart was in front of me, but I could not seem to focus on it. From the corner of my eye, I watched Devlin make his way to his office. It was next door to Mr Ruttman's. No doubt it once belonged to the son portion of the *Ruttman and Son* firm. Devlin settled at his large desk, with three big screens in front of him. There was also a plant in one corner of his room. It was the only plant in the entire office. Devlin looked serious as he bent his head down to make notes in some ledger, glancing up periodically at the screen. Hell, he looked sexy in his serious, hard-at-work-lord pose.

'Viiiic! In my office!' Mr Ruttman shouted

I was expecting it, yet I still jumped in my seat. 'Bloody hell, I'm not deaf,' I muttered.

'Good luck,' Fred whispered from the side of his mouth. 'Don't let him push you around. He is a sweetheart really.'

Once again, I sat on the edge of the chair in front of Mr Ruttman's desk, and once again he took some pink tablets before turning to speak with me.

'You are late again. That's twice this week. You are slipping. I know how it starts. You come in late, you start to arrive drunk, then you start dressing like...' His eyes took in my appearance and he turned pink, then red. He thought about it for a moment, then wrapped his fingers together. 'Now look here, Vic. I am going to give you some advice as man to...' He blinked and stared, tilting his head ever so slightly. His gaze dropped to my crotch, then quickly shot back up. 'Well, never mind that.'

I blushed. Victoria slinked away, leaving me alone to face his anger. *Coward.*

'Well, this is how it is,' he said patiently. 'I know you youngsters live in a time that is different to how it was in mine. And some of you seem to be confused about what you were born to be. It is unnatural I say, these modern-day proclivities. All laws of nature tell us that men must be men, and women must be women. There is a reason for it, you see. Survival. However, I am outgrowing the times, and there is nothing I can do to stop this degeneration of... shall we say, natural order. Now, I do not care which one you are. But if you want to keep working here, you are just going to have to pick a side and stick to it. Either be a proper man, or damn it, act a proper woman. Look at Lucy. Now she is what I would want my own daughter to be, if I'd had one. A proper lady. And Devlin! He is what my son should have been!' He pointed a finger at me. 'I will tell you this only once, Vic. Make up your mind, and then arrive here as one or the other! And be clear about it.'

I was mortified. I had to fight not to shrink into my seat. Mr Ruttman had a booming voice that carried, even when he was not shouting. I could hear the silence outside. Worse, I could hear the silence next door where Devlin sat.

I could have walked out, slammed the door, swore at him and told him to mind his own business. But I was late on my rent. And this was the first proper job I had managed to find in three years, and I was afraid my next option would be to sell my body to some pervert that Li brought over. Besides, I liked it here. For all his insulting beliefs and outdated opinions, I rather liked Mr Ruttman. I even felt sorry for the old codger, whose son wore a tongue stud instead of a neck tie. More than anything, I felt at home here. More so than I felt in my tiny, lonely flat, which I shared with an empty fridge and a small TV that did not work.

Besides, I don't think I could have stormed out or ranted even if I'd wanted to. My tongue felt like it had swelled to double its size. I did not know what to say, and even if I could have found the words, I was certain it would have come out all jumbled. So like a limp fish, I just sat there staring at him.

'You may go now,' he said. And I did.

When I left his office, the keyboards were busily clicking away as they never do at any other time. No one met my eyes. I went back to my desk and pretended to care about the wheat chart still plodding its upward course to my demise. I checked on the storm in the Indian Ocean, my one lifeline. It was still heading south, just as the forecasters had predicted.

'So, coffee time,' Fred said, as if he had not heard Mr Ruttman just tell me to work out whether I was a man or woman, and just stick to it.

'Sure, why not,' I said, and followed Fred to the kitchen.

'Hello Vic, would you like your usual; black with one sugar?' The coffee machine piped cheerfully... too cheerfully. *What was she up to now?*

'So, you are talking to me again?' I said sullenly.

'Please reply using the following commands, 'Yes' or 'No'.'

'Better do it her way, Vic. I think she is giving you another chance.' Fred nudged me in the ribs.

Poor, naive elf. This was no 'another chance'. I knew evil intent in the brewing when I heard it.

Fine, let Victoria handle her. I smiled sweetly. 'Sure honey, I'd love a cuppa,' I said cheerfully in my Victoria voice. 'It is too kind of you to offer. Now don't dally, do be a love and pour me a cup.'

I swear, the lights on the machine blinked. 'I beg your pardon.'

'No need to beg, darling, just coffee will do.'

Fred's mouth hung open. 'You are good, Vic. If trading does not work out for you, I'd recommend acting.'

'Please reply using the following commands, 'Yes' or 'No'.' The machine repeated stubbornly.

I glanced at the plug in the wall.

'Don't,' Fred whispered frantically. 'Don't do it.'

Victoria spoke up then. 'Now, darling, I am afraid you are simply not listening. You see, I have nothing but big red numbers awaiting me at the desk. In fact, I refuse to go back to face them without a shot of coffee. And I can quite happily stand here and chat away to you until you give me one of your best cups of black your little nozzles can sprout. And bear in mind, I will not move until you give me one. Not even for your darling Devlin. So, my dear, how about it? Look, I will even put the cup in station four for you, so you don't overload your precious circuit boards trying to work it all out.'

'I did not ask you to do that yet,' the machine snapped.

'Of course, you did not,' I said soothingly. 'No need to fret over it, hey darling. You see, I've been standing here for five minutes, and still you don't seem to grasp what I am saying. Perhaps if I told you the sad, long story of my childhood, and how I came to be here...'

Coffee poured into my cup, followed by a drop of sugar.

I picked up my cup, smiling. 'Aren't you a darling. You will let me know if you do want to hear that story.'

'Bugger off,' the machine replied.

'Now, now, there is no need to use inappropriate language, machine.'

Steam came out of all four nozzles.

Fred jumped back. 'Oh, well done, Vic, I think you just pissed off the coffee machine.'

'Oh, don't mind her, Fred, she is just pouting.'

Fred cautiously placed his cup in station two and jumped back again. 'Ahem, machine, do you think you could...?' Angry steam came out. 'Never mind, you take all the time you need.'

The machine poured him the coffee silently.

Ha! Know your place, serving appliance. No one pulls the high and mighty over Victoria.

Lucy came in then, all pink and smiling, her hair tied back with a pretty ribbon into a cheerful ponytail.

Oh hell, I forgot about her. In her hand, she held a small plate covered with the rose-patterned towel.

Oh hell. No, please! No!

She gave me a small smile. 'Thanks for making sure I was alright last night. I thought I'd bake you some cookies as a thank you.'

Arghhh! This is your cue, Victoria.

'Don't mention it, honey.' I waved a hand at her, then lifted the towel and took a cookie. 'Ooh, these look almost tasty. Thank you, darling, these will go great with my coffee,' I said, and bit daintily into the cookie. 'Hmm. Remind me to give you my own cookie recipe, hon.'

Fred's cup rattled. 'Oh shit!' He was looking down at his groin where he had somehow managed to spill his coffee. He tried to wipe it with a towel, then mumbling something, dashed out to the office toilet.

'Though perhaps Devlin may need the larger share of your thanks,' I said lightly to Lucy. 'Wasn't he just such a gentleman, all chivalrous taking you home alone like that.'

Too obvious, Victoria, tone it down.

Lucy looked confused for a moment, as if trying to recall. 'Oh yes. He paid for my cab home. I remember now. I should really thank him, too. But these cookies are for you.'

Had the fluorescent lights just brightened? So, she and Devlin did not spend the entire night rearranging her bed sheets with their sweaty bodies. My smiled widened until my cheeks hurt.

She suddenly blushed, very prettily, like a maiden of old. 'No need to smile so happily. They are just cookies. But I'm glad you like them.'

What? Why am I holding a plate of cookies? I quickly put them on the counter.

'Oh, and about... you know, the kiss...' she began shyly.

I waved at her. 'Don't worry about it, dear. Everyone was drunk and...'

'No, I meant... I liked it.'

Yes! Take that Devlin Knightsbridge. No! This must end.

'Erm,' I said.

Reply. Reply quickly. Anything!!! Just say something! I did not like it... except for the cherry flavour, which I loved by the way. Where do you buy your lip balm? Oh, and lets never speak of this again.

'Erm,' I repeated.

'Do you want to have a beer later?' she asked sheepishly.

No. We must realise that we both made a terrible mistake last night. I like you as a friend. You are a lovely girl, but I'm not interested in you romantically.

'Umm.'

A large predatory shadow was approaching. I felt him draw closer. I glanced sideways to see Devlin stride towards us. His slick, black hair caught in the breeze of Paul's desk fan. His hot gaze was fixed on me and Lucy. He must have seen me talking to Lucy, and thought to make his move again. Looks like the battle was not over, after all.

My attention snapped back to Lucy. 'I would love that, darling,' I said smiling pleasantly. 'Maybe you can tell me all about the latest celebrity gossip I missed out on this week. We could drink cocktails and just chat, like the best of friends?'

Tone it down, Victoria.

'Oh, I'd love to tell you all about it.'

'All about what?' The lion said in his deep, hungry voice. He was looking from me to Lucy suspiciously.

'Oh, Vic and I are going on a date today,' Lucy announced happily.

I choked on my coffee. Did I just agree to a date? I guess I must have. Though hearing it made it seem weird somehow, and wrong.

'Oh?' Devlin raised an eye brow at me, but his eyes glowed hot and angry.

Ha! He thought he would be the one to ask Lucy out. Wait, no. This was over. Well, maybe just one more rub to fluster the lion. Just to make sure he feels well and truly defeated.

I smiled benignly. 'Yes. Lucy and I are off for a few drinks.' I picked up a cookie and bit it. Then offered Devlin the plate. 'Yum. Want one? Lucy made them for me.'

He scowled. 'Fancy that, Victoria. Did not think you the cookie type. I think I will pass. Not one for cookies, myself.' He turned to the coffee machine. 'Hello, darling. Miss me?'

'Oh, Devlin, you devil, why have you kept me waiting so long?' the machine purred.

'Maybe if Lucy is agreeable, you and the coffee maker could join us for a double date?' I said and chuckled into my cup.

He looked at me over his shoulder, then his face changed to pure evil 'Sure why not, we'd love to come.'

My smile fell away. 'What?'

'I said, I accept your offer, Victoria. If that's fine with you, Luce?' And he gave her such a charming smile, men and women the world over would have agreed to anything he asked.

Lucy was not immune to it. She beamed up at Devlin. 'Oh, sure, Dev, why not? The more the merrier.' And she giggled.

'On a date?' I asked incredulously. I was certain she had lost track of what was being said.

Devlin gave me a smug smile.

'What date?' Fred came back in, his groin wet from where he had washed away the coffee.

'My date with Vic,' Lucy informed him.

His head snapped back to me. 'What! But... no!'

'And me,' Devlin said casually.

Fred now looked from one to the other of us. 'Are you having a laugh at my expense. Did Tim put you up to it?'

'Not at all, 'Devlin replied. 'Vic just invited me.' He winked at me.

I scowled back.

'Why would Vic invite you to a date with Lucy?' Fred's voice rose a notch.

Devlin shrugged. 'The more the merrier, I'm told. Maybe Victoria will invite you too if you ask.'

Fred now looked at me, his face pleading and hopeful, and I could swear his pointy ears curled in fear of rejection. 'So, can I come on this date too, Vic?'

'Oh, hell, why not.'

'Ahem, what was that Victor?' Devlin the devil said, his eyes laughing. 'Victoria does not strike me as the swearing type.'

Damn him, he was on to my ploy!

I cleared my throat. 'I said, it would be lovely if you would join us, dear,' I said in my Victoria voice and patted Fred's arm. 'Oh, yes, it would be delightful indeed.'

Fred stared at me. 'Something wrong with your voice, Vic?'

Devlin chuckled.

Lucy just sipped her coffee, watching me adoringly.

6
The Wrong Date

'When was the last time you went on a date?' Li asked. She sat back on her lounge, swirling a glass of red wine. She was dressed up for Mark in his favourite cherry-red gown and a ruby necklace.

I did not want to answer that. It was too humiliating.

'Let me guess. Alex,' she said anyway.

Li knew me too well. It was useless trying to hide my shame from her.

'Alex,' I agreed, staring up at her ceiling, sipping my wine.

'That was two years ago. You have not had sex in two years?'

At that, I looked at her. 'Of course I've had sex since then.'

'I meant with another person. You do not count,' she said dryly.

Damn her, she knew me far, far too well. 'Thinking about it, I had two dates a year ago, *after* Alex.'

'One night stands don't count as dates. You meet in the bar, chat as a formality, then have sex. In the morning, one or the other of you sneaks out. No, my friend. That is not a date. Now, this.' She ran her hand down her dress. 'This is a date. Mark is taking me to a restaurant before the theatre. He will likely make love to me before we leave. Definitely make love to me after we return, then maybe pass out in my bed for the night. After I make him coffee and breakfast in the morning, he will kiss me on the cheek, promising to see me soon, and leave for...' She frowned, then waved her hand in the air. 'Whatever it is billionaires do during the day. Now *that's* a date.'

'I don't' think Lucy and I will be making love before or after the date,' I said.

'You are kidding no one, Vic. I happen to know Lucy is not your type.'

I sighed. 'No, she is not. Nice girl, though.'

I did not like to be fussy in any aspects of my life, but in truth, I preferred men. Being shy around strangers, however, was not conducive to being approached at the bar. I would sit there, slouching, hoping not to be noticed... except by the one sexy bloke chatting away to his mates, whom I actually wanted. I wanted him to see me and approach boldly, offer me a drink and tell me he liked the shy, nervous types. Pah! Fantasyland. No one ever approached slouching wall-flowers hiding behind their drink.

So I tried a few dating sites. I posted my picture online and decided I would not be fussy about who asked me out. Any date was better than the lonely nights in my tomb-sized flat. Unfortunately, I felt self-conscious having to tell them whether I was a man or a woman. So I did not. Besides, I simply did not feel like either one or the other. I was just Vic.

A part of me wanted a man to simply look at me and know straight away, without going through the awkwardness of trying to work out what lay between my legs.

The only date I had from the dating site was a disaster. Alex was charming, attentive, handsome in his own way. He seemed comfortable with me and made me laugh with his quirky humour. We went on a few dates before he finally took me home, kissed me senseless, put his hand on my groin... then touched again, just to be certain he had not misunderstood... and freaked out.

'What the fuck! You are... you are... fuck! Why didn't you tell me? Get the fuck out!'

'I thought you knew!'

He had shouted more vile words at me as I fled. I guess I was not his type, after all. It cut deep. I had actually cried. I hated tears. I did not blame him, though. I liked Alex. It was my fault. I should have been more forthcoming. But I thought he knew. Just once I wanted someone to look at me and simply know without a doubt. In that moment, I hated being an 'it'. As Mr Ruttman had said, men were men, and women were women. If I chose neither one side nor the other, did I have the right to complain? But then, I had not chosen to be so unclear about my gender. I was born with just enough masculine and feminine features that I never had a choice about how I was perceived. My body was slender, yet lacking feminine curves. A strong jaw dominated my face. I was tall for a woman, average for a man. I was a perfect androgyne in appearance.

I never saw Alex again. It took me a while to return to the dating scene in bars and night clubs. This time, however, I pretended to be confident and open to attention. Women and men approached me. More women than men, in truth. I became Victor for a while. Victor did not care what people thought of him. Victor was adventurous. Victor liked women.

After a year of celibacy, I decided not to be fussy and took a woman home. It left me unsatisfied, and miserable. Some nights later, I shagged a man in the toilet cubicle of a nightclub. It was sordid, hollow, and in the end, depressing. That night I discovered I wanted more than just sex. I wanted to have a laugh together and share breakfast. I wanted... hell, I was not certain what exactly I wanted. I guess I wanted what my mother and father once had together.

I drank more of the nerve-fortifying wine, thinking of my coming date with Lucy. I was dressed as Victoria, in purple velvet trousers, frilly white shirt, and broad-heeled boots. As Vic, I also liked frilly sleeves and collars, and bright colours. And since I left the Wild Riders, I discovered a liking for jewellery. I did not think in terms of dressing to display or hide my gender. Nor did I dress to make a statement. I simply wore what I liked. Sometimes it was labelled women's clothing, sometimes men's. I shopped in both departments.

The door bell rang and Li bound to her feet. 'Mark is here. You better go to your own date, Vic. I won't let you hide here all night.'

I was already on my feet. She accompanied me to the door. Outside stood a grey-haired, trim man holding a fine silver cane, grinning like a besotted fool. He ignored me, his eyes running down Li appreciatively. 'You look dashing, my dear.' He stepped in as I stepped out. The door closed behind me.

'Come here, my little oriental Lilly,' he growled behind the door.

'Oh, you randy old rascal,' Li laughed.

I pulled out my wallet. Not enough money for both the cab and the beers. So I caught the bus. It was late, so I was late arriving at the *Dish and Dirty Cloth*; a cosy little tavern which served good, honest pub food of pies and chips. There were fifteen different types of pies on their menu, involving every common animal and bird, and combination thereof.

The bar was full. Every table was taken and groups of people were blocking the walkways.

My eyes quickly found Lucy, happily chatting away to Devlin, cosily tucked away in the booth in the corner. My ire rose. This was my damned date, not his. Never mind that I wanted to end it with Lucy before it got out of hand. And where was Fred? He should have been chaperoning them until I arrived.

Lucy's glass of wine was running empty, and so was Devlin's pint. I could see his hand reaching for his wallet in his inner jacket pocket. But Lucy was saying something to him and he could not leave without appearing rude. This was my chance. Neither of them had seen me. I weaved through the crowd to the bar, pushed in surreptitiously behind a man chatting up a woman next to him, and ordered before he realised the barman was addressing him.

'A pint of *Evil Dick* and a glass of rosé,' I said quickly, keeping an eye on Devlin, who was now making his way to the bar.

I threw a banknote at the barman, and without waiting for my change, grabbed the glasses. Ducking my head, I made my way the long way round, keeping the crowd between me and Devlin.

I slid next to Lucy into the spot occupied by Devlin a moment ago. It was still disturbingly warm.

'Sorry I am late, honey,' I said smoothly, sliding a glass of rosé to her. 'The queue at the bar was simply terrible.'

'Oh, hello, Vic. I'm glad you made it.'

'Wouldn't miss it, Luce. Now, why don't you tell me all about yourself? We've never had a chance to talk, and I always wanted to know all about you.' That always got the women talking, and it took the effort of making conversation away from me. I only needed to nod and ask pertinent questions now and again.

'You did?' Her eyes grew wide with happiness.

Oh, hell. Well done, Victoria. 'Of course. I like to know everything about all my friends.'

And so Lucy told me everything about herself. Her happy childhood. Her well-to-do parents. At school, she was popular and named the most beautiful girl in school five years running. She did some modelling work after university.

'Well, you have the face for it,' I said distantly, nodding away whilst watching Devlin's back. There were two layers of bodies between him and the bar. I grinned. The man did not know how to push in. Or was too polite to do so.

'That's not the type of modelling we are talking about here, Vic,' she said sternly. 'Aren't you listening to me? I was talking about computer modelling work on the economic effects of increasing import tariffs, specifically in relation to the Gross Domestic Product forecasts for the next ten years.'

That got my attention. 'I thought you said you were a beauty queen at school,' I said lamely, stupidly. That was my problem, when put on the spot some rubbish would roll out of my mouth and land like a lead weight into the silence.

'What has that to do with GDP?' she asked, confused.

'I really don't know. Anyhow. After you did the modelling work...' I prompted quickly, hoping to recover my ground.

'Oh yes. I went on to write a thesis on the economic benefits of the artificial trade war with China, while simultaneously encouraging consumer spending with targeted incentives. I believe the government has finally decided to implement the strategies in my thesis.'

'You sound like you have an interest in economics,' I said in what unfortunately came out as a resentful voice. Who was this cookie-making, giggling economist before me?

'It was my degree, Vic. And as I said, I've always had a passion for economics and markets, which is why I work for Mr Ruttman. He went to school with my father. I think they wanted me and his son to get hitched at one time. Well, that was never going to happen, now was it?'

I frowned. 'I thought you liked fashion and celebrity gossip.'

'I have more than two interests, Vic,' she said slowly, as if explaining to a child. 'I am an educated woman, you know. I also happened to like the series, *How I Got Away With Cold-Blooded Murder*.'

I blinked. Then tilted my head, squinting, defocusing her edges. Try as I might, I could not quite grasp the kind of person she was. Was she some genius with a crazy streak who laughed at the world with her feminine facade, or an educated cookie-baking homemaker, with a crazy streak.

She leant in. 'Do you have something in your eye? Here, let me see.'

'No, I am fine.' I waved her away.

Devlin was now ordering. Hell, he was going to hijack this 'date' when he returned.

'I was thinking,' I said abruptly, grabbing the first malformed plan in my head. 'How would you like to go to... erm...' *Think quickly. Where do people on true dates go?* '...A restaurant and a theatre?'

'Right now?'

I had to get her away from Devlin. More importantly, I had to get Lucy alone so I could tell her that there could never be anything between us.

'Yes, right now. Just you and me,' I said hurriedly, keeping an eye on Devlin as he gave a bank note of the colour I had never seen before to the barman. The till probably did not stack enough notes to break that bill. I hoped they'd give him his change in coins. I smiled to myself.

The barman frowned at the note in his hand, turned it over a few times, and was now examining what was in the till.

I stood up and grabbed Lucy's hand. 'Let's go, hon.'

'But Devlin...'

'Fred will keep him company.' I pulled her up to her feet.

'Oh sure, why not?' She giggled. 'You are full of surprises, Vic.'

Grabbing our coats and her hand bag, I pulled her towards the door. She scurried awkwardly behind me in her tight skirt and high heels.

At the door, I could not help myself, I looked back.

Devlin was standing at the table two drinks in hand, looking thoroughly flummoxed. Another couple had already taken our abandoned seats. I chuckled.

He looked around and saw me. I pushed Lucy through the door, winked at him, and darted out just as his face turned thunderous.

'Come along, Lucy.' I dragged her by the hand towards the cab that just pulled up. A couple was getting out one side, while Lucy and I got in the other.

'Where to, ladies?' the driver asked.

'Can't get this belt to work,' Lucy said looking down at the seat belt clip.

'Just drive!' I shouted, as Devlin burst through the door onto the street. His cold blue eyes fell on the cab, and he strode towards us like some angel of vengeance hungry for blood.

Oh hell. 'Drive!' I shouted at the driver. 'That man wants to kill us!'

The driver did not need any more prompting than that. He pressed his foot down and screeched into the traffic. A horn sounded behind us.

'What man?' Lucy asked curiously, looking outside her window.

'Oh, just some thief,' I said, secretly sighing with relief.

Well, that was close. The man was frightening when he was furious. I grinned and settled back into my seat. I was finally alone with Lucy. Now we could go to... My heart plummeted into my stomach. How the hell was I going to pay for a restaurant and a theatre?

'Stop here!' I shouted before the meter added another zero to our fare.

The taxi screeched to a stop. We got out into the street in Chinatown, not far from where Li lived. The cab took the last of my money. I was officially broke, with not a penny to my name, and stranded in the heart of the city.

'Oh, the *Angry Dragon*!' Lucy pointed at the restaurant in front of us, and I knew this was the Universe's punishment for stealing Devlin's woman and doing a runner on him. 'I always wanted to go there. The president of China dined there once.'

Just my luck. That was the restaurant Li's parents owned. It also just happened to be the most expensive restaurant in the city. In the last ten years, it had become the most iconic Chinese restaurant outside of China. I had tasted every dish on the menu, having spent many of my evenings there with Li when we were kids, doing our homework in the office room next to the kitchen. Later, when I was older, I worked there every evening, trying to save up enough money to buy my bike.

'You have to book three months in advance to dine there,' I said, shaking my head sadly. 'How about we try that one over there. The *Old Dragon* does the best dumplings in Chinatown.'

Outside of the Angry Dragon, *of course.* And the owner there knew me well enough to give me a meal on credit.

Lucy looked across the street to a darkened restaurant with no one inside. 'It looks closed,' she said.

'It's just quiet... at this time of the day.'

She checked her watch. 'It's seven-thirty. And there is a homeless man sleeping against the door. No, let's ask in the *Angry Dragon* if they have a table. You never know, we might get lucky. Devlin told me the food there is superb. He took some woman named Francesca there.'

Of course, he did. A meal there cost more than my bike. He probably just pulled out gold bars from his pocket to pay for it.

'Who's Francesca?' I asked.

Lucy shrugged. 'Some woman who lives with him. He only mentions her in passing. And I never remember what he tells me. He is so dull.'

Her words hit me deep in the gut. Devlin was living with some woman named Francesca? He was in a relationship? Of course, he was. There was, no doubt, a queue of women waiting their turn to date him.

'Maybe she is his sister?'

Did I just say that in a pathetically hopeful voice?

'Oh no, he does not have a sister. Just Francesca. I think he had a brother once, but he died.'

I felt oddly hollow and miserable. He was living with Francesca. Then why the hell was he so keen to pursue Lucy? Or was he? He flirted with everything and winked at everyone. Did I imagine his interest in Lucy?

Lucy pulled me by the hand. I followed mindlessly.

Did I get all this terribly wrong? Was Devlin simply flirting with Lucy as he flirted with the coffee machine? This meant he would not care whether I dated Lucy or not. He would not care whether Lucy rejected him. He had the gorgeous Francesca at home, whom he took to the most exclusive restaurants in the city. I had never seen her but, of course, she would be gorgeous, a proper bikini model, rather than an economic modeller like Lucy. A sickness of sorts settled in my stomach.

We walked up three steps and Lucy suddenly pulled me through the double doors marked with a giant dragon, and into the warm bowels of the *Angry Dragon*.

Wait... no!

'Erm, Lucy...' I began.

But it was already too late. Bob, the maître d', had seen me and beamed. 'Vic! You come back! It is good to see you!'

He was dressed in crisp starched whites and black trousers, and shoes so shiny I could see my reflection in them. Bob's real name was Jing, but he liked Bob for some strange reason. It seemed to amuse him.

'Hey, Bob,' I said miserably. Bob was always good for a pat on the shoulder and the 'there, there Vic, all will be well'.

'I know this is probably very hopeful of me,' Lucy said with a pretty begging tone and a fluttering of eyelashes at Bob. 'But you don't suppose you have a spare table for us?'

I shook my head urgently behind Lucy, miming 'no table, no table.' I waved my hands to emphasise, 'no table'.

But Bob only smiled and nodded. 'Of course! We always have a table for our friend Vic. Come, come, I will show you to the best table in the restaurant. It overlooks the stars and the river.'

By the 'stars', Bob meant the lights from the skyscrapers across the river.

Lucy was gaping at me. She snapped shut her jaw and hit me playfully on my arm. 'Shame on you, Vic, pretending that you needed a reservation here.'

I thought I did. I had no idea that being friends with the boss' daughter when we were kids, and later washing dishes in the kitchen, automatically gave me a table whenever I wanted it. Or perhaps Bob was simply having a laugh at my expense. Pranks such as bankrupting someone would amuse him greatly.

'Um, Bob? Honestly, I don't want to put you out.' I was begging now. 'I'm certain you are fully booked, like always. And I am sure Lucy would not want to inconvenience some celebrity who has booked a table three months ahead, only to find at the last minute that they have lost it to a little nobody like me.'

Please let Lucy feel guilty and back me on this.

Her eyes lit up. 'Oh course, I want this! Whose table do you think we are stealing?'

Bob turned around, solemn and very proper, like some English butler. 'The lead singer of the *Vampires Suck* band, and his... ahem, special friend Tom the drummer. But worry not, we will reschedule for them, or perhaps they might wait. We will give them the best champagne on the house.'

My stomach grew even more unsettled. The best champagne here cost more than my monthly wage. I hoped they were not thinking of recouping the costs from me, as per their usual tradition of settling a table theft.

As Bob led us through the crowded restaurant, I noticed Li and Mark at another table. Li was laughing as his wrinkled hands fed her pieces of fruit from his plate. Li then fed Mark back with some morsels from her plate. She looked like she was truly enjoying herself, whilst I plodded along behind Lucy like a sulky adolescent. I was definitely on the wrong date.

Bob gave us the best window seat, overlooking the river and the city.

'And may I offer you something to drink, maybe a glass of champagne, while you peruse the menus?'

I quickly grabbed the wine list before he suggested something 'special'. I opened it and could not breathe for a moment. The numbers next to the French dialect were of the magnitude I would never associate with food or drink. The numbers swam before my eyes. Lucy smiled at me expectantly. I began to sweat.

The cheapest was always at the top. My eyes shot up to the top line. Was I seeing double? I rubbed my eyes. It did not help. The price of one glass still cost more than the most expensive bottle of wine I had ever bought.

'Two glasses of... Lavez-Vous... La...' I tried to read the French name.

'*Lavez-Vous la Bouche Avec Cette Boisson Avant D'essayer de la Vraie Champagne,*' Bob said in perfect French. 'A very good choice. Except, may I recommend a slightly better vintage...'

'No! I mean, no thank you, Bob. *Laves-Vous la Bouche* will do.'

Bob's face was impassive. He bowed slightly in the waiter-style, took the list and went away.

'Just two glasses, Bob, not the whole bottle,' I shouted after him.

At the table next to ours, a matron of middle years wearing jewellery designed for queens, tsk-tsked at my poor manners.

Victoria snorted in their direction and looked away haughtily.

Lucy was looking at me moon-eyed. 'I never realised you were so well known in such high circles. You must be very rich to dine in a place like this often enough that they would give you *Vampires Suck's* table. You are a true mystery. Why don't you tell me all about yourself?'

Oh, hell. Women loved mysteries. Devlin might be living with some woman named Francesca, and this game might be pointless, but I still had my pride. I was not going to tell her I used to work here, rather than dine here.

'Ahem, yes, well. I don't like to talk about myself.' Which was true. I hated it when people asked me personal questions. It always felt as if they were trying to undress me by slowly peeling away one layer of dirty clothing at a time.

Bob returned then with a bucket of ice and a bottle of champagne.

'I said two glasses,' I hissed at him.

He smiled and nodded. 'Yes, a bottle and two glasses. I understand, Vic. I do exactly as you ask.'

And now I knew for certain that he was playing one of his pranks on me. Before I could object, he quickly poured the glasses for us, put the bottle in the ice bucket and rushed away.

Hell. That bottle alone would take my weekly wage off me. I sighed and downed the glass.

Lucy was perusing her menu with intent interest and excitement. I dreaded even opening the menu in front of me. However, overtaken by curiosity as to how much I was going to owe the restaurant, while I ran away to a new life on another continent, I lifted the leather cover to peer at the starters. I felt instantly dizzy. The starters were the price of my average weekly food shop. The mains were the price of my weekly rent. Worst of all, I was not even hungry... no, the worst was that I did not even want to be on this date. I should have just left Lucy at the bar with Devlin. I wondered whether he was home now, making love to his gorgeous Francesca.

'This all looks so delicious, I simply cannot decide,' Lucy said.

I downed another glass of champagne. 'Take your time, dear,' I said in my Victoria voice.

Bob came over again, and Lucy cheerfully recited an order to him. It seemed to take an eternity. How much could a pixie eat? It included the starters of duck liver purée and lobster entrees, followed by shark fin soup and bread, and sides of vegetable and flower petal salads to go with her main.

Bob turned his smile on me. 'And what would you like today, Vic?'

I wanted to ask only for water... tap water. Instead, I picked the three cheapest dishes on the menu and gave Bob an evil eye that promised retribution. He bowed, smiling smugly, and went away, his shoulders shaking with his ill-concealed chuckling.

An awkward silence followed. Lucy was looking at me expectantly, waiting for me to tell her all about my ugly life.

'More champagne?' I said quickly and poured full glasses for both of us.

I fidgeted in my seat, itching with indifference and boredom. I was uncomfortably warm and my shirt was sticking to my back. Lucy began talking about things she'd read recently in celebrity gossip columns. I listened with one ear, smiling and nodding, and occasionally asking pertinent questions. In the distance, Mark laughed at something Li was saying. I suddenly wished I was sitting closer to their table where I could listen in. Li was always fun to be around.

Lucy suddenly leant in and whispered. 'Don't look now, Vic, the lead singer of *Vampires Suck* and Mr Ruttman's errant son have just come in. They are looking our way, and they look pretty angry.'

Good. I hope Bob gets a full-blown unhappy customer tantrum.

'Are they shouting at Bob?' I asked hopefully.

'No... No, they are smiling and nodding. Bob is showing them a bottle of champagne. They are heading for the bar. Oh, look, they are waving to us and thanking us! I think Tom recognised me.' Lucy waved back.

I wanted to bang my head against the table. Looked like their complimentary bottle was on me after all.

Our meal arrived. Tiny portions on very large plates decorated with colourful sauces, strange smelling herbs and bright orchid flowers. The whole meal felt like a starter. Thankfully, I had no appetite, else I'd still be ravenously hungry.

Lucy had colourful morsels of dessert I could not identify. I decided I was not drunk enough to face the bill yet, and fortified myself with sherry. Victoria drank sherry. She thought it a proper lady's drink. Victor hated it. He was a bourbon man. I preferred a good scotch whisky myself.

Then came the moment I had been dreading, and I was still far too sober for it. Bob was coming towards us, a spring in his step, and a black wallet in his hand, holding my prison sentence on a single sheet of bill-sized paper. The whole world slowed. He placed the black wallet on the table in front of me, asking from far away whether we enjoyed our meal.

'Yes, everything was perfect,' I replied from far away. *You evil bastard.* 'Thank the chef for me.' *I will get you back for this, Bob.*

Then Lucy reached across, and for an instant, I thought I was saved. She placed her hand on my arm. 'Thank you so much, Vic. This was the best meal of my life. It was so kind of you to treat me and make me feel so special. I will be sure to bake you more cookies.'

I managed a strangely serene smile. 'Anything for you, honey.'

Victoria stood up gracefully and took the bill to the till. I did not bother to look at it. The numbers might cause a seizure. I could not pay it anyway. Hell, I could not pay my bus fare home.

Bob crossed his arms when he saw my face. 'Let me guess, you thought to take advantage of our friendship, and treat your lady friend to a free meal. Well, it won't do, Vic. You will pay or else you will work to pay.'

I sighed and held out the bill to him. 'I will work to pay for this. You've got a good one on me this time, Bob.'

He chuckled. 'Didn't I?' His smile ended abruptly. 'That was for the soup you and Li poured over my head as a prank.'

'That was ten years ago! We were children.' With only the greatest force of will and rather impressive muscle restraint did I manage to stop a smile from escaping my lips.

'No excuses. You thought it was funny. Admit it.'

I held my features stony and grave. 'I don't remember.' *It was hilarious.*

'But Bob never forgets. Bob gets his own back.' He nodded proudly and shoved the bill into his pocket. 'You can start tomorrow evening in the kitchen. And you will work every day until you pay it off.'

'Every other day,' I said.

'OK, but also the weekends.'

'Fine. Weekends too,' I said resigned.

I looked around. Li and Mark were long gone. Maybe Li had the right of it. Say what you might about the old man, he looked like an entertaining dinner companion. He was not too bad looking either, for an old man.

I went back to Lucy and pulled on my coat.

'So, the theatre next?' she asked, brightly.

I suddenly remembered why I did not date. It was too bloody expensive and tiring. I was ready for bed, and not in a vigorous sort of way either. Just curl up and sleep sort of way. 'It's quite late. We've missed the shows, I am afraid. Dinner was so enjoyable, I lost track of time,' I lied brazenly. Never before had two hours dragged like two days.

'So what's next, then?' Lucy asked, wrapping her pale pink scarf around her neck.

I was broke. My wallet was limp in my pocket, and I had a long walk back home. I yawned and stretched. 'It's been a long day. I'd best go home and sleep. Last thing I want is Mr Ruttman sacking me for being late again.'

'Oh.' She sounded disappointed. 'Right, sure, Vic. Well, it was such fun today.'

We went outside. I put her into the cab, and as she moved over to let me get in, I said quickly, 'Well, see you tomorrow then,' and closed the door. I waved cheerfully, turned and walked away.

It took me over an hour to get home, and plenty of time to think of how I was once again screwing up everything in my life.

Victoria failed me, just like Victor. Devlin was living with another woman, and there I was trying to make him jealous. And Lucy still planned on baking me cookies, while I had no interest in eating them. I was certain I had bankrupted my client portfolio, and perhaps the firm. And, as if I did not have enough to worry about, for the next month or two, I was going to have to work in the kitchens of the *Angry Dragon*.

It was time to kill Victor and Victoria for good. Never again would I resurrect them. From now on, I would work quietly, stay out of trouble, recover my losses on the wheat futures, and think no more of Devlin or Lucy. Ever. I would simply be the quiet, sensible Vic no one noticed... but for the curious quirk of nature that made people stare and wonder; *is Vic Victor or Victoria?*

7

The Question of Femininity

Femininity was beautiful. Not just in women, but also in men. Lucy was the gem of femininity. I respected her for it, admired her even. I just did not fancy her for it.

Today, my plan was clear. I was going to politely decline Lucy's cookies and explain that I simply did not like her that way. I would do it gently, privately, maybe during the first coffee break. No more Victor or Victoria. I would have to do it myself. Today I was back to being just Vic.

When I arrived at the office, Lucy was surrounded by Fred, Devlin, Paul and Sally, as she merrily recounted our entire date, start to finish, with plenty of embellishments. That was something else I forgot, the need for beauty and femininity to share itself. Apparently, my secret riches and prestige were such that the staff of the *Dangerous Dragon* bowed to me, and *Vampires Suck* band offered me their table.

She saw me and waved, calling out, 'Vic! I was just telling them about our dinner date last night. It was wonderful.' She sighed and her expression turned dreamy.

Everyone turned and stared, as if I was something freakish they had not seen before. Well, there goes my chance to slip in unobserved and bury myself in the appearance of industrious work.

Fred was looking morose again. Clearly the moody sort, I thought, one moment happy, the next miserable. I guess that was just Fred.

I waved back politely, and lowering my head, quickly walked past the grey cubicles, hoping to reach my desk before Lucy could embarrass me further.

'Where are we going tonight, Vic?' she called out cheerfully. 'You promised me theatre, and I intend to keep you to it.'

Oh hell. I looked up again. They were still all looking at me. Devlin crossed his arms, leaning on Lucy's table with his hip, giving me that annoying raised eyebrow look, as if asking, *Oh really? And how are you going to pull this one off? Because you have not fooled me at all. I know your game, and you are losing. Ha! Take that Victor-Victoria.*

I had a chilling feeling he was not fooled by Lucy's recounting of our last night's meal and my riches. How much could he possibly know? His piercing gaze said, *Everything. I know everything, Vic. You can't hide from me. I can read your cringing mind, and see your soul squirming under my gaze.*

I shuddered.

'Erm,' I said. 'I... umm... have something tonight... a prior engagement...'

Devlin's eyebrow rose higher. Fred's jaw dropped in disbelief, and I realised how that must have sounded.

Lucy's smile wilted. 'You have another date? Oh Vic, how could you cheat on me like that.'

'No! Not a date...' Wait, how the hell could I cheat on her when we had one date and it was a disaster... at least from my end? 'I am not cheating on you...' That did not come out right either. 'I meant to say I would not...' *No, that is not what you meant to say, Vic. What you meant to say, is, 'there is nothing between us, so how could I possibly cheat on you?'*

She brightened again. 'Oh, I am glad. I thought that was what you meant. Perhaps we could go tomorrow then, and you can tell me all about your mysterious engagement tonight.'

They would have to pull out my fingernails before I confessed to having to work off the meal from last night.

'Erm, how about we talk about this later, Lucy? Maybe privately?' I ducked into my cubicle, hiding behind my screen. *Hold it together, Vic. They will lose interest as soon as nine kicks in... and why is Devlin here before nine? And why do I care?*

Fred sat down behind me. He was silent for a while, his mouse button clicking in that repetitive, regular rhythm of restless fingers waiting for the mind to return to work.

'Lucy tells me your date went well,' he said abruptly. 'When I came to the pub last night, Dev told me you and Luce did a runner on him.' Fred sounded peeved. 'I thought we were going to have a drink together. I thought this was meant to be a date for all of us.'

That is way too creepy, Fred.

'Lucy wanted to be alone with me,' I said, and cleared my throat from the lie lodging in it.

'Lucy said you are rich,' Fred continued, trying for a lighter tone. 'Fancy that. Never took you for a secret Midas, myself. Guess there is much we don't know about each other, hey Vic.'

'I guess,' I said noncommittally, staring at the wheat price. Having shot past the all-time high, the price had now levelled off into its usual flatline. Well, at least it plateaued before the firm had been bankrupted by my outrageous losses.

'Want to go for a beer then? You know, to catch up on everything we don't know about each other.'

'Erm, I'm not the catching up type of person. You know that, Fred. Besides, we work together. We can catch up any time in the office.'

The wheat price marched on, straight ahead, neither up nor down. *Drop, damn you, drop.*

'But I thought we were friends, and friends go out for drinks together,' Fred said in his kicked-elf voice.

'I suppose,' I said. I forgot about things friends did together. Li was too busy with her whirlpool of champagne-for-breakfast lifestyle to go out with me like we used to. And I guess Fred was a friend. So why not? 'Maybe next week, hey Fred?' I promised.

There was a dull clinking sound of spoon on cup. 'Right, everyone,' Mr Ruttman boomed. 'Before we start work this morning, I have an announcement.' Everyone turned. Devlin stood next to him, looking like a king being announced in court.

'What now?' I murmured to myself.

'Can't you guess?' Fred whispered. 'Mr Ruttman's been building up to this for years.'

Mr Ruttman cleared his throat. 'I would like to announce a new partner in the *Ruttman and Son*.

Devlin and I spoke long and hard about it, and I have accepted his offer to purchase a substantial amount of shares in my firm. From today, we will be known as *Ruttman and Knightsbridge.*'

A round of applause and cheers went up. I could not bring myself to clap. Once again, the Universe realigned the celestial bodies to make the golden boy shine even brighter.

Devlin was looking at me. But not in a satisfied sort of way. Just looking. I had no idea what was going through his mind. Maybe he did see me as a rival for Lucy's affections, after all. Maybe he and Francesca came to a 'natural' end of their relationship, no doubt due to Devlin's propensity to flirt with everything that moved. Maybe my interest in Lucy, and more importantly her obvious interest in me, had forced his hand, and he'd dumped his live-in lover. Hell, maybe Lucy was using me to make Devlin jealous so he'd do just that. Was that even possible? Lucy did not strike me as the type to play someone like that. She was... nice. Either way, I could not compete with a partner of a trading firm. I suddenly found I did not even want to try. If Devlin wanted Lucy, he could have her. He wins, I thought morosely.

I was not sure how I felt about Devlin's elevation. For some reason, it made me feel inadequate. Trying to teach Devlin humility suddenly felt as laughable as trying to teach that lesson to a god. Mere puny humans like me would get smitten trying.

Mr Ruttman patted Devlin on the shoulder. 'How about a few words, my boy?'

'Thank you, Sir. As you know, I love this firm. I have worked here for the last four years. They have not been easy years. We have seen many ups and downs...'

Ha! Only ups for you, I'd bet.

'But we have always been a small family here, thanks to Mr Ruttman and his generosity towards his people.'

Ha! That's why I have to work in a kitchen to pay off a meal. Alright, it was a very, very expensive meal only the rulers of wealthy countries could afford, but even so.

'And I am honoured beyond words by Mr Ruttman's trust in me. I hope never to disappoint him, and I hope most of all not to disappoint any of you. Our firm has risen a long way to become one of the most respected in the city...'

Something painful and sickly churned in my stomach. He sounded so sincere, so humble. He looked so gorgeous standing there, all serious, his suit crisp, his hair dashing black, his eyes strikingly blue and intense.

Don't look down, Vic, don't drop your eyes to his crotch... oh hell, yes, a lump... and swelling? Good god, did it just move? Maybe he keeps a pet ferret in his pocket.

'... and I can assure you, I will do everything in my power to make it rise further under the close gaze of...'

What? My eyes flew to his face. He was still delivering his speech, but he was looking at me again. *Oh, no. Did he see me looking at his groin? No, he is too far away. No, don't turn red, Vic! Or he will know for certain. Oh hell.*

'... the trading community,' he finished.

More cheers and applause. Someone shouted, 'Way to go, Dev! Knew you would be partner one day.'

Everyone gathered around him. Patting him on the back, shaking his hand. Sally gave him a kiss on the cheek. Followed by another one from Lucy. I turned away, feeling oddly hollow and depressed.

'Vic! I want a word in my office,' Mr Ruttman shouted.

I sighed. Of course, he did. There was a natural balance in the universe. For every good deed, there was bad. For every rise, there was a fall. I was Devlin's other universal half. For each of his successes, I had been dished out failures in equal proportions. Well, enjoy your rise, Mr Perfect. I might have failed to humble you, but the Universe will not be so generous to you forever.

Hell, it probably will. I sagged in defeat and entered Mr Ruttman's office.

Mr Ruttman bade me sit down. He steepled his fingers. 'I will come right to the point, Vic.'

Oh, good. Just get the kicking over with.

'Your accounts are a shambles. Devlin will be reviewing them more closely. We have never before had such astronomical losses on our books. If not for Devlin, I would have lost the firm on them. Thank my lucky stars I have Devlin. He has put up the profits from his own accounts to offset your losses. We may be forced to close off your disastrous position, and simply take the hit. Devlin told me he will review all the information, and let me know what he thinks.'

'Yes, Sir. I understand,' I said lamely.

'And I am placing trading restrictions on your portfolio. You will not be able to invest more than a tenth of its value at any one time. It will cut down on possible commission, but it will protect the firm against reckless trading.'

Perfect, just what I needed.

He waved me away and I left silently.

Devlin popped his head out of his office as soon as I closed Mr Ruttman's door. 'Vic. A word with you.'

Oh, here we go. More kicks. And now, he has a perfect chance for revenge on my stunt last night. Fine. Let him gloat and scold, and call me all manner of idiot for selling wheat when I should have been buying. And chastising me for ignoring his Midas tip. I could have been rich by now, instead of broke and working off my meal in the kitchens of the *Angry Dragon*.

'Take a seat.' He patted the back of the chair facing his desk.

I sat down, feeling worse and worse by the minute, while my whole body was buzzing with some energy I could not understand. My stomach was fluttering, and I could not look at him without the fluttering increasing. This, at least, I could recognise as the acute anxiety that would tie up my tongue.

He sat behind his desk, then rose again. 'Sorry, do you want coffee first?'

I shook my head. 'Just get this over with.'

He sat back down. 'This is not an execution, Vic. I just wanted to have your take on the wheat portfolio.

No one knows it better than you, and Mr Ruttman has asked me to look into it. So I thought I'd simply consult with you and see what you think we should do with it.'

I stared at him, waiting for him to start laughing. But he remained serious, waiting for me to answer. My heart bolted in my chest.

'It's losing money,' I said. 'A lot of money.'

His lips quirked in a smile. He looked dashing. 'I know that. I simply wanted to know whether you think it worthwhile holding onto your trading position, or buying back and taking a loss.'

I cleared my throat and shifted in my seat. 'Hold on to it.'

Devlin sat back in his plush, leather chair, looking completely at home. 'And why would you think that?'

Why would he care what I thought? He knew the markets inside out. He already knew what should be done, I was certain. The man could not become this stinking rich and successful by not knowing. This must be some kind of test to see whether I was actually aware of the markets, rather than randomly choosing between two buttons on my screen, like a monkey with a keyboard.

I sighed. This must be the Universe teaching me my own lesson in humility. Maybe I deserved it. Well, there was no escaping this unless I wanted to throw my job in his face. I could not do that. I needed this job. It was clean and respectable, and in the heart of the city, where I could wear suits every day. I did not want to let it go. So I humbled myself to tell him what he already knew.

'China's own wheat production is strong,' I said dully. 'They have full stores of it. I think the announcement was meant to drive up the wheat prices so they could sell their own stock high, or perhaps they simply overestimated their national demand in the years to come. Either way, this morning their agriculture minister has been sacked, and the new minister will review their contracts over the weekend, before they are signed. I think they have overcommitted, and they know it. There is also that storm in the Indian Ocean. It's growing larger, turning into a cyclone.'

'Yes, I saw that. The meteorology office thinks it will head south rather than east,' he said.

I shrugged. 'Some models suggest that, yes. Others believe it will turn east. Australia's wheat fields may get a drenching by early next week. The only path for the price of wheat now is down. You might not reverse all the losses, but I think we can recoup most of them within a week.'

He nodded. 'That's all I wanted to hear. I will let Mr Ruttman know that I agree with you, and think we should keep the position open for at least another week.' He looked like he wanted to say something else, but at the last minute, firmed his lips tight.

I left his office feeling strangely sick and light at the same time.

That day I worked late. I did not want to go all the way home, only to have to go back out again to the *Angry Dragon* for my evening shift. I might as well head from here. I had never stayed late before and watched everyone leave one by one.

Lucy walked past me on her way out. 'I will see you on Monday then, Vic,' she said and kissed me on the cheek.

I was so startled I could not muster a response. Oh, damn. I completely forgot to break it off with her after my chat with Devlin. He was watching us through the glass wall now, his eyes unreadable, cold. I guess that clarified whether he was pursuing Lucy. My plan had succeeded, after all. I could not bring myself to gloat. For some reason, I was feeling the loser in this game.

Fred put on his coat soon after. 'Beer after work on Monday,' he said as he departed. 'I'm keeping you to that promise, Vic.'

'Sure, why not.' I waved him away.

Mr Ruttman left when all the cubicles were empty. He stuck his head in Devlin's door to bid him farewell. 'You work too hard, my boy. Go home to Francesca and get some rest.'

My heart sank.

'She is out with some girlfriends tonight,' Devlin replied. 'Besides, recently, it seems I can do nothing right. I hate arguing with her, so I thought I'd put some space between us for a little while.'

My heart sank further. Definitely in a relationship and pursuing Lucy. *The cheating scoundrel. Reprobate.*

'Women, hey,' Mr Ruttman said sympathetically. 'Just tell her how pretty she looks. That always works with my Barbara.'

'I think she is sick of hearing it from me,' he laughed.

Snake of a man. Swine.

Mr Ruttman did not see me as he left. A small, pitiful part of me, eager for his approval, was disappointed. I had hoped to at least raise myself a little in his estimation after my second, and utterly disastrous, week at work.

I ran my hands through my hair. *I'll do better next week*, I promised myself.

The office was dark and silent, and eerie. The presence of its occupants seemed to haunt the space long after they had left it. I felt like I'd stepped into a secret world of phantoms and echoes no one else knew about.

I passed the time reading the news and weather pertaining to wheat, and desperately trying not to be aware of every movement that Devlin made in his office. At six, I gathered my jacket and helmet and went to the elevator.

Devlin rushed up behind me, as if he was waiting for me to leave. Last one in, last one out? I did not acknowledge him. His nearness was unsettling and heady. It occurred to me that this was the first time we had ever been alone together. I became uneasy. We did not like each other, that much I knew. The tension was palpable. I suddenly found it hard to breathe.

Just ignore him, Vic. Don't say anything you might regret. He is your boss now.

'So what's your thing with Lucy?' he asked me bluntly.

I almost jumped out of my skin, as the sound of his voice snapped the taut string of silence between us.

The cad was actually jealous. I should have been thrilled, instead, I was annoyed. Living with one woman, and pursuing another. *Libertine.*

I shrugged. 'What's your interest in Lucy?'

'I just asked you that,' he retorted irritably.

The lift doors opened and we stepped in. They closed. Silence.

'Well?' he demanded.

'Why do you care?'

'Lucy's a nice girl. Don't want to see her hurt. So whatever game you are playing, end it.'

I spun on him. '*Me* playing a game? You live with one woman while pursuing another, and you are worried *I* will hurt Lucy? Does your arrogance know no bounds? Or does it sting that Lucy fancies me instead of you? Can't take a beautiful woman looking at someone else, hey Dev?'

He moved so quickly, I was still speaking when he shut me with his mouth and tongue. He slammed me against the wall of the elevator, his erection pressing into my stomach, his mouth ravenous, his tongue hot and coffee flavoured. Coffee. Yum. I sucked it. He groaned. And moved his hips to rub his hard cock against me. I sucked his tongue harder and heard the lift doors open... then close. Then reality came at me like a train.

What the hell!

I pushed him away. 'What the hell, Dev!'

His lips were swollen. He gave me an angry smile. 'Thought so. I think Lucy is just too much of a woman for you, Vic.'

'No she isn't!' I objected stupidly. My lips, still wet from his kiss, were throbbing... as were other parts I did not want to pay attention to.

Oh, sweet god, he tried to shag me in the lift. And I nearly let him!

He grew angrier, his eyes darkening. He put both his hands either side of my head on the mirror wall, glaring at me. I knew he was tall. Taller than anyone else in our office. Mr Ruttman stood to his shoulder. But until now I did not truly realise how tall and overbearing he actually was.

My fear must have shown. 'What's the matter, Vic, too much of a man for you. Is all this masculinity too frightening for you that you hide behind Lucy's skirts?'

'I do not hide behind her skirts,' I said, affronted.

'You know what I think?' He bent closer and closer until his hot breath whispered into my ear. 'I think she is far too feminine for your tastes. I think you really want me. Admit it. You are trying to make me jealous with Lucy.' He nipped my ear.

Oh hell, I wanted to collapse, to drag him closer. *Be in control, Vic, he is baiting you.* Why on earth would he think I was trying to make him jealous of Lucy?

'Ha! Nice try at trying to bait me, Dev. You are right, though. I was trying to make you jealous... of me, not her! I know you fancy her. I can see you gritting your teeth every time she comes near me. Well, she does not want you. So, Mr Perfect, you'll just have to lick your wounds, and accept that not every woman wants to fall at your feet when you wink at her.'

He looked stunned. 'What the hell does that mean? Why would you want me to be jealous of you? And why would you think I want Lucy? Why would you want me to be jealous at all?'

'Because you are an arrogant arse, Dev, that's why.' I shoved him hard in the chest. Hell and damnation, he was like an unmovable rock. He stepped back, but not from my effort. 'Because the sun rises for you, and someone should finally show you that life is not all sugar and light.'

I hit the button to open the lift door, and tried to shove past him. He grabbed my arm. 'You don't fucking know me, Vic. And you know nothing of my life. Have you even once stopped to consider that you might hurt someone with your childish games?'

He stormed away, leaving me watching his back.

Damn him! That was meant to be my indignant exit. He would not give me even that much. I strode to my bike, shoved on my helmet, and as he was pulling out of his car space, I wheel spun and swerved in front of him.

He slammed his breaks. As I raced out of the car park, I heard his belated, angry horn.

Ha! Take that, Mr Perfect.

I rode blindly, racing and swerving through the traffic. Horns sounded in my wake. I did not care. I replayed our argument, over and over. Then I replayed our kiss. I could still taste him. I no longer understood what he was, what he wanted. He had some woman named Francesca. He was pursuing Lucy. He kissed me. And I sucked his tongue like some candy. I did not even like him. No, I bloody hated him!

8
Game's End

I pulled up at the back entrance of the *Angry Dragon*. I was fuming. Worse, I was hurt. Why was I hurt? I hated Devlin, and he hated me. He thought to trick me with that kiss into betraying my apathy towards Lucy. And like an idiot, I confessed my callous ploy to wound him. He was right, I had not considered what it might mean to Lucy. I had to break it off with her. Monday. I'll do it on Monday.

'Get in here, Vic! You are late.' Mr Chen, Li's father, shouted through the open window.

The familiar smells of his cooking wafted through the air. Those comforting smells of spices that reminded me of the better parts of my orphaned years, when I had sat in the back of his kitchen doing homework with Li. Since the death of my father in a freak construction accident that left me an orphan, Mr Chen was the closest I had to a father.

'Coming, Mr Chen,' I said, as I locked my bike.

I guess I was lucky, in the way many orphaned kids weren't. I was placed with a rather nice foster family. An elderly couple with religiously driven goodwill, who were never blessed with their own brood. So they took on everyone else's abandoned ones. They were old, and there were too many of us, so they left the older ones mostly to their own devices, while they cooed and ahhed over the younger ones. As long as we were kept off the streets, and fed when we wanted to be fed, the social workers were happy enough. There were eleven of us in one giant house. Boys and girls, toddlers, and adolescents on the cusp of adulthood.

It was alright, I guess. Better than the streets. I had my own room, toys and plenty of food on the table. I was never chastised or sent to bed. I was left alone to do what I wanted. It suited me fine. Most of the time, however, I hated my housemates. They were either too young and pathetic, or too old and angry with their lot, which they expressed through hitting or fucking. I was neither too young, nor pathetic. I was one of the angry ones.

I had sex for the first time with one of the older boys when I was thirteen. Like in any society, there was a hierarchy to our group. Lock had been at the top of it. He was seventeen, a man to my eyes, good-looking, and broody. I fancied him. Many did. But I was thirteen, and he paid no attention to me. He hung out with older kids. I knew he shagged them, boys and girls. He rarely bothered to close the door when he did. I saw him at it once. I don't really know what I thought of it. It did not look pretty or pleasant. But I fancied him, and I guess I wanted him to notice me.

I had no idea how to make someone notice me, other than to make fun of them. So that's what I did. I began taunting and goading him with childish insults. Lock cuffed me on the ears a few times, then hit the back of my head. Once he punched me in the shoulder. Then, one day, he simply pushed me against the wall, pinned me with one hand, and pulled down my pants with the other. I did not fight him. I don't know why. I was afraid, but did not want to appear a coward. I was curious perhaps, and I fancied him. Either way, I just stood there and let him force himself into me. He was not gentle. That was fine with me. I was one of the angry kids, I welcomed pain. It made me forget the pain of grief. At least, I found out what sex was like. I did not think much of it. I thought it would be more arousing than it was. I was a teenager, I knew about arousal. I felt it when I watched him shag Debby. Now that it was my turn, I did not feel the same excitement.

Afterwards, he once again lost all interest in me. When I taunted him again, he pretended I did not exist. That hurt me more than the sex itself. It made me feel dirty and used, and ugly. It was then that guilt and shame swarmed over me. What he had done suddenly felt wrong. I should not have allowed him to do that to me. I thought about my mother and father, and how horrified they would have been to see me get fucked by some boy up against a wall. I wept in my bed and hoped there was no heaven, and I hoped my parents were not watching over me, as our foster parents were fond of telling us.

I decided to put Lock out of my mind, and spend more time after school with Li, which invariably involved spending time in her parents' restaurant. Being there, reminded me of what normal family life was like. Li was fussed over and scolded when she did something wrong. It was strange to miss being told off, and yet I did, to the point of tears. No one now cared enough about me to tell me off, except Mr Chen, Li's father. He treated me no differently to Li, and for a time I found comfort, and security. I did not have sex for some years after that, though Lock tried to corner me for more now and then. The thought of it shamed me each time.

When I had confessed to Li what I had done, she nodded and simply said, 'Don't know why you are ashamed. It's just sex. I can't wait for it myself. I'm planning to sell my virginity on my sixteenth birthday. There is a market for it, you know.'

I thought she was joking. Then, when we were sixteen, she showed me her new apartment in the city. We compared notes on our experiences. She too, she had told me, felt a little ashamed. 'But then I thought of never having to work in the kitchen again, and suddenly, it did not seem so bad. It hurt at first, but the next time it was better. I think I like it. It was just business in the end.' And that was that. After leaving school, Li moved out of her parents' house into her apartment. A year later, she owned her current mansion.

After I left school, I fell in with Lock and his gang of Wild Riders. Lock and I had been sleeping together for over a year by then, and I was well and truly in his power. I believed all the crap told us about being a family, and how we could do anything we wanted. And after I grew too old for foster care, and Li left to pursue her glamorous new lifestyle as a courtesan, I was too lonely, and too afraid to face the world alone.

In the Wild Riders, I was not Victor or Victoria or 'it', I was simply Vic. We rode bikes, drank, partied, took drugs and had group sex with men and women. For a time, I thought I enjoyed it all. Then one day, three years later, I had woken up to the reality of my life. Flashes of the previous night's orgy flashed through my mind. My mouth around a cock, another man pumping me from behind. There were women bouncing on men, and men bouncing on women, and men on top of men, and women wedged between two men. We switched partners, and drank, and laughed, and fucked some more.

I was hungover and ill with drugs. I threw up, showered, and scrubbed myself clean. Then I left and never looked back.

Li took me in. I was a wreck. The alcohol and drugs took their toll. But it was the shame and disgust with myself that broke me. I was depressed, angry, tearful, and utterly lost. Li looked after me. For a time, it was just the two of us. Then, when her boxer lover turned her into a piece of bloodied meat, I looked after her. Her pain and grief brought me out of my own melancholy. I guess that was when I finally woke up from my past and decided to forge a new life for myself.

I returned to work in the kitchens of the *Angry Dragon*. I cleaned up. I took to reading books, like I used to when I was younger. Then, I began to notice the type of people who came to dine in the place where I served. 'The suits', Li and I used to call them. They looked fresh and sharp, like a new bank note. I suddenly wanted to be one of them. I wanted to be on the other side of the divide, and to know what it was like to dine in a restaurant rather than clean one. I could not sleep for the wanting of it.

I decided to become one of 'the suits'. It was easier said than done, however. I had no university degree and no past that I could speak about to prospective employers. And when I did manage to reach an interview, I found I had a deeper problem of anxiety and articulacy. Three years later, Mr Ruttman was the first job I was offered, and two weeks into it, I was already making him regret his decision. Two weeks into it, and I was back to working in Mr Chen's kitchen.

I walked up the stone steps, and the heat from the kitchen drenched me. Inside, five staff were preparing food on massive stoves, three washed dishes. Food runners rushed in to drop dirty plates on the counter, and rushed out again taking the newly prepared ones. Mr Chen did not look up from the plate he was speedily decorating as he shouted instructions to the staff around him. I always thought it uncanny how he saw everything at once in his kitchen. For a moment, I stood there, feeling like I was home.

I forgot about Devlin and Lucy, and the dismal start to my new job. I grabbed the white uniform shirt from the shelf in the cupboard by the back door and, after quickly taking in the situation in the kitchen, went straight to the sink. I peeled vegetables, helped with the plate settings, stirred the sauces on the stove when they were neglected too long, and scrubbed pans. Mr Chen, like many busy chefs, did not hold on to staff very well. So I knew no one else in the kitchen from the time when I last worked here.

The restaurant was always busy. I worked nonstop all night. No one spoke apart from shouting basic instructions or requests. Mostly, it was Mr Chen who shouted.

When I next looked up, the kitchen was clean and tidy. My legs were aching and my feet were swollen and blistered from the office shoes I still wore. I was the last person, besides Mr Chen himself, to leave.

We sat on the back steps, the restaurant silent and dark behind us. The cold night was crisp and fresh after the heat of the kitchen.

Mr Chen took a long inhale from his bong. He preferred old-fashioned remedies for his joint pain, he had told me a while back, and the mellowing side effect of his 'herbs' was just another boon.

'It's good to have you back, Vic.' He handed me his small porcelain bong. It was a Chinese antique from two hundred years ago. A family heirloom, according to Mr Chen.

Usually, I would decline, but today I felt an itching need. Guiltily, I took a long draught, choked and gave it back to him. It had been a while.

'Things run smoothly when you are here. Want to come back for good?'

I thought about it. It would be easy. Life in the kitchen was simple. I simply did what I was told, worked hard, then went home. There was no confusing Devlin, or obsessive Lucy, or Mr Ruttman's disappointment in me.

I sighed. 'I am trying to make a fortune in the city, Mr Chen. You know, become one of them 'suits' who eat out every night.'

He took another draught. 'How's that going?'

'I just lost a fortune... except it wasn't my own fortune, which makes it worse, I guess.'

'Youngsters today think there is a trick to getting rich quickly. I am rich now. Very rich. See what I have. It was not easy. Took me forty years to get here. It's hard work, and slow. Last to win is the man who rushes to the end.'

'Is that some kind of Chinese saying?'

'No. One of mine. You like it? It is wisdom I gained through life, and I pass it to you now, like I passed it to Li.'

'Thanks, Mr Chen. I appreciate a bit of wisdom now and then.'

'Good. Now go and sleep. I will see you tomorrow morning. Long days, Saturday and Sunday. But you will earn plenty of money you owe me.' He shook his head. 'And this is another wisdom you will finally learn from me by working off that foolish meal you could not afford. Rashness is the mother of Misery. How many times have I told you this?'

I smiled. Mr Chen was always a harsh taskmaster in teaching life's lessons. He also taught me to owe no one what could be repaid. 'See you tomorrow then, Mr Chen.'

I put on my helmet and rode home. It was long after midnight when I showered the oils and food smells off myself and crawled into bed. I passed out from exhaustion, and awoke feeling achy and still tired when my alarm reminded me it was time for another shift.

I dragged myself out of bed, fortified myself with two cups of coffee, and went back to the restaurant. And so my weekend passed in Mr Chen's kitchen, and come Monday morning, I was tired, sore all over, and cranky.

I put on my suit and was halfway through breakfast when someone pounded on my door, rattling it on its hinges.

'Vic, you owe me rent!' Mr Gruleman shouted from the other side.

Oh hell. I was counting on some commission to get me the two weeks' pay I owed him. My week's wage would barely cover this week's rent, and maybe some fuel and bills, and leave me next to nothing for food or drink.

How was I going to explain to Mr Gruleman that I could not pay him two weeks ahead again, especially after I'd promised him I would? He would kick me out.

I could not face that conversation now, so I remained quiet, holding my breath.

He banged on the door again. 'Vic! You will pay me today for two weeks, or you will leave tomorrow.'

I heard his feet stomping down the stairs.

Soon after, I snuck out, silently closing the door behind me, and tiptoeing down the stairs past his flat. Outside, I jumped on my bike and was off.

As always, Devlin arrived at nine fifteen. I did not look up as he flirted with Sally the receptionist, and gave his usual debonair greeting to everyone he passed. He stopped to praise Lucy about her keen trading sense, since the copper futures had risen over the weekend, earning her a very handsome commission. He then complimented Paul on a report well done.

'Oh, and I really enjoyed watching the game with you and your brother on Saturday,' he added. 'Let's do it again sometime.'

'Sure thing, Mr Knightsbridge,' Paul replied almost breathlessly.

I ignored Devlin, whilst straining to hear his every move, his every word. The memory of his kiss came back to me with a jolting force. I remembered his arousal pressing against me. Was that for me? Or was it just masculine anger manifesting itself below his waist? I grew hot thinking about it. I thought I could feel his eyes on me, but when I glanced up, he was striding into his office.

'Still watching the lion?' Fred said with a huff.

'Only to make sure he does not pounce,' I replied.

'Hey Vic,' Lucy said brightly behind me. 'Fancy a coffee with me this morning. I was about to grab one. I thought we might discuss what theatre you want to take me to today.'

Fred turned at that, his mouth downturned. I knew I had promised him a beer after work today.

I ran my hand through my hair, exasperated. I had to end it with Lucy, and now was as good a time as any. She would not make a scene in front of all these people, and I would be safe from her advances, or pleading, or anger, or whatever other possible embarrassing ways women reacted to being dumped... or scorned. Bloody hell, the woman never missed an episode of *How I Got Away With Cold-Blooded Murder*.

I shook my head at that. *She is just a pretty butterfly, Vic, stop thinking crazy thoughts.*

As I got up to follow Lucy, my cup in hand, Fred gave me one of his wounded looks. I gave him a shrug that said, *What can I do? It's her not me.*

The machine gave Lucy hot chocolate from station two. 'I hope you have a happy, sunny day, Lucy,' the coffee machine piped, and I felt like the lowest type of scum who crushed a butterfly under my boot.

Oh well, best get my own coffee before I piss off both Lucy and the machine. The coffee machine was courteous, and I received a good cup from station four. I was not fooled, however. The machine was up to something again after that putdown by Victoria.

Lucy turned to me with a bright smile. 'I've missed you so much over the weekend. I can't wait for our next date today. I was thinking maybe we could go and see something romantic, like the *Pirate King's Sword*, or perhaps, *The Phantom and the Rock Star*. I have not seen either of them.'

'Erm.' There was no way to do this gently. I just had to say it. 'Lucy, we need to talk.'

There, I'd said it. The words to end our relationship. It was hard, but I got them out.

'We *are* talking, Vic.' She giggled and patted my arm.

I sighed. 'No. We need to talk,' I repeated slowly, meaningfully.

I watched her face change from surprise, to shock, then disbelief.

'No. I refuse to talk! You promised me the theatre.' Tears appeared in her eyes.

Oh hell, not that. I glanced around to make sure no one was watching.

'No, No. We definitely need to talk.' *Quick, make her feel that it's not about her but you.* 'It is not me but you.'

'What do you mean it's me? Of course, it's not me. How could it be me?' Her voice rose into shrill notes, and I glanced behind us. Eyes began to rise in our direction. In his office, Devlin sat back with his hands behind his head, watching us. 'We are in love, and you just throw me aside!'

'Erm. We are not in love, Lucy,' I said quietly, trying to pacify her.

'Of course, we are in love!' she screamed, and the office stilled; the silence so deep I heard someone's paperclip hit the carpeted floor.

Good god, she *was* a mad cookie-maker with murderous tendencies.

'And don't deny it, Vic. Not after all your efforts to dress nicely for me. And you took me to the best restaurant in town. And you kissed me in the street!'

'You kissed *me*,' I objected.

'All your efforts to woo me, and make me fall in love with you. And now you simply dash my hopes and dreams. Oh, how could you be so selfish and cruel, Vic!' And with that, she burst into tears and run out of the office, towards the stairs.

Everyone was staring at me. I wanted to sink through the floor. Working in the kitchens suddenly seemed like a wonderfully simple way to live. A week ago, I thought my plan was so perfect. It never occurred to me that I might actually hurt Lucy. It seemed it was me who needed a lesson in humility, not Devlin. He never made Lucy cry. No, he made everyone laugh, and feel good about themselves... everyone except me. He made me feel... Hell, I did not know. I guess he made me feel not good enough, inadequate. This was what my plan was truly about. Not teaching him humility, but the inadequacy of the type that I had lived with all my life.

'Viiiic!' Mr Ruttman shouted from his doorway.

I took a deep breath, and without meeting anyone's eyes, went into his office and sat down. His face was red with anger. 'You come in late. You lose this firm money, and now you have upset poor Lucy. Vic, I am putting you on notice. I have no choice in this. It's the firm's rules. Three gross misconducts and you are on notice. One more, and you are out. I am giving you just one more chance, Vic. Just one. So you'd better get yourself sorted out.'

With that, he dismissed me.

'Hell, Vic,' Fred said when I sat down at my desk. 'On notice! Mr Ruttman's never put anyone on notice before. Not even when Rick Smarty threw his computer through the window in a fit, after his trading went a bit sour. Mind you, not as sour as yours, but still pretty bad. Mr Ruttman simply patted him on the back and bought him a new computer. What did you say to Lucy anyway to make her cry like that?'

'I told her we needed to talk.'

He flinched. 'Ouch, that's brutal. Could you not have let her down easily?'

'I thought I was. Or else I would have said, 'I don't want to date you'.'

'You know, that one doesn't sound as bad. Sort of direct and to the point. I think I would have gone with that one. But why did you do it in the office? You could have waited till you were in a restaurant, or somewhere nice, where you could make her feel special. You know, a special break-up for a special girl.'

'It's a break-up. What does it matter where it's done? And how can you make someone feel special when you are breaking up with them?'

He tilted his head at me. 'So, never been in a relationship before. Never been dumped either. Look, ask anyone. Hey, Paul,' he shouted across the office. 'Where do you dump your girlfriends?'

'Oh, somewhere special,' he shouted back. 'Either in bed after sex, when they are mellow, or in a nice restaurant. Maybe a sunset cruise with a glass of champagne. They don't feel so dejected and ugly then. You know, make it special for them. Why, who are you dumping?'

'Just asking.' Fred turned to me again. 'See? You need to work on your sensitive side, Vic.' He shook his head sadly.

I crossed my arms. 'So, where do you want to be dumped?'

'In bed, after sex,' he replied instantly, without thought.

I thought about it. 'I guess you have a point there.'

'So, beer after work?'

'Sure, why not. My only other plan has just fled out the door in tears.'

At the end of the day, Fred and I made our way to the *Goat and Frog*. Fred paid for the beers, and I was grateful for it. I was mostly broke. At least, I would be after I paid my rent.

Fred sat back, stretching his arms over the back of the cubicle seat, one arm behind me. I felt a little uncomfortable, but hey, he was watching the crowd. If he did not notice, why should I?

I drank my ale. My thoughts drifted to my predicament. It was Monday night of the third week of my new, respectable life as a 'suit', and I was on notice. From now on, I would be a model worker, get in early, work hard, speak to no one, make no one cry. I drank more of my ale.

Fred began telling me about his life. Why did people always feel compelled to tell me about themselves? Li thought it was because I would sit in silence, and it made them uncomfortable.

'Erm, the ale is good in this place,' I interrupted his tale and sipped my pint as if to demonstrate.

'Oh, yes, it's delicious. I always marvel at how many things we have in common, hey Vic?'

'I suppose,' I said absently.

His hand twiddled my hair. 'You hair is very soft. It must be the shampoo you use.'

I yanked my hair out of his fingers. 'Stop that. We use the same shampoo. You told me that the day we met.'

'Oh, yes. I remember,' he said.

The inn door opened, and Devlin walked in with Mr Ruttman. Oh damn. Fred had not seen them. He began to touch my hair annoyingly. Devlin saw us then, and his eyes turned to burning ice. And once again, his kiss invaded my mind.

'Quit that, Mr Ruttman is here,' I hissed at Fred.

Mr Ruttman saw us, and his eyes went wide with horror. Fred quickly snatched his arm from the back of the seat. 'Mr Ruttman, come and join us!' He shouted, waving. 'Vic and I were just going over the latest market trends.'

'Go ahead, Sir,' Devlin said to him. 'I will get us some drinks.'

'Oh, if you are sure, my boy. Very generous of you.' Mr Ruttman approached us, suspiciously casting his gaze from me to Fred and back. 'Hope I am not interrupting anything?'

'No, not at all,' Fred said. 'We were just comparing notes. It's hard to get time to do that at work, what with so much work to get through during the day.'

Devlin returned with a pint for himself, and a gin and tonic for Mr Ruttman. 'Well, this is a pleasant surprise.' He smiled meanly at me. 'Out for a friendly drink?'

If Fred was a cockerel, he would have fluffed up his feathers and pushed out his chest. His change in demeanour was not too different to that. 'Oh yes, very friendly.' He shrugged one shoulder.

I stared at him. What the hell was he implying?

This was becoming weird and awkward. I suddenly wanted to be anywhere else but here. Mr Ruttman looked thoroughly uncomfortable. Fred was posturing, a cockerel against a lion. Devlin was clearly annoyed, giving me and Fred dark looks. He looked dangerous beneath the charmer facade.

I downed my drink. 'Well, I'd best get back home. Up early tomorrow.' I stood up. Fred and Devlin rose to their feet with me.

'I should be off too,' Fred said quickly.

It was the last thing I wanted. I actually fancied a quiet drink by myself in the *Lonely Lizard* up the road. 'No, no. I think you should stay here and keep Mr Ruttman company. You can tell him all about our notes, and compare them with his.'

I grabbed my jacket and helmet, and without looking back, left the three of them there.

9
Confrontations

The *Lonely Lizard* was a dark, green pub in the basement under the main street level.

'The usual, Vic?' Tony, the owner of the pub, rasped. He spoke in a strained, throaty way. Years of smoking had given him throat cancer, which had to be removed, along with his voice box.

I sat in my usual seat at the bar. 'Sure.'

He put a shot of whisky in front of me. Good scotch was my secret sin. I loved it, but it cost me a fortune.

'On the tab?' he asked, seeing my face.

'You know I'm good for it.' I looked around. 'Quiet tonight. Where's the usual crowd.'

'Bill's at a funeral. Meggy's off on some over sixty-fivers' romp cruise. Jenny is getting ready to be married for the seventh time. Sam's still in hospital with his liver problem, and Pete's out the back on the bog.'

'Oh.'

'Long day?' he asked, while polishing the glasses with a towel.

'Long week. Third week on the job, and I'm on notice. One more transgression and I am out.'

'Really? That's quick even for you. Who did you kill?'

'My boss, almost... more than once.'

'Huh. If you want, you can come back and work here. It was a lot more fun when you were behind the bar.'

I sighed. 'I'm trying to make myself rich, Tony.'

'Oh? How's that going for you?'

My head fell into my arms. 'You don't want to know.'

I heard the door open and close.

'Ooh, don't look now, but god has just come to earth to take me away.' Tony rasped in gay wonder. 'My, my.'

I shook my head and lifted it up to down the whisky. 'Top me up then before you go, hey Tony.'

He slopped some more whisky into my glass, and turned to the man behind me. 'And what can I get for you today?'

'Just whatever Vic's having,' said the deep voice that reached places no voice should touch.

'No, don't, Tony. Go away, Devlin,' I said without looking at him.

Both ignored me. Tony poured him a drink and Devlin sat on the stool next to me. We sat in silence for a while.

'Meant to apologise,' he said. 'For the other night.'

'Which part?' I asked surlily.

'All of it... except for the kissing part. Not sorry for that one.'

'Fine. I forgive you. Feel free to bugger off now.'

Silence. I drank to fill it. He drank too.

'So, what did I do to make you hate me, Vic?'

From the far side of the bar, Tony kept giving me those unsubtle looks that told me not to be stupid and drag the god home.

I ran my hand through my hair in frustration. 'I don't really hate you, Devlin. Only your bloody perfection. Everything comes easy to you. Everyone loves you. Everything you touch turns to gold. God, just look at yourself in the mirror. Hell, you probably do every morning and kiss yourself. No man should have that much share of scant good fortune, while the rest of us scrape shit from the floor. You walk on sunshine. I bet you never fucked up in your life. Fine, call me selfish, arrogant, self-absorbed. I've heard worse in my time. But you asked and I answered. Now leave me alone.'

I did not look at him as I spoke, and he did not look at me. So I could not judge his reaction to my long-winded whine. Hell, I hated myself for sounding like I was a moaning child who did not have the toys the other children had.

'Had it rough, hey, Vic?' he said quietly, and it did not sound like mockery.

I did not reply. I'd be damned if I was going to lay out all my woes to him. He was silent for a long time, but I could hear him thinking, chewing things over.

'I was where you are now some years ago,' he said over his drink.

I snorted. 'I truly doubt it. Let me guess, born to well to do parents, went to a good school, and a better university. Loved by everyone all your life. Never a night alone in your bed. Sure, maybe you went off the rails once or twice, had too much to drink, passed out, shagged the wrong person. Daddy probably pulled some strings and you landed a good job. Bet you've never known the true meaning of degradation. Or wanted something so bad, you try and try until your soul bleeds, and still never get it. Hell, do you even know what it's like to lose someone? I bloody doubt it. You were weaned on privilege and success. People like you have good lives, and good for you. But you and I are not the same, Dev. We are worlds apart. Now spare me your hard luck story and I will spare you mine.'

'My, you certainly paint a colourful, idyllic picture of my life. No one has it worse than you, hey, Victor-Victoria?'

His mockery raised my ire further. I wanted to shock him, to throw the grief and shame and vileness of the world at him. 'I was raped by a grown boy when I was thirteen, and I did not even try to fight him off. I just stood there and took it. Hell, I wanted him to do it. I was so mad at Ma and Pa for dying on me, I wanted them to be sorry for all that was wrong in my life. Later, when I was older, I hung out with him and his sordid, wastrel gang. We had one hell of a party. Did things pretty city boys like you would cry to their mothers about.' I downed the last of my whisky. 'And these were just the better parts of my life. So spare me your wounded boy, and how I made it better for myself speech. I've heard them all. One day, I will get there myself.'

'It wasn't your fault,' he said softly.

It was the worst thing he could say. A lump lodged in my throat. I stood up and staggered.

He gripped my elbow. 'Let me take you home,' he said.

I ripped my arm away. 'Let go. I don't need your chivalry and charm.'

Tony was shaking his head at me from the far side of the bar.

'See you later, Tony,' I called out to him.

'Sure thing, Vic. Take care. And think about my offer. I can make you manager if you want.'

I waved at him and went outside. Devlin followed me.

'Why are you following me?' I span round on him.

'Just want to be sure you get home alright,' he said, and again tried to take my arm.

I snatched it away. 'I'm fine.'

He walked beside me back to the car park of our office building where I kept my bike. I knew I was in no state to drive, but I just could not bring myself to care.

We walked in silence. Then a thought occurred to me. 'How did you know where to find me?'

His lips quirked up without humour. 'You drink there every other night. I thought it a safe bet you'd go there after you left us.'

I stopped again and poked him in the chest. 'How the hell do you know where I drink? And why?'

He shrugged. 'I have my sources. As to why, I just wanted to know what you got up to in the evenings. Who you saw, were you single? You are not very forthcoming about yourself, you know.'

'Why the hell do you want to know that about me. What's it to you who I date?'

'Like I said, I just wanted to know,' he said looking at me intently, meaningfully.

I spun on my heel. I had no idea what his game was. Did not want to know. 'Go home to Francesca and leave me alone, Dev.'

I marched to the car park and began to put on my helmet. He took it out of my hand. 'No, you don't. The bike's a bloody death trap even without adding alcohol to the mix. I'll take you.' He fished out his car keys.

'I'd rather walk.' I turned to go.

We heard the sound of breaking glass, and looked to the far end of the car park where two youths were trying to unlock the door of one of the cars.

Devlin charged at them. 'Hey! Get away from that car, you bastards.'

They squared up to him. 'Mind your fucking business, neck-tie.' One of the youths spat at Devlin.

Oh hell, two against one. I ran up behind him. I had only been in a fight once or twice in my life. Mostly, I preferred to keep away from them. I was slight and did not take a punch well.

'Get out of here, before I call the police,' I said.

They looked me up and down, and laughed, 'And what the fuck are you supposed to be? Hey, let's see if you have tits.'

'Sod that,' his companion said. 'His kind might have tits and cock. Let see if he has a cock?'

Both of them moved towards me. Devlin threw a quick, hard punch without warning that floored one. Bloody hell, he punched like a boxer. For a moment, as I watched the guy's nose bleed through his fingers, I was too stunned to move. I remembered Li's battered body, and felt sick and afraid at once. I suddenly wanted to run away from the fight. Devlin pushed me back, and took the fist in the stomach from the other youth meant for me. He recovered quickly, and turned to reply, but the lad was faster. He kicked out viciously at Devlin's leg. To my horror, his leg buckled and bent in the ugliest and unnatural way. He fell to the floor, his leg at a frightening angle, twisted and dislodged. The other thug was up now and kicking him.

I threw myself at them, hitting and kicking wildly where I could. One of them punched me. I fell to my knees. He went for a kick when the sirens sounded at the entrance of the car park. The thugs turned and fled.

'You alright, Vic.' Devlin crawled to me, fear and concern on his face.

His bent leg was dragging behind him, yet he showed no sign of pain. It could only be shock.

'Hell, Devlin, your leg's broken, we need to get you to a hospital.'

I shook my head and rubbed my jaw. Not too bad. I'd deflected the direct hit, as Lock had once taught me. It saved my teeth on more than one occasion.

'I am fine,' he said gruffly. He sat down, dragging his leg in front of him, and pulled up his trouser leg.

I stared in shock. It was a prosthetic, going up to above his knee. The fastening on his leg stump was ripped off when the youth kicked him. Welt marks appeared on the flesh of his thigh. I had never felt a bigger idiot in my life.

'I'm sorry,' I blurted out, staring at the stump of a leg. I don't know what I was sorry for, only that it felt like being punched in the gut to see him like this. He was supposed to be the perfect Devlin Knightsbridge.

'What for, you did not kick me.' He was adjusting the metal leg and straps. I remembered how I had seen him limping slightly in the car park. I remembered his anger when he saw my bike.

'How did you lose it?' I asked, though I already suspected the truth.

'Bike crash. Got drunk, got stupid, lost a leg, killed a man, left a little girl an orphan.' His voice was thick with suppressed rage and pain.

Grief like that never leaves you. It dulls, and sometimes you forget it's there, but it never goes away.

'Are you two alright?' A police officer loomed over us.

'Fine, thanks to you, officer.' Devlin pulled down his trouser leg and stood up awkwardly. I tried to give him a hand, but his pride would have none of it. As soon as he found his feet, he bent over and threw up.

'Need a doctor there, buddy? Looks like one of them was giving you a good kicking,' the officer said.

'No, just give me a moment.' Devlin put his hand on my shoulder to breathe. 'Hell, that hurts.'

'I'll need the both of you to give me a statement and a description.'

'How did you get here so fast, anyway?' I asked.

The officer pointed at a camera. 'Remote monitoring. Got a call about a car break-in.'

Devlin leant on the bonnet of his car while we gave our statement. One of his eyes was purple and swollen shut.

'Can't let you drive in your state, Mr Knightsbridge,' the officer said to him. 'If you won't go to a hospital, then I'd better take you home. '

'I'll give him a hand,' I said.

Devlin was not walking well. His ribs took a beating. He said nothing was broken, yet he could not straighten. He claimed that he was just sore and stiff. I thought he was underplaying the damage. I had to get him home safe, where his woman could look after him.

His woman. My mood soured, if that was even possible. I did not want to see the gorgeous Francesca who shared his bed. But what choice did I have? I would just walk him to the door and leave.

In the back of the police car, Devlin gave the officer the address of his home. He was looking better, straightening somewhat.

'Slowing up, old man,' he said under his breath, shaking his head at himself.

I turned away, smiling. He could not have been older than his early thirties.

The officer took us into the most expensive part of the city. We drove past mansions with enormous gates and large, sculpted gardens. My jaw hung open. I knew Devlin was rich. But this was beyond rich. Can one really earn that much at trading?

The cad read my mind. He grinned. 'In case you are wondering if you can earn that much in trading, then yes. It's not easy, though. Need the right combination of smart and gut. Too much smart usually means not enough gut. Too much gut means recklessness and large losses.'

'Yes, I know. I screwed up my accounts. No need to bring it up again.'

'I wasn't,' he said.

We got out in front of a mansion fit for a king. I helped Devlin up the steps to the front door. He fumbled in his pocket for a key.

'What, no butler?' I said dryly.

'Now, now, Vic, play nice. Though to be honest, I had considered one. Then I thought it might be taking new wealth a little too far. Besides, Fran did not want a butler. Thinks it's weird and outdated.'

I felt another kick in the gut hearing him speak of his ladylove in such an affectionate way.

He unlocked the door into a marble hallway. *Oh, for the love of god!*

'A cosy, humble home you have here, Dev.'

He slanted me a look. 'Jealous.'

'Of this museum?'

A sprite in a white silk nightdress ran down the central stair. She looked about twelve. Black haired and blue-eyed. Bloody hell, he had a daughter! The burn of jealousy this thought brought to me was startling and unwelcome.

'Uncle Dev! Uncle Dev!' She stopped when she saw me. She turned back to Devlin and saw his bruises. 'What happened to you?'

Uncle?

'Don't fret, Fran. Just some thugs stealing a car. They got worse from me,' he lied smoothly. He stood straight in front of her, gritting his teeth against the obvious pain.

'Oh good. I should hope so,' she said.

'Francesca, this is Vic, a friend of mine from the office.'

My world spun. So this was the mysterious Francesca. Not a lover but a child. His niece, if it was to be believed. She looked too much like him to be believable.

'Hi,' she said dismally to me, and crossed her arms.

'Hi, yourself,' I replied, and ignoring her, looked around. You'd never catch me cooing over some snotty child.

'Is that all you've got to say?' Francesca demanded.

'That's twice more than you've had to say, kid,' I replied. My eyes fell on a man-sized statue of an angel by the stair, with a leaf covering his private parts.

Devlin coughed to cover up a laugh. 'Why don't you go to bed now, love. I'm home and all is well. I don't want you oversleeping school again tomorrow.'

'I only overslept because you forgot to wake me,' she replied sulkily, then gave him a kiss on the good cheek and darted up their grand marble staircase.

Devlin limped up the stairs after her. 'Fancy a drink before you go?' he asked without looking back.

As if pulled by an invisible chain, I followed him. 'Sure, just one. Just to make sure you don't pass out in your own blood.'

He chuckled at that, and my insides tightened.

As we climbed the stairs, I looked around at the portraits on the walls. I wondered whether they were expensive masterpieces of some famous dead painter. I knew next to nothing about art. I suddenly felt gauche. Maybe I should visit one of those art galleries that Li's clients always take her to.

We came to a small sitting room, with a connecting door to another room. There were bookshelves stacked with books of all types, and a large study table, as well as a sofa facing a fireplace.

Devlin opened a wooden panel to reveal a cupboard. A golden collection of dozens of whiskies shone into the room. I was instantly beside him.

'Sweet lord,' I breathed in awe. 'There are vintages here which are rarer than kings.'

'I am a bit of a collector of scotch,' he spoke close behind me, his breath stirring the hairs on my neck. Goose bumps run up and down my spine.

Then I saw a rare red bottle of whisky, as dark as the peaty earth it came from. I could not help myself. I picked it up, reverently. 'You have the one-hundred-year-old Glen Elfick! I thought it was just a legend. It is said to have been made by Scottish elves!'

He chuckled and took it out my hand, his fingers brushing mine. It felt as if an electric shock passed through me, and lingered there. I snatched back my hand. He did not seem to notice. 'Want a try?'

'No! Don't open it on my account. It's worth more than this mansion.

'It's already open. I don't keep this collection for show. Life's too short to let good things pass.' He was looking at me as he said that.

I took a step away from him. 'Sure, I'll have a tumble... I mean a thimble worth.'

He chuckled and poured me a double measure.

'You can't be serious,' I said when he handed me the glass.

He poured his own. 'It gets lonely appreciating all this fine stuff alone. Call me arrogant, but I want to hear admiration in your voice when you taste my collection,' he said the last words in a lowered, suggestive voice.

Bloody hell, he was flirting with me. The man just could not help himself.

'Arrogant arse,' I said, and smiled.

'Go ahead try it, before you call me names.'

I did. If ever I came close to orgasm without being touched, it was in that moment. 'Oh good god.' I closed my eyes. 'This is heaven.'

He was sipping his own drink, watching me with a heated gaze. 'I thought you'd like it.'

Oh, hell. I knew that gaze. I have seen it on other men, but on him it was devastating. I was instantly aroused. I sat on the sofa and crossed my legs.

He got the fire going in front of us, and sat away from me watching the flames. We sat in silence brimming with tension, sipping our whisky. I could not believe I was in Devlin Knightsbridge's home, sitting cosily by the fire, drinking the whisky that most believed existed only in legends.

'Whose daughter is she?' I asked suddenly. The question had been torturing me since I met Francesca, who looked too much like Devlin to be another man's.

'My brother's,' he answered with a catch to his voice.

'And where is he.'

He put his head back on the sofa, closing his eyes against the memories that twisted his face into pain and self-disdain. 'Killed in the same crash that took my leg.'

I felt like scum at the bottom of his shoes. And after my hard-luck rant in the bar. I was an idiot. He probably thought me an idiot now if not before.

'I'm sorry,' I said again. I had to stop apologising to him. It sounded hollow even to me. 'Where is her mother?'

'Died birthing her,' he said. 'And I made her an orphan.'

There was such devastation in his face, I felt I had to say something. 'It was an accident.' Empty words, but no doubt true.

'No, it was not. It was my stupidity. Nick raised me after our mother died of an overdose. I'm not sure if we shared the same father. Unlikely, I think. He was seven years older than me, practical and driven. Wanted more for both of us. Got himself a job in a small shop, rising to shift manager. Took care of me. Never said no to any of my whims. I did not do so well. I was always angry, reckless. Angry at our mother, the way she was; drugged up, passed out. Angry at the men who made use of her, and beat me and Nick. And once or twice made use of us too. Nick tried to protect me, and suffered more than I. We never really spoke of it.

'He found a woman he loved. They did well together for a few years. She got pregnant. He bought them a small house to raise a family. Then she died in labour, leaving him to look after his newborn daughter, as well as me. I was a man by then, but he made my life easy, and I wanted it to remain easy. So I tried various ventures, some not so legal. Got beaten up a few times for not paying up debts promptly enough. My brother bailed me out too many times to count. He tried to convince me to get a proper job. Told me there was no quick and easy path to riches. Naturally, I wanted to prove him wrong.

'It was my twenty-fifth birthday. I was lonely and wanted to celebrate. My brother told me he could not go, for he had Fran to take care of. She was six then, and old enough to look after herself, or so I thought. We did when we were kids, and younger than that too. But Nick was anxious. Always anxious for his precious little princess. But for just one night, I wanted Nick back for myself. I told him we'd only go for a few drinks nearby. I lied. I got the rounds in and added shots into the mix, reminded him how it used to be, just the two of us. Reminisced. Plied him with more drinks. Managed to make him forget Fran, then took him to the city on my bike, where we hit bar after bar. It was like the good old days, before he had Fran. Just him and me against the world.

'I grew wilder. At some point, Nick lost his wallet, with all his cards and ID. Neither of us had any money for a cab. I told him I'd drive him home. He was too drunk to argue with me. He just wanted to get home to Fran. His precious little princess, I thought, hating her, then hating myself for hating that part of Nick.'

Devlin downed his whisky and got up to pour another double measure. He did not face me when he spoke again. 'I wanted it to be just me and my brother again...'

He shook his head and glanced at me, then looked away, as if ashamed. 'I rode like a maniac. I flew across a red light. I don't remember if I saw it or not. But I remember the blinding light coming at us, and an awful screeching sound. I tried to swerve around something large.'

He drank some more, and his hands trembled slightly. He gripped the glass tighter to still them.

'After that, I remember little. Not the impact itself. Just shattered parts. Pain. Flashing lights. My brother's broken body underneath a truck. His feet at ugly angles. Lots of blood. Then, I was being rushed through the hospital; bright lights overhead, blurred faces, urgent voices. Someone jabbed my arm with a needle. I awoke three days later missing a leg. My brother was dead. The police came to speak with me. They confirmed the identity of the dead man, for there was nothing on him that told them who he was. Then they told me I was under arrest. I nodded numbly to all their charges, wishing for death.'

He faced me again, his lips curling in self-contempt. 'It must have been days later when I remembered Francesca. I woke up in a sweat and panicked. I tried to rise out of bed, forgetting my missing leg. I could still feel it there, you see. I fell on the floor. The nurses rushed in and dragged me back to bed. I tried to fight them off, but the police guard outside my hospital room cuffed me to the bed. When I was calmer, he told me that Francesca was safe in care. They were looking for a foster family for her. It was only then that I felt the soul ripping grief of my brother's death. I wept and wept until I was hoarse from it.

'Later, I learned how Fran woke up the next morning after the accident, and found herself alone and afraid. Four days she had sat by the window, waiting for her daddy to come home. It was the school that alerted the police about a missing child.

Four days she waited, before the authorities came to tell her that daddy was dead.

'I admitted to all the charges in court. Told them everything. How much I drank, how I'd sped through the streets. I went to jail for two years. I was furious. Was that all my brother's life was worth to them? Two fucking years in jail for his murder.

'It was the longest two years of my life. Every hour of every day, I imagined the worst sort of foster home for Francesca, where she was beaten, neglected, abused, unloved. I imagined her in the type of home my brother and I grew up in. It tore me to pieces being trapped in prison, imagining the worst happening to my brother's child, until I could not breathe for the fear of it.

'When I left prison, I immediately went to find Francesca. I was not allowed to contact her. So I spied on her and her family. She was in a good home, with good people. She had more than I could have offered her, but she had grown, and matured beyond her years. Her eyes were sad, world-weary. I did that to her. I should have walked away, but she was all I had now, and I was all she had. I owed Nick, more than I could ever repay him. And I knew he would have wanted me to take care of his child.

'So I got myself a job in a workshop. Worked hard for months, doing long shifts, saving every penny. Got a nice little house in a good area, next to a good school. I filed for the right to adopt my niece. I was denied. Unstable home, criminal offences, a prison sentence in my recent history. I went to see a lawyer. He laughed, and said the only way I would get her was if I was as rich as a king, and could offer her more than her foster parents... as well as afford the exuberant court fees to go with the claim. So I came to work for Mr Ruttman. I told him where I came from, what I'd done, and that I had just come out of prison. He gave me a job anyway. Every man deserves a second chance, he had told me.

'I stared at market charts until my eyes could no longer focus. Went home only to wash and sleep. I read everything there was to read, every gossip, every scrap of news. When that did not earn me the riches I needed, I made contacts with key people in the city who got information before anyone else. I bribed, threatened and blackmailed them for insider information on markets. What they did not give willingly, I stole. Once, I broke into newspaper offices to find out key news before the markets opened in the morning. I began to make money, and money makes money.' He looked at me then and laughed bitterly. 'Bet you thought it was simply luck or brilliance, hey Vic? My Midas touch? A small part of it was. The rest was just downright information. The more I made, the easier it was to buy information. I had blokes working for me. Those who knew how to get what I needed. Still have them, you know.'

'Bloody hell, you are a crook,' I mumbled, looking at him in the whole new light. This was not the man I knew.

He looked me in the eyes frankly. 'How else is a man to get as rich as a king from nothing? I did it for Fran. I did it because I owed Nick. I did it to defeat the system which divided our family.' He took a good sip of his whisky before continuing. 'I thought I was set. I bought this mansion. I appeared on TV, hoping Fran would see me. I went to court and paid an enormous amount of money to get custody of my niece, signed the adoption papers, and rode up to her foster home in a limousine. Thought she would be overjoyed to see her rich uncle come to get her. There would be nothing she might want that I could not buy her. I was so confident when I strode up to that house, doll in hand.'

I cringed. 'Ouch. That would have hurt.'

He gave a reluctant laugh. 'Indeed. I was an idiot, of course. Her foster parents opened the door. They were upset. Devastated, really. I did not care. She was my niece, my blood. She belonged with me.

'Fran refused to see me. The police had to break down her locked, barricaded bedroom door. They dragged her screaming and kicking, and biting like a wildcat. Her foster parents were in tears. She screamed that I killed her daddy, and wished me dead. She pleaded with her foster parents to allow her to stay, promising to be good and tidy her room. Anything, as long as they did not let me take her away.

'My heart broke into a million pieces all over again that day. I almost turned away and gave her what she wanted. But I knew my brother would not want that. We were family. He looked after me once, and I would look after his daughter. I steeled myself, closed my ears and my heart to her screams, and dragged her to the car.

'For two years we battled. Twice she ran away. I showered her with gifts, and gave in to her every whimsical wish. She called me names, told me she hated me, and wished I'd died instead of her father. I wished the same, every bloody day since the accident. I told her that one day. After that, she was sullen, watchful. It was a fragile peace we had for a while. It is better now. Though she still has her moments of depression and anger.'

He downed his whisky and brought back a bottle. Topped up my glass and his. Drank some more.

He sat down again, looking at the fire. 'Not such a perfect prince after all, hey Vic.'

'It's the imperfections that make a man perfect. My friend Li always said that.'

'Your friend sounds wise,' he said.

'Wiser than me,' I said sadly, and for a long moment, our eyes locked. 'I was an arse to you, Dev, I know it...'

He moved quickly. His hand dug into my hair and his mouth found mine, fierce and hungry. He was overwhelming, his heat, his size. Oh hell, he tasted like a very expensive whisky. I sucked his tongue, desperate to strip it of every delicious flavour of whisky and man. His smell drugged my senses. I gripped him, pulling him closer, then realised what we were doing. I turned my head away. He kissed my throat. My hands tangled in his hair.

'Dev. You've had too much, I don't think this is a good idea,' I said breathlessly.

'I want you. I fucking want you, Vic,' he breathed against my neck.

'I thought you wanted Lucy.'

He lifted his head to look at me. 'Why on earth would you think that?'

'You always flirt with her,' I reminded him.

'I always flirt with *you*. I just was not certain if you...'

I pushed away and leapt to my feet, remembering the horrified expression on Alex's face that time. 'If I was a man or a woman? Do you know now? Are you sure you did not make a mistake? You would not be the first.' I was unreasonably angry. In that moment, I realised I wanted no one more than him to know, to simply know.

He laughed. 'It's bloody obvious, Vic. Of course, I know. I just did not know whether you liked men or women. Then, when I saw you with Lucy, when she was throwing herself at you, it became obvious you did not fancy her. I'm not blind or stupid. I know when someone watches me, and the bulge in my trousers.' He grinned, and I heated with embarrassment. 'You want me, Vic.' He was on his feet advancing.

I backed away until I hit a wall. This was a mistake. I should leave now. Sweet lord, when had I began to want Devlin's heated gaze on me. Even with his one eye purple and shut, it was still hypnotic. Then he pulled me to him, and kissed me fiercely.

'I know you,' he whispered into my ear as he pulled my groin to his. 'You think I do not see the core of you. You are like me. I saw you the moment I met you.' He kissed me again, his hands in my hair, on my body, pulling me closer.

How many times have I been there, hot with need and want? Tomorrow he would be done with me. They always were. But tonight, just for tonight I could have him. He was pulling off his shirt and then ripping at mine. His teeth nipped my chest, my nipples, he licked me all the way down, pressing me against the wall. He pulled down my trousers, and an instant later, his mouth was on me, sucking, licking, gently biting. His tongue licked and lapped as if I was his last meal. I dug my hands in his hair, thrusting forward into his mouth. I was shuddering uncontrollably, my legs shaking. I closed my eyes, and only his hungry, greedy mouth existed.

'Bloody hell, Dev,' I gasped. The building tension was unbearable, and in moments, I came harder than I ever had in my life. My head exploded, my legs nearly buckled underneath me.

He stood up, wiping his mouth, and kissed me again. A moment later he pushed me through the door of the sitting room into his bedroom. It was a masculine bedroom, smelling of manly musk. Before I could take in the surroundings, he was kissing me again. No, Devlin did not kiss, he devoured. He pushed me down on his bed, and standing above me pulled off his pants to free his erection. It was a masterpiece, like the rest of him. I was dimly aware of his false leg, but only for a moment, before he was on top of me, rubbing his erection against me, as he kissed every inch of me. He growled, bit my shoulder.

'I want you so fucking bad, Vic.' And he spun me around underneath him, and entered me with one fierce thrust.

'Oh god, yes!' I cried out.

He was inside me, hot, hard, eager. Devlin Knightsbridge's cock was inside me! I was aroused and aching again. I pushed up against him as he entered me again and again. His false leg was as hard as the rest of him. It pressed against me with each thrust. It was erotic. I arched my back, turning to kiss him. He met my lips.

I'd had sex too many times to count, but this, with Devlin on top of me, his cock sliding in and out of me, was unlike anything I'd ever known before. It felt as if we were not simply fucking, but making love. He kissed me so hungrily, and yet so tenderly, I almost wept with the wonder of it. His hand gentle and exploring. A man had never felt so right before... as if we belonged. I had never known such bliss. He reached around me to touch me, as soon as I felt his hand on me, I came again. He was wild now, his rhythm stronger, faster. He roared and I felt his cock throb and pulse. He collapsed on top of me, breathing raggedly.

'Vic,' he muttered by my ear and passed out.

I lay there for a while, before elbowing him. He grunted sleepily and rolled off without waking up. I could not sleep. The moment was too precious to waste on sleep. I lay there watching him for a long time. He lay on his front, his face turned towards me. He looked even more handsome in sleep, if that was possible. There was a rawness to him. Naked in sleep, he was not a fine-tailored charmer. The day's stubble on his face, along with his tousled hair, gave him a wild, untamed look. He was an imperfect man. Ironically, it made him even more perfect.

My eyes fell to his leg. I sat up and unfastened the straps holding it in place. It was an expensive design, making him walk without a limp, unless he tried to move fast, like he did that day in the car park. On another man, the false leg might have seemed a weakness, an insecurity, an embarrassment perhaps.

But not on Devlin. It suited him. It was who he was. It was his strength. On him, it looked sexy. I took it off and put it by the bed, where he could reach it. The scar on his leg was ugly, as scars tend to be. It did not bother me. I traced it with my finger. The scars inside him were uglier, as they were in me. But Devlin was not a man to feel pity for, so I did not.

I remembered how I had accused him of an easy life, a life of privilege. He was right, I spun a great tale without knowing a thing about him. I looked at his surface and judged him. Made assumptions based on nothing but the cut of his suit. The same assumption people made about me. I set out to humble him, except it was I who needed to be humbled. I was wrong about him, just as I was wrong about Lucy.

Yet he saw me. He knew me. At least in that, I was right. Men like Devlin saw men and women, no matter their guise. But it had nothing to do with his masculinity. He simply looked closer at people than anyone else. He saw the core of them, who they were, what they wanted. Though I always wanted to be seen so thoroughly, to be understood and not judged, in the end, I was no better than anyone else. I did not take the time to study or look beneath the surface of people. Devlin did. Once again, I felt insignificant beside him.

I did not deserve Devlin's regard.

I lay down beside him again, and after a while, fell asleep. I woke up at dawn, shivering. It took me a moment to remember where I was, and what had happened the night before. Devlin's arm was around me. He was breathing into the back of my neck. My bum was pressed against his arousal. I was suddenly content and safe, as I had not been since I'd had a home, with a mother and a father. Home. I felt home. Dangerous thoughts, and I suddenly knew the real threat to me here. Devlin could destroy me. He was the one man with whom just sex would never be enough.

I slipped out of bed, dressed quickly, covered him up, and left.

I walked home in the icy spring dawn. We lived a few miles away, and yet worlds apart. The walk home gave me time to think. He said he wanted me. Lock often told me the same. I knew it meant little. But Devlin bared his soul to me as Lock never had. In one night, I had come to know Devlin better than I had known any man before. And I told him things I had never told anyone, except Li. In return, he had shown me a man far more devastating than the perfect Devlin I thought I knew. I could not hate that man. What now, then? I was not delusional enough to think that Devlin might want more than sex, or that he'd want me more than once. Gorgeous, perfect men like him were never serious about someone like me. I did not have the looks, the wealth, the success. I was awkward and gauche. I was a duck to his swan.

I had seen Li broken-hearted. I could not allow my illusions that there might be more between us drive me into that pit. Already, I could feel the lurking pain in my chest waiting for the chance to cripple me. I shook it off vehemently. *It was only sex, Vic. Stop having crazy thoughts.*

Then this was it, I guess. We'd go back and pretend nothing had happened between us. It would be hard to see him and not remember, but I would try.

I got home, undressed, and stood in the steaming shower for a long time, washing away Devlin's kisses, his mouth on me, and the delicious musk of his body. I began to ache for him. Then the pain, true and sharp, struck where my heart beat. I did not want just sex, I wanted Devlin. I wanted him to hold me and love me, as I was. I wanted the impossible. I leant my forehead on the wall of my shower.

Oh, hell. Now I've gone and done it. Just what my disastrous week needed. I went and fell in love with the man I hated.

10
Coffee Machine's Vengeance

I was the first to arrive at the office. I sat there, watching the wheat chart dip lower. It was not much of a dip, but it managed to wipe another zero from my tear-inducing losses.

Like everyone else, I had believed in Devlin's Midas touch, some magical gift no power of science could explain. Last night I had learned the truth. He drove his success by its ears, as Li would say. It was not magic, just sheer will and determination. He simply did not allow rules, or laws, or men to stand in the way of what he wanted. Men like him were rare. Men who would break into the press offices to steal tips that would sway the markets come morning. He would open his trading positions overnight, and wait for the morning rush to push the markets where they would inevitably go. He deserved his success. Unlike me. What had I done to earn it? What had I sacrificed? More importantly, what had I ever fought for?

'Long night?' Fred said when he saw me. 'I thought you meant to retire early.' He gave me a suspicious look.

'Couldn't sleep,' I said.

'Is that a bruise on your cheek?'

Damn. I forgot about that. I thought about lying, then realised the uselessness of it. Everyone in the building would know about the attempted car theft.

'Devlin and I confronted some thugs breaking into a car downstairs,' I said dismissively.

'Devlin caught up with you?' His face was suddenly stony.

'Yes, in the car park. He floored one of the men. He's got a good right hook on him.'

I had hoped that would be the end of it, but Fred seemed intent on interrogating me. 'So, what's the deal with you and Dev?'

Oh, for the love of elves and their inquisitive natures! 'There is no deal with me and Devlin. Why the interrogation, Fred?'

'He left as soon as you did. Looked like he was running after you. Had a look to him, you know. A man in pursuit, if you get my meaning.'

Perfectly, I thought grimly. *He pursued and he caught.*

'No, not really. Look, Fred, I'd best get back to work. I've had perhaps the worst week of my life. I just want to get through this week without incident. I can't give any excuse for Mr Ruttman to fire me.'

'No need to snap at me. I'm just asking questions that any friend would ask.' *Why do you keep kicking me?* his sad face asked.

'Sorry. Did not mean to kick you... I mean to snap at you.'

'Oh, Devlin! What happened to your beautiful face?' Sally cried out at her desk.

I turned just in time to see him wink at her with his good eye. 'Nothing to worry about, darling. Caught some thugs breaking into a car. Taught them a lesson they won't forget. There were only two of them, so the odds were high in my favour.' He leant on her counter with his elbow. 'So, you are worried for me, hey darling?'

She chuckled. 'Oh, you devil, with your stories.'

'It's true, my love. So, Sally, now that I know your true feelings about me, how about we get hitched.'

Bloody hell, the man just cannot help himself.

'Oh, be off with you. You know why, because my Billy would hunt us down and shoot you.'

He sighed. 'Oh, Sally, you crush me.'

She chuckled again.

I saw it now, his mask. It was not a false mask. That was Devlin, alright. It was just shallow. It simply showed one facade of his nature, the one he wanted the world to see. The charming rogue. The perfect alpha male people loved and wanted to please. The man who could make anything happen. As him, Devlin was whole. He had both legs. He did not grieve. He did not have responsibilities beyond those of this office. He had never been to prison. He had never been a boy at the mercy of grown men, nor watched his mother suffer abuse. Here, he was the perfect man.

He saw me watching him and winked. I shook my head. *Impossible man.* I fought back a smile. I'd be damned before I fed him more of the slush these poor fools were feeding him.

Our wild night together flashed through my mind. I was growing hot already, wondering whether it was truly possible to have a quick shag in the bathroom, with no one knowing about it. Quickly, I turned away before he saw my thoughts.

'Hey, Devlin.' That was puppy Paul's voice. 'I've done that report you wanted, and left it on your desk.'

'Great. I look forward to reading it.' I looked up to see Devlin patting the young man on the shoulder.

I caught sight of Lucy then. She was staring daggers at me. I guess I deserved every crumb of her scorn. I tried to look closer at her, to see her as Devlin might. Then, as if a fog had cleared, I saw Lucy in a whole new light. I saw a lonely, smart woman who wanted romance in her life, who wanted to be swept off her feet, who wanted to be loved above all else, and one who was not afraid to love back. A sting of envy passed through me. I glanced at Devlin again, and wished I could be as brave as Lucy in showing him my feelings. What would be his reaction? A pang of ache and hope went through me.

Get a grip, Vic, he would only laugh at you. It was just sex... at least for him.

The morning was interminable. I was acutely aware of Devlin, his every move, his every word. I watched him from the corner of my eyes as he strode through the office, speaking with individual traders. Later, I watched him in one of his rare, unguarded moments in his office. He sat with his hands behind his head, thoughtfully looking out the window. His face changed then, and I saw that rawness about him that spoke of a life-worth of grief and regrets. How had I missed it before? As if he felt my eyes on him, his gaze flicked to me. Our eyes held. He did not smile, did not wink. Something deep and meaningful passed between us in that moment, I just did not know what it was. Was he remembering last night? Did he regret it?

I was the first to look away, feeling very unsettled, and afraid. I felt like running and hiding. Devlin was just too much. A man like that could crush you, break you with the want of him. No. I had to stop this obsession with him, before it crippled me.

Work, Vic, focus on work.

The weather... ah, yes, the cyclone is shifting course...

'Vic, can I speak with you in my office,' Devlin's deep voice spoke from his door.

Oh, no.

He closed the door behind me and went to sit behind his desk. I perched uncomfortably in the chair in front of it.

'Let me guess, we need to talk,' I said dryly.

'What? No! That is, yes, but not like that.' He sat back in his chair, then lowered his voice. 'You left.'

Oh hell, this was going to be awkward.

I cleared my throat, and glanced at the glass wall, behind which all our co-workers were pretending to work, whilst really reading our lips to confirm what they no doubt already suspected; that Devlin and I had sex last night. I was certain it was stamped onto my face like some tattoo.

'I thought it best,' I said, trying not to move my lips too much. I glanced again to the office. Everyone was pretending to be occupied in their work. *Ha! They did not fool me. Could they hear us whispering?*

'I was disappointed. I do a great breakfast, you know.'

And there it was again, the jolt of hope that made my chest ache and my stomach flutter sickeningly. I searched his face, trying to see the core of him. Could he possibly have feelings that went beyond the want to bed me? I looked and looked, but saw only his inscrutable face. His eyes did not glow with warmth as my father's had when he looked at my mother. He did not love me. I was an idiot for even trying to imagine that he could. I looked away, hurt rising afresh.

'Erm. I don't think we should be talking about this here,' I mumbled.

'Fine. Let's talk about it after work. We'll go for a beer.'

I tried to squash the fresh surge of hope and excitement at the prospect. Maybe if he got to know me better, he would fall in love with me. *Stupid, stupid, stupid, Vic* But what did I have to lose, anyway? Just one drink could not harm anyone... Damn it all. I had to work in the *Angry Dragon* tonight. 'I can't... not tonight.'

He looked suspicious suddenly. He tried to disguise it with humour. 'Another date already? Truly Vic, you are insatiable.'

'Erm. No.' I would hang myself with my computer cord before I would admit that I had to pay off a meal by working in a kitchen.

'How about Friday or this weekend? We could go out for dinner. My treat,' he added quickly.

My heart sank. I promised Mr Chen to work all weekend. And he included Friday in the weekend. 'Erm. I have plans this weekend... and on Friday.'

That sounded much worse out loud than in my head. Oh, hell, I was mucking it up in my usual kamikaze style, as Li would say. *Tell him... tell him... something!* Nothing came to mind but the truth I could not bear to share. My throat contracted, as my mind blanked.

'All weekend?'

I cleared my throat. 'Yes.' My voice came out squeaky. Mr Chen ran his restaurant from midday to midnight at the weekend.

Devlin looked unshaken, but I could see hurt in his eyes.

'I see,' he said dully. 'Let me guess. You have plans tomorrow and the day after too.'

Tomorrow, I promised to take Li to the dentist. She was terrified of them, and needed me there to make sure the dentist did not secretly sedate her and remove all her teeth to sell on the blackmarket of second-hand teeth. Afterwards, I would have to stay with her until she felt certain the dentist did not follow her home with his evil teeth removing kit. And Thursday was, of course, my alternate-day shift in the *Angry Dragon*.

'I'm sorry... it's not... I meant, it's just that... I have plans.' My tongue tripped over itself and bruised as it tried to explain that it was not about him. 'It's not you, but me.' *Wait, that's not how I meant it.* 'I meant to say... I can't... I have plans.'

His face was blank, his expression unwavering. Was he just going to sit there and let me make a fool of myself?

He must have seen the desperation in my face and took pity. He lifted his hand, but there was a listless quality to it. 'Enough. I've heard enough. You'd best get back to work, hey Vic.'

I left his office feeling like my heart was slowly peeling into bloody shreds. I went back to my desk and worked until Fred said cheerfully, 'Coffee?'

Maybe a cup of coffee was all I needed. I picked up my cup and listlessly followed Fred into the kitchen.

'Why hello, Fred. Would you like your unusual today, black with one sugar?'

'Yes please, machine,' he replied, and placed his cup in station two. A moment later, he had a thick steaming cup of coffee which was making me giddy just smelling it on the air.

I approached the machine. She remained silent.

'Ahem, machine. I'd like my usual today, too,' I said.

The machine remained silent.

'Hello, machine.' I tapped her on the top with my palm. 'Hello. Anyone in there?'

'Don't hit her, you might break something,' Fred said, taking a step forward. 'Hey machine, are you alright?'

'I am perfectly fine, Fred, thank you for asking.'

'Oh, you evil bitch!' Well, I knew how to deal with one of those. 'Either you give me some coffee, or I swear, I'm going to pull the plug on you. See how you like being in the dark.'

'I don't think you should threaten her, Vic. That's not how you make friends.' Fred sipped his syrupy coffee. I could smell it, dark and delicious.

I slammed the cup down on station four. 'Coffee. Black. No sugar. Please,' I added as an afterthought.

'I am sorry, but we are out of coffee in station four. Please try again later.'

'OK, I will have it from another station.' I slammed the cup into station three.

'I am sorry, I do not recognise your command. Please press one for assistance, two for technical support, three for...'

I grabbed the cord and yanked the plug out of the wall. The coffee machine powered down and went dark.

Ha! Now who is laughing! Technical support my arse.

Fred was gaping at me, his jaw slack. 'No one has ever done that to her before. Why did you do that, Vic? What if you killed her?' He sounded distressed.

'You heard her!' I waved the plug in the air. 'She would not give me coffee!'

'That's not a reason to pull the plug on someone! Just because she's run out of coffee. Here, have mine.' He held out his cup. 'No need to be mad. Someone will refill her overnight, and you can have your coffee tomorrow.' He spoke calmingly, as if trying to pacify a lunatic.

Perfect, now the coffee machine was making me look like an unreasonable git.

I took his cup anyway, and downed his coffee. *Ha! Now we will see if she is really out of coffee.*

'Oh no!' That was Lucy's voice. 'You broke her! How could you, Vic? Must you be so destructive.'

'She was already broken,' I snapped. 'She would not give me coffee.'

'She was *out* of coffee,' Fred the traitor explained patiently.

'So you unplugged her!' Lucy was outraged.

Then Paul was there. 'Did I hear you say the coffee machine is broken?'

'What!' Sally came running over. 'Not our coffee machine.'

The rest of the office followed her.

'What's wrong with the coffee maker?'

'Vic broke her.'

'Why did Vic unplug her.'

'Tantrum. Apparently, the machine's run out of coffee.'

'Is the machine alright?'

'Plug her back in. See if she comes back.'

'What if she reboots and we've lost her?'

Seven accusing gazes were now directed at me. In my hand, I still held the cord with a dangling plug like some murder weapon at a crime scene.

'What is going on here.' Mr Ruttman elbowed his way past the mob.

'We think Vic just killed the coffee machine.'

He turned his gaze on me. 'Vic, is this true?'

'I just unplugged an appliance,' I said in exasperation. 'What's the big deal?'

'In my office, Vic,' Mr Ruttman commanded and turned on his heel.

There were angry mumblings around me.

'Let us all be calm here,' Fred said soothingly. He then turned to me. 'Look, maybe if you plug her back in, she will be fine and no harm's done, hey, Vic? How about you give me that cord before you do any more damage.'

Then Devlin pushed through the crowd. 'Big queue for coffee today,' he said jovially. 'Is there a party here I was not invited to?' He grinned and everyone's faces relaxed and turned to him, like children eager to have an adult mediate a dispute.

'Oh, thank god you are here,' Paul said.

'We think Vic has killed the machine for running out of coffee.'

He quirked his eyebrow at me in that annoying way of his. 'Really?'

'Vic pulled the plug out and won't plug it back in.'

'Fred just asked nicely for the plug back, but Vic won't give it to him.'

Devlin turned to the machine, placed his cup in station one, and her lights came on, as if by magic. 'Hello, Devlin.' Her sultry voice came out. 'And how may I please you today?'

'Just my usual, hey darling. Nice to see you are not as dead as everyone seems to think.'

I stared at the plug in my hand. Then looked behind the machine for another cable at the back. 'She has a battery backup! Oh, you deceitful little...'

Fred clasped his hand over my mouth. 'Don't do it. I think you've had a lucky escape. Let's just leave quietly, whilst no one is looking.'

He wrestled the cord out of my hand and handed it to Lucy, who rushed to the wall to plug it back in.

Everyone was gathered around Devlin, watching as his cappuccino was being poured. A collective sigh of relief went all around.

Fred dragged me out of the kitchen. 'That was close. I was certain they were thinking of stringing you up by that cord.'

I shook him off. 'The bitch set me up for a fall,' I snapped at him.

He shook his head sadly. 'That's not how it appeared to me back there, Vic. I think perhaps you are getting overwrought with the adjustment to a new place. Maybe you just need to take a few days off and recharge *your* batteries, hey.' He chuckled at his own pun.

I strode off. Mr Ruttman was waiting for me in his office, his expression stern.

Oh, hell. He might just give me those days off Fred recommended.

I sat in the chair in front of his desk and found my hands were shaking.

'Now, Vic. I will get straight to the point. You were on notice, as you know, and all you needed to do was get through the week without any more incidents. That included not starting a riot, or damaging company property...'

'She is not damaged... battery backup. Devlin made her work...'

'Yes, Devlin is very good at fixing things. And don't interrupt me when I am sacking you.'

'You are sacking me for unplugging a coffee machine!'

'And starting a riot. Yesterday you upset poor Lucy. Today you upset the entire office. And don't think that I am blind. I can see Devlin watching you. He should be courting a nice girl like Lucy, rather than panting after...' He waved a hand at my body. 'You! An unnatural creature, neither man nor woman. I know your type. I've heard of them, and I feel sorry for you.' He shook his head. 'But whatever you are, I simply cannot allow such a disruptive influence disrupting the smooth running of this distinguished firm. I am afraid I will have to let you go.'

Two weeks and two days. I managed to keep my dream job for two weeks. I could taste the ash of my dreams in my mouth. It had taken me years to get this job, and it was only Mr Ruttman's pity that had given me this chance. I knew I would never have another.

'I am sorry I disappointed you, Mr Ruttman, and thank you for the chance you gave me.' I stood up and walked out.

'Now wait there, I did not finish sacking you...' he called after me.

But what more was there to say? I went to my desk. Picked up my jacket, helmet and my cup.

'Vic?' Fred's voice sounded concerned.

I was afraid to look at him and see more pity. I was only barely holding it together.

'See ya, Fred. Thanks for being a friend,' I said without looking at him. And with that, I left the office without meeting anyone's eye. I knew they all watched me go.

I got on my bike, feeling strangely free, yet broken, and raced out of the car park. In my mirror, I saw Devlin run out of the elevator and watch me leave.

11
The Morning After

I woke up to the pounding on my door. 'Vic, I know you are in there, open up.'

Fred? What was he doing here? And how did he know where I lived?

I turned, resettled, and tried to ignore him. I did not know what time it was. It did not matter. I worked until after midnight, then smoked with Mr Chen, then went to a grotty late-night bar, where I drank myself into numbness, and staggered home through the empty streets without getting mugged, or worse. An achievement in my neighbourhood, and I was pleased with myself.

I had to get up soon and go back to Mr Chen's restaurant to work for free, at least for another week, while not having enough money to pay the rent I owed. I would now have to apply for more jobs. The thought of another job interview tied my stomach in knots. I pushed back the rising queasiness. Mr Ruttman had taken pity on me, had given me a chance, and I blew it. It was all Devlin's fault. If he hadn't been so bloody perfect, none of this would have happened.

The door pounded again. 'Vic! I can do this all day.'

Devlin would have probably just picked my lock. But he was not here. That made me want to curl up even more.

'Vic!'

He is not going to go away.

'I'm not going to go away, in case you are wondering.'

I hate it when they read my mind.

I got out of bed and staggered to the door, blurry-eyed. I yanked it open. 'What do you want, Fred?'

He blinked. 'You look sexy all tousled up like that from sleep. It's past eight, you know.' He walked past me uninvited and looked around my flat. 'Cosy.'

Past eight. That meant I had three more hours of sleep before I had to go to work, if you could call unpaid labour that. Penance, perhaps, would be more accurate. I told Mr Chen that since I had lost my job, I would work every day for him until I paid off my meal... and the complimentary bottle of champagne someone else enjoyed on my behalf.

Fred took off his coat and threw it over the back of my worn, two-sitter sofa. The table in front of it was littered with empty bottles of beer from last night. I drank more when I got home, just to be certain I'd remain passed out until I had to go to work again. Now, thanks to Fred, that too was a wasted effort.

I closed the door behind him. 'Why are you here, Fred?'

He went into my kitchen and began opening the cupboards. 'Coffee?'

The thought of coffee made me ill, and not just because of the machine who set the office mob on me.

'No. Thank you. I think I might switch to tea.'

'Was thinking of doing the same myself,' he said and pulled out a box of stale old teabags.

I sat down, rubbed my face, and watched him make tea. 'Don't you have work to go to?'

'I've got time before I need to be there. Milk?' He looked inside my fridge.

'I don't have any.'

He studied the contents of my fridge. 'Nothing for breakfast either.'

'There is some bacon, and bread in the freezer if you are hungry.'

'Was thinking of you, Vic,' he said. 'But don't mind if I do.'

The smell of cooking bacon slowly stirred my senses awake. My mouth watered and my stomach rumbled.

Fred made toast and put a plate of bacon in front of me.

I ate.

'Better?' he asked over his own mouthful.

Before I could reply, another knock sounded on my door. My landlord, Mr Gruleman, no doubt, demanding the rent I still owed him. Well, there was no point in avoiding him now.

I opened the door and my heart leapt, then plummeted. Devlin.

God, he looked perfectly tailored, crisp, and out of place in this rat hole of a building.

For a moment, I just stared at him.

'Hey, Vic.'

'Dev,' I said.

'Just came to see how you were.'

I shrugged. 'Fine. Will find another post, I expect. Not that hard, you know.'

I saw that he did not believe me.

'I came over last night, but you weren't here.'

'I was out.' *Stupid thing to say. Of course, I was out, if I was not here.*

'May I come in?'

I suddenly felt deeply ashamed of where I lived. I did not want him, of all people, to see what a loser I truly was. He could not see from the door how small and run down my apartment was. How untidy, after last night. It probably stank of last night's stale alcohol, and other smells ingrained into the stain-mottled carpet, which itself was older than me.

'Now's probably not a good time,' I hedged.

'Hey, Devlin.' Fred came to stand behind me, his toast in hand. 'Fancy seeing you here this early.'

Oh hell, I forgot about Fred. I suddenly realised how this must look, with me still in my pyjamas, and Fred here so early.

He lifted his slice of toast. 'Vic and I are just having breakfast. Want to join us?' The smile he gave Devlin was full of meaning and lies.

'Fred!' I exclaimed, horrified at his insinuations.

'Oh, sorry. I guess it might be a bit awkward, since we are out of bacon.'

Devlin looked from me to Fred, and back to me. 'I see.'

Fred winked at him.

Devlin turned and strode off.

'No... no, you don't see,' I shouted at his back. Devlin was hastily walking away, his limp now apparent. And I knew he would never come back. I wanted to curl up and cry.

He did not even give me a chance to explain.

I rubbed my forehead, which pounded harder than ever.

Fred bit off the toast. 'So, what did he want? Condolences from the management?'

I spun on him. 'Why the hell did you make out that there was something between us?'

'What do you mean?' he asked innocently. 'We are friends, right? I was just making sure he knew that and did not say or do anything that might hurt you. People like him prey on weakness. So I just backed you.'

'He is nothing like that!'

"Cause he is. That's why you hate him. Right, Vic?' He bit the last of his toast and chewed it.

There was no getting through to Fred. His heart, I guess, was in the right place. In his own misguided way, he was trying to protect me.

'You'd better leave. I have things to do today.'

'I thought we might spend the day together. Might cheer you up a bit, hey Vic?'

'You've got work,' I reminded him.

'I can take a day off. Haven't taken a day off in two years. Guess I'm due for one.'

'Maybe another time,' I said, and was suddenly weary of his company. Weary of any company.

I managed to push him out, thrust his coat into his hands, and shut the door in his face.

I went back to bed and pretended to sleep, while pretending not to think of Devlin. When my alarm went off, I got up, dressed and left my flat.

Mr Gruleman flung open his door when I tried to sneak past. 'Where is my rent, Vic?'

I fished in my coat pocket for this week's rent. 'It's all I have.'

He snatched the money out of my hand, waving it at me. 'This is not enough! You owe me two weeks.'

'I will move out tomorrow,' I said, and with that, I continued on my way down the stairs.

By the time I got to the restaurant, it was already crowded with lunchtime custom.

'You are late!' Mr Chen waved a soup ladle at me. 'You know how I hate it when my staff are late. Don't make me shout at you, Vic.'

'Sorry, Sir, won't happen again,' I mumbled a weak apology and a promise I was unlikely to keep, no matter how hard I tried.

I worked all day in the kitchen. Mr Chen gave me a few hours off during the quiet time between the end of lunch and dinner. During those hours, I wandered listlessly around the city, ate a sandwich on a park bench, then went back to work.

I tried to keep my head down and work so hard I wouldn't have time to think of Devlin, or the look of raw anger and hurt in his eyes when Fred came to stand behind me. Yet try as I might, Devlin invaded every secret pore of my thoughts. Worse, I could not forget our night.

It was over and done with, I told myself. Better sooner than later. But those thoughts were useless. I wanted Devlin. I wanted his arms around me, his body on top of me, inside me. I wanted to taste whisky and man on his tongue. As I scrubbed a pan I wondered when I had begun to feel like that. I had been aware of Devlin more than anyone else since the moment I saw him. Had I wanted him all this time?

Was my ploy with Lucy not some sort of revenge, or a lesson to be taught, but another misguided, childish attempt at making a man notice me? I just did not know anymore. I did not know what had happened with Devlin and why. He kissed me and said he wanted me. But then so did Lock... now and then. Hell, I would not insult Devlin by comparing him to Lock. But just because a man wants you does not mean he loves you. *Face it, Vic, he is gone.*

Kitty, the waitress, ran into the kitchen. 'Mr Chen, Mr Chen. Jules has just thrown down his apron and left!'

Jules was a sullen, young waiter who hated his job, and complained about it to anyone who would listen. He also complained about how few 'proper' jobs there were for young people who had spent a fortune on their university degrees.

Mr Chen quickly looked around his kitchen and pointed at me. 'Vic, put on a floor shirt and get out there. You'll be on the floor for the rest of the night.'

Oh no, anything but that. I would rather scrub vomit and shit from the toilets. 'I would be more help here, Sir.'

'You know the menu better than anyone here. Now go. You owe me, Vic.'

I sighed. I did, and more than just for the meal that I had not paid for, though I knew that was not what he meant.

'Table five are waiting to order,' Kitty told me hurriedly. 'And table six are angry about something. They shouted at Jules, which is why he left. And table four...'

'I've got the picture,' I said sullenly, threw on a crisp white shirt, and went out there.

The restaurant was a large hall, at the end of which a skinny, long-legged musician played the grand piano. Every table was taken, and eight waiters rushed between tables. Bob was greeting new arrivals, directing them to the bar where they could have a drink while they waited for their table. I had worked the floor before, and hated every moment of it. I was never comfortable in such a public display. I hated to have to ignore their confused, questioning stares as they tried to work out my gender. More than anything, I hated to be on this side of life, serving the side where I wanted to be. Each time I walked that floor, I walked on the edges of my dream. And like a dream, I could not touch it, could not grasp it, and as soon as I turned my back, it faded into just another childish wish.

Well, there was nothing for it but to get the night over and done with.

First thing first. The angry table six. I saw them immediately. A plump woman with crossed arms, ranting at her husband. You could always spot couples who have been together for a long time. They shared the same body shape, mannerisms, and facial expressions. There was also a young, sheepish looking girl at their table, looking embarrassed by her mother's indignation.

I took a deep breath and pushed every fear aside to become Victor. Victor could talk to angry people and pacify them with his charming, brazen ways. Feeling more confident, I approached them.

'Hello, I am your new waiter,' I said in my charming Victor voice. 'The last waiter has been sacked for his terrible manners and incompetence, so please accept our deepest apologies for any distress he may have caused you. I will be here to make sure your meal is enjoyable and you lack for nothing.' *There, that came out better than I'd hoped for. Thank you, Victor.*

Instantly, the woman's posture eased. 'Sacked, you say? Well, I *am* pleased about that. The boy was far too snotty for a waiter. And when I told him not to take that arrogant attitude with me, for he was nothing but a waiter, he stuck up his nose and informed me that he was a historian. Who's ever heard of historians working in a restaurant?'

'Who indeed, ma'am,' I said in a deep husk.

She looked pleased. 'Well, you are much better, young man. Yes, I think we will keep you.

'I am very happy to hear that,' I replied smoothly.

'Ahem, darling, I believe this young man is a woman,' said her husband.

The woman leant in to take a closer look at me. 'No, no. I am certain she is a man. What do you think, dear?' She looked at her daughter. 'He seems about your age, you should be able to tell.'

The girl looked up, squinted and tilted her head. 'Oh, um... I think it may be a transgender, you know, once a man — or a woman — now the opposite.'

I simply smiled politely. I did not care whether people thought of me as a man or a woman. Neither was an insult to me.

'Well, are you?' The woman turned on me accusingly.

'No, ma'am, I am not,' I replied dully, trying to sound bored by the conversation, as Victor would have done, rather than affronted like Victoria.

'There, see? The young man said 'no'. Now, shall we get back to our dinner.'

'May I bring you anything else? Perhaps more drinks?' I asked. 'On the house, of course.'

'Oh, well, if you are offering, maybe another bottle of the red we are drinking.'

'Of course, ma'am.'

Now that that was sorted, I turned to table five and froze. *Oh hell, no. Will the Universe never give me a bloody break?*

Devlin was staring up at me from his menu, shock and surprise on his face. His face quickly reordered into a neutral expression. His lips pursed tight. I tried and failed not to squirm under his intent gaze.

Victor retreated and was hiding. *Coward.*

The little Francesca was looking down at her menu. 'I think I will try something different today, Uncle Dev. Hong-Kong style steamed duck with rice and Szechuan sauce.' She slammed shut the menu, looked up at me, and narrowed her eyes. 'Aren't you the one who came home with uncle Dev, then snuck out at dawn like a thief? Didn't realise you worked here.'

Snotty little miss.

Victor emerged to smile patronisingly at the silly child. 'There is probably much you don't realise at your age.'

Her eyes turned to daggers. 'You are supposed to be nice to customers. Even someone of *my age* realises that.'

'You are right, of course, Miss Know-It-All. I do humbly apologise.' My tone could not have been less humble or apologetic. 'Are you ready to order, Sir, little miss?' I said blithely, though my heart was in my throat.

Devlin's lips twitched, as he held back a smile. 'Yes, of course, thank you, Victor,' he replied smoothly.

I shot him an icy look. 'It's just Vic.'

'Sure it is,' he said indolently, giving me a knowing look, which made me blush.

'Your order, Sir,' I repeated in my bored waiter voice.

After I took their order, I went straight to the kitchen. Once there, I could breathe again. I leant against the door feeling a funny kind of sick in my gut. He must have heard me act like some snivelling idiot to the table next to his. Worse, he would have heard the confusion about my gender. When had it begun to matter? And now he knew me for the loser I truly was. He saw where I lived. He knew I could not have paid for the meal, as Lucy had boasted.

'Vic, table three are ready for their desserts,' Kitty stuck her head around the door to hiss at me.

I straightened my shoulders. Too late to hide now. Might as well just do my job. So I went out there, and took orders, and cleared tables when the food runners were overloaded with orders, and was most gracious and polite to every customer. I avoided Devlin's eyes. I knew he was watching me. I wanted to sink through the floor, but Victor kept his head up high and did his job, and earned a pocket full of tips, which was more than the commission I had earned in two weeks of trading wheat futures.

When I returned to Devlin's table to clear the plates, he tried to catch my eye. I refused to meet his. When I picked up his plate, his hand moved towards mine, but at the last moment, he diverted it to pick up his glass.

Francesca was busy ogling the dessert menu with childish delight. I took the plates away and came back some minutes later to take their order.

'Are you ready to order your desserts?' I asked politely.

Francesca gave me a pert look. 'I will have ice cream... and brandy.'

'Francesca,' Devlin intervened. 'You can't have brandy, we've discussed it before. You are too young to drink.'

'But I like it!' she objected.

'When the hell did you learn to like it?' he demanded.

She shrugged. 'When you were out. You have been coming home late recently, and I wait up for you, you know.'

'Well, don't,' he snapped.

Her face fell, and she was suddenly a small girl again. 'I'm afraid to go to sleep, in case you don't come back.'

He looked stunned, then hurt. 'I will always come back, Francesca,' he said gruffly.

Tears welled in her eyes. I have never seen a more perfect performance. And indomitable Devlin was crumbling into a puddle under it. 'I still want brandy.

I'm twelve now. And you did promise that I could have anything I wanted.'

The poor sod was actually thinking about it.

'Excuse me, Miss Know-It-All,' I interrupted, sickened by such a man being brought so low by a manipulative snot of a child. 'You may, of course, realise this already, amongst your wealth of deductive reasoning, but it is actually illegal for us adults to serve little children like you alcohol. You may end up going to prison if we do.'

She gaped. 'Uncle Devlin would never let them take me to prison.'

'If he is complicit in allowing you to drink alcohol, he will join you there.'

'How would they know?' she demanded.

I smiled evilly. 'I'd tell them, of course. It would be the right thing to do, as a good citizen. Now, shall I bring you that brandy, little miss snot, followed by a police officer with an arrest warrant?'

Her eyes narrowed. 'I don't think I like you.'

'And yet you are so certain of everything else.'

Devlin chuckled.

'Uncle Dev! It's not funny.'

'I'll just have the whisky,' he said to me, smiling. Then, as if that was a key word to unlock a flood of memories, his smile fell away. He abruptly turned back to Francesca. 'Ice cream for you then, pet?'

I took their order, and soon after brought it out. Later, I cleared their table and did not return. Bob took over the end of meal duties.

As I took the empty plates from another table, I saw Devlin talking to Bob while settling the bill. Bob seemed too friendly and familiar, but then Devlin was a regular here. The thought opened the gates of bitterness and dejection I'd held back all night. When Devlin left, the restaurant seemed a darker, lonelier place. The man was wrapped in light.

I worked the rest of the shift until only Mr Chen and I were left, sitting on the cold backstairs, smoking his medicinal pot. My back hurt, my legs hurt, and my feet were blistered and sore where my shoes have been rubbing all day.

Mr Chen pulled out an envelope. 'Here are your wages. Two evenings and three full days.'

'I'm working off the meal I owe you, remember? You don't owe me anything.'

'I did not, but now I do. Your tab was settled.'

'What! By whom?' But I knew. It was just another blow to my already shattered pride.

'Mr Knightsbridge. He asked Bob how long you've been working here, and Bob told him since you ran out on your bill. So he paid it, in full. Which means I owe you wages now.'

Like the wheat futures, it seems my shame found new heights. Now Devlin knew the type of fraud I was, and a liar, and pathetically broke.

'I don't want it.' I shoved the envelope back to Mr Chen.

'And I don't want to owe anyone money. If you don't want it, then give it to Mr Knightsbridge. This is between you and him. I have my debt, and you have your pay. The rest is not my problem.' He inhaled deeply from his bong. 'And by the way, Vic, you are sacked.'

'Why? I did nothing wrong, and you are short of staff.' I did not think I could have sunk any lower than losing two jobs in two days.

'I do need staff, and yes, you are good. But this is not what you want. You must follow your own path, else you will get trampled on another man's path.'

'Another Chinese saying?'

'No, my own. Li taught me the wisdom of that. She is a girl, but she is smart. I wanted to leave her my restaurant. But she did not want it. Said it was not her path in life. And I know working in my kitchens is not your path either. So I do you a favour, because I love you like I love Li. I am pushing you off the wrong path. You want more, you told me that. Go out there and get it. I will not allow you to hide here in my restaurant.'

'I was sacked from the firm, Mr Chen,' I said sullenly. 'There is nothing out there for me.'

He waved it away. 'Then go find another firm.'

I inhaled deeply and breathed out, lowering my head. 'I'm not sure I can. I'm not even sure what I want anymore.'

Devlin. I wanted Devlin.

'Sounds like you are in love,' Mr Chen said wisely. 'If so, follow your heart and it will find your path for you.'

He was wrong, I thought morosely, there was nothing there for me either.

12
The New Path

'Mark, you are a darling.' Li glowed as he took one of my boxes from her hands. The old billionaire smiled as if she had just offered him a giant candy.

I strained under my own box, carrying it down the four flights of stairs from my flat on the top floor. There was no lift in the building, for it was built hundreds of years ago, and had probably never been redecorated since then.

'I'll take the last box,' Li said and picked up the box consisting of one pillow and some bedding.

Three boxes, one suitcase and a rucksack in the boot of Mark's limousine was the sum of my life. The furniture, the cutlery, and even the filthy shower curtain, all belonged to Mr Gruleman. It was depressing. Yet I was still going to miss this flat. It was small, run down, but it was my own place.

'Got everything, Vic?' Li asked.

I nodded and closed the door behind me.

'I am looking forward to you coming back to live with me. It'll be like the old days.'

That's what I was afraid of. I wanted to leave those old days behind. Yet each step forward seemed to propel me back two.

The driver of the limousine held the door open for us as we climbed into the back. I watched Li sit beside Mark and reach into the fridge cabinet for some drinks, and I realised that it could never be like the old days. Li was not the same woman she had been when we last lived together. She doted on Mark, her eyes were just for him. And I was not the same Vic that I had been two weeks ago. Between now and then I had gained all that I had always wanted, and then lost it all. I lost my job, my pride, the man I loved. Yes, I could admit it to myself. I could not hide from it. I could not hide in Mr Chen's restaurant. That much became clear to me overnight. Yet I did not know where to go from here.

'So, how did you manage to lose your dream job?' Li asked, handing me a glass of red wine.

'The coffee machine set me up for a fall,' I replied sullenly. 'The little fake played dead to set an angry mob on me, then got me sacked.'

Li laughed. 'Only you, Vic.'

Mark chuckled too. 'This sounds like a conversation one has after many more drinks than I've had.' He drank his wine happily, whilst patting Li on her knee.

I knew how ridiculous it sounded, yet I did not think it funny. I told Li about Mr Ruttman's last words to me.

'Wait... did you say he was annoyed with Devlin's interest in you?' Li asked, intrigued.

Not caring if Mark listened in, I told her about Devlin and me, and how Fred accidentally gave Devlin the wrong impression about us.

'So, while you were trying to make Devlin jealous of you, he was actually jealous of Lucy, and now he is jealous of Fred?'

'I don't know. Li, honestly. He did not even give me a chance to explain. We are done.'

'Yet he paid for your meal with Lucy?'

'Probably to let me know that he knows what a loser I am,' I said and turned to look outside.

'Is he like that?' Li asked, affronted. 'I don't think I like him.'

'I don't know anymore. It does not matter. I just need to get back on my feet, and forget all about him.'

'Sure thing, hon. Like I said, it'll be like the good old days.'

Li's mansion was not as palatial as Devlin's house, but it still allowed me to have the whole floor to myself, far away from Li's amorous liaisons. Although, Mark seemed to be taking up most of her time. Li has been turning clients away in preference to spending time with him; going on walks during the day time, entertainments in the evenings, and private excursions on his yacht at the weekends. It was nothing like the 'good old days'.

I was mostly left alone in the huge house with nothing to do, except apply for jobs, to be only met with silence from the other end. There was no cleaning to be done, for Li hated cleaning, and a lady who did not speak English came in once a day to dust and scrub, and do Li's laundry.

Li hated cooking, so each evening she dined out, mostly with Mark. She liked to make breakfast and we competed for that one chore. Considering how little time she spent and ate at home, her cupboards and fridge were always fully stocked. Her housekeeper came in every other day to make sure all of Li's basic supplies were taken care of. She also organised any necessary maintenance on the house, and took Li's more expensive dresses to the dry cleaners.

So I wandered restlessly around the massive house and its many empty rooms, longing for my cosy flat.

The day after I moved in, I stuffed the money that Mr Chen had given me into an envelope, added most of my left over wages from Mr Ruttman, and borrowed the rest from Li. I addressed the envelope to Mr Knightsbridge and posted it to his address. I would rather die of hunger than owe him a single penny.

I imagined him laughing in the office, as he recited how Lucy's meal was paid for by my kitchen duties. The fact that I knew Devlin was not like that, did not lessen the sting the imaginary laughter caused me. I tried to pretend it did not matter, and I hated him. He assumed the worst of me and Fred, and did not even give me a chance to defend myself.

Good riddance! Forget him, Vic.

Once I had posted him the money, I forced myself not to think of him, or Fred, or the office... no matter how much I missed them all.

A week ago, I was 'a suit'. Now, I was back living on Li's charity.

I could not complain about Li. She was easy to live with. On the rare occasion I saw her, she dispersed my gloom, like a butterfly in a dead garden. Her laughter and joy were contagious. She was like that. She enjoyed life and made you enjoy it with her. When she was around, I could almost forget Devlin.

Each day, however, I was aware that I was living on borrowed time. Though Li would never throw me out, I could not live on the edges of her life forever.

So I applied for jobs each day. Most were in trading — for those sticky tatters of dreams of riches still clung to me. After weeks of silence, and one failed interview, I decided to apply for other office jobs: a clerk, a receptionist, a PA, an office assistant — anything that required me to wear a suit.

I fumbled and stumbled through three more interviews. Neither Victor nor Victoria were any use to me when I was faced with the stony face of the person deciding my future. I felt inadequate, desperate, and I was certain that all my ugly past was written plainly in my face.

One night, some four weeks later, I found myself walking into the *Lonely Lizard*.

Tony greeted me from the bar. He saw my face and poured me a double measure of whisky. 'On the tab again, I guess,' he said.

'You know I'm good for it.'

I was broke and had too much pride to ask Li for more money. I was already living in her house and eating her food.

'Rough times?' he asked.

'Lost my job at the firm.' I picked up my whisky glass and drank half of it. 'Is your offer still open for a manager... or even bar staff?'

He looked guilty. 'Sorry, Vic, if you'd come round a week ago, I would have had something for you. But I just hired Rachel. She is a nice lass and eager to work behind the bar. I gave her all my spare shifts and she wants more. I like her. I think she is a long-termer. I would not want to sack her for someone who did not have their heart in it, if you know what I mean.'

I nodded. 'I understand. Just thought I'd ask.'

'A week ago I would have been good for it. You know that. Right?'

'Don't stress, Tony. I understand.'

He cleared away some glasses and wiped the water rings off the bar. 'Glad that you came round, though. That gorgeous god has been round asking after you. Comes in every few days asking if I'd seen you, or heard from you.'

'Oh, hell,' I sighed, as my heart leapt in my chest. 'What did you tell him?'

He looked puzzled. 'What can I tell him but the truth. I have not seen you since the night he was here with you. He asked me to let him know if you happen to come in.'

'Don't,' I said. 'Don't tell him.'

He winced. 'You know I'm crap at lying. And he is so handsome. And his eyes... they see things. He will know. And did you see his size! He will crush me. Don't do that to me, Vic.'

'Fine, just don't tell him where I am staying.'

'I don't know where you are staying!' He put his hands over his ears. 'I hear nothing. I don't want to know.'

'Right. You don't.'

That night Li was waiting up for me. There you are, she drifted into my room like a red swan. 'I think I've solved all your problems.'

'I hate it when you say that,' I said, throwing my jacket down on the chair by the old fireplace.

I took off my shirt and fell backwards onto my bed of red satin sheets. Li loved reds. They suited her, and her life: vibrant, dangerous, alluring.

'Mark is hosting a party on his yacht in a few weeks. He is taking me, of course, though for this one night he says I am forbidden any tricks with other men.' She shrugged, 'Fine by me, I told him. The old goat is randy enough as it is. I don't think I will have any energy for the others. Anyway, you know how it is with these billionaire playboy events. Everyone will be bringing consort dates.'

I could see where this was going. 'No.'

'Wait, you have not heard me out. It's not like that. No sex. Just let me finish. Mark has a business associate, a sharp bloke, old. Maybe as old as fifty. He is getting divorced due to his... ahem, inability, if you know what I mean. Can't get his prick to stand to attention. Tried all kinds of drugs, acupuncture, and even anal...'

'Yes, yes, I got it.'

'Anyway, he wants a consort, but he is after a very specific type. Wants an androgyne. Doesn't care whether it's man or woman. In fact, he specifically asked for one so good that he would not be able to tell. Willing to pay ten thousand for the night.'

'Oh, hell, Li. No man would pay that and expect nothing in return, and I don't mean just looking pretty next to him.'

'Told you, he can't get it up. At most, he might grope you a bit, but he can't do anything to you. You get these types of rich blokes who just want what no one else has, and will pay for it. You know, like one of them expensive paintings. What use are those, I ask you? Half of them are too boring to even look at.'

'Not ten grand. I'd have to give him my virginity for that.'

'Ha! Shows how little you understand about the sex market. Only idiots sell their best and single commodity for so little money.'

'Either way...'

'Just sleep on it, Vic. I know you are bust broke. And I know you won't take any more money from me. One night, with nothing but looking good on some rich man's arm, and you will be sorted for cash. You never know, you might even like it.'

'I won't,' I said gloomily. But I was strapped for cash, and what other choices did I have?

'Besides, it will put that Devlin rat out of your mind.'

'He is not a rat,' I said quietly.

'All you do is brood and sulk. You need another man to show you how many rich fish there are in the sea.'

'Fine, one night.' I agreed. My gut already told me I was going to regret this. No one paid ten grand for a date without something else being on offer. Money just did not flow that easily.

Li turned to go, looking pleased. 'Oh, and another thing. Pa told me Mr Rat Knightsbridge has been asking after you, and where you were staying. Pa wanted to know if you wanted him to know.'

'No,' I answered quickly. Nothing good could come out of that either.

'Thought so. It's what I told Pa. Night, hon.' She blew me a kiss.

'Night, Li.'

She breezed cut of my room, and I felt alone and lonely. Devlin was looking for me. What did he want? Probably nothing I'd want... nor dare to give.

Either way, I could not bear to see him. I had to forget him. Move on with my life. Maybe this date with Mr Soft Steel was just the thing I needed. Or maybe I just needed sex with someone else, to wash Devlin's memory from my skin, to purge him from my pores once and for all. The plan might just work, I told myself, and felt even more depressed.

13
The Mistake

Li had been away for a week with Mark. He took her on his private jet to Venice. I was not envious... much. Though I did indulge a few nights imagining what it would be like to have such adoration all to myself.

The cleaner had come and gone today already, and I was again alone in a dark, silent mansion. I picked up a random book from the old library Li had purchased with the house, and sat in my personal living room, adjoining my bedchamber, sipping one of Li's better wines. She had a whole cellar of them. She preferred red wine, so she instructed me to drink the whites to make room for more reds she was going to send from Italy. So I obliged.

I heard a knock on the front door and ignored it. Must be one of Li's jilted lovers. Her housekeeper — if she was here — usually sent them away.

The knock came again, louder, more persistent.

Bloody hell, she does not want you. Go away.

I sipped my wine. It was good. A ten-year-old vintage from some castle in France. It was early afternoon, and I planned to have another bottle before dinner, and maybe one with dinner. What else was there for me?

I was reading a play by some French writer to go with my French wine.

Click, creak.

What the hell was that?

I sat up. There it was again, soft steps outside in the hallway. A door creaked open, then softly closed.

Oh, hell. It was definitely not the maid. I crept to the door, put my ear against it and listened. One set of surreptitious footfalls, slow, meticulous.

A thief!

Li locked away her jewels in a secret safe. But she still had a lot of silver and all kinds of fancy-looking pieces around. I'd rather drown in a vat of liquid manure than allow any of Li's possessions to be stolen on my watch.

I tiptoed to the fireplace and picked up a poker. I weighed it in my hand; heavy and nicely pointy. I took a few practice swings and hid behind my door. Someone stopped on the other side of it, listening. Could he sense me here? Could he hear me breathing, or my pounding heart? The handle moved. I tightened my grip on the poker. The door opened slowly, silently.

I raised the fire poker.

Someone large stepped in.

I swung.

With lightning reflex, an arm blocked the poker from descending on his head. 'Argh!' he cried. Then yanked the poker from my hands and threw it aside. 'Damn it, Vic, you almost killed me.' He grabbed his arm and bent over it. 'Bloody hell! That might have been my head.'

'Devlin? What the hell are you doing here? Who let you in? Damn you for scaring the shit out of me.'

'I let myself in at the back,' he snapped. 'After you clearly ignored my knocking. And you nearly broke my arm!'

'You broke into Li's house and snuck around like a thief. Of course I almost broke your arm.'

'Hell, Vic, why didn't you just answer the door?' He flexed his arm and fingers experimentally.

'There is no one I want to see. And that includes you. How the hell did you find me anyway? I'm assuming you are not here to burgle Li.'

He gave me a look. 'Money buys information, on top of everything else. You can't hide from money.'

'Who ratted me out?' I demanded.

'I'm not likely to betray my sources, now am I? What kind of a businessman would I be?'

'Fine. You found me. Tell me what you want and leave me alone. I sent you the money I owed you.'

He sobered then. 'You did not need to...'

'Yes, I did. I am not going to owe you, Dev. So why are you here?'

He looked around, saw the bottle of wine I was drinking. Picked it up and whistled. 'Li is doing well for herself. This is one of only three bottles from that year from *Château De Millésime Moyen*. He sniffed it. 'Mmm. Nice.' He fell back on my sofa and drank out of the bottle.

I crossed my arms, standing where I was. 'Help yourself.'

'Now, now, Vic. Share and share alike.'

'What do you want?'

'You,' he answered quickly, gruffly.

I looked away. 'I can't.'

He drank again, deeply. Then put the bottle down and run his hand through his hair. 'Vic... I don't know what's between you and Fred, but...' He shook his head. 'I don't know what happened that night between us... I mean I do, but not why you left, and why you've been giving me the cold shoulder ever since. Fred swore he did not know where you have moved to... I did not believe him.' There it was, that raw hurt in his eyes.

'He does not,' I said, angry with him all over again. Maybe I did not deserve his trust, not after the way that I acted with Lucy. But Mr Flirt here was not one to preach about trust. The bloody man proposed marriage to a married woman every damned morning.

He looked thoughtful. 'Seems I owe him an apology for that black eye.'

'You hit him! Why on earth would you hit a defenceless elf?'

He shrugged. 'Like I said, I did not believe him. Thought a bit of pain might make him tell me the truth. Besides, I felt like I owed him that one.'

'You are his boss!'

'I was not at the time. It was the weekend. Doesn't count.'

'Of course it does,' I said outraged.

He looked annoyed suddenly. 'Why are you defending him anyway. I'm here to discuss us, not him.'

I looked away. So, he thinks that I bedded Fred the day after I bedded him. Now his cock was chaffing in his pants, and he needed me to chafe against. Hell, the idea did not sound so bad. In fact, I began to ache just thinking about it.

'You don't have much of an opinion about me, do you?'

'It's not like that, Vic. Honestly, I don't know what it's like. I just wanted to talk to you,' he said frustrated.

'You came to bed me, Dev.'

'No...well, maybe that too.'

'Fine. Let's go to my bedroom.' I led the way next door.

'Vic... wait.'

I did not, so he followed. I stopped by the bed and took off my shirt. His arms were around me. 'It does not have to be like this, Vic. This is not sordid between us.'

'Sure it is,' I said softly, bitterly.

We have not had a single date. Not even a drink together. This was no different to anything else I ever knew. Except, somehow, with Devlin it was.

He kissed the back of my neck, then gently, slowly down my shoulder His erection was pressed against my bottom. Feeling it there, I suddenly wanted to rip off my trousers and have him inside me. I fumbled with my belt. His hands stopped me. He kissed my neck, his hands unhurriedly stroking my hips, my waist, my stomach, my chest.

I did not have his patience. The smell of him was making me drunk. His heat was all-enveloping, soothing, safe. God, have I ever been this blindly, dizzyingly aroused. I turned in his arms and kissed him fiercely. I pushed my tongue into his mouth, he sucked, then his own explored my lips, my mouth. I groaned husky and deep in my throat.

His arms tightened around me, and I could feel his leashed fierceness. His body was buzzing with his raw need to throw me on the bed and pound into me. He contained it, restrained it, like a beast on a chain. He kissed me slowly, his arms exploring, pulling me closer. He kissed my neck, my jaw, his hand stroking my bottom, then pulling me close to grind me against him.

I pulled off his coat and worked on the buttons of his shirt. My hands were clumsy, shaking.

'God, this is torture,' he whispered and ripped off his shirt over his head, threw it aside and unbuttoned his trousers. I was there, eagerly waiting to grab him. He sprang free into my hand, and I crushed him in my grip.

'Easy there, tiger,' he whispered and chuckled. He kissed me again, removing my trousers, his hand reaching down to stroke and caress me in return. I began to throb, and move against his hand, blind with want. I wanted him, now, inside me. I fell to my knees and took him into my mouth. Oh god, no man ever tasted so good.

'Vic...' he gasped, his hand tangling in my hair. He was big and full in my mouth, and growing harder. My tongue explored his every ridge and vein. I grew frantic with my own building need. He was gasping, growling mindlessly, pulling my hair to bury himself deeper in my mouth, my throat. My hand massaged his testicles, and I felt them tighten. His cock began to throb. He came hard, gripping my hair until it almost hurt.

'Good god, Vic,' he breathed through gritted teeth. 'Don't ever leave me.'

I chuckled. He was still semi-erect as I kissed his stomach, his chest. My hand was still massaging his testicles, his cock. A moment later, I felt him grow hard.

Bloody hell, the man was insatiable.

He pushed me on the bed, spread my legs wide and crawled over me. He hooked my legs over each arm and thrust into me. I arched to meet him. He was slow, deliberate, savouring each thrust.

'Stop torturing me... harder,' I begged.

He smiled, wicked and evil, and drew out each thrust, knowing how it was driving me mad. 'Now, now, Vic. You must learn patience.'

His hand moved between us, his fingers brushing me gently, slowly, just enough to make me almost scream in frustration.

I grabbed him and pulled him down on to me, gripping him tight with my thighs wrapped around his waist. He chuckled and thrust in earnest. His rhythm increased, growing more urgent. I flipped him over on his back and mounted him in turn. I was in charge now. I was making love to him. Making love... I never made love before. The thought at once made me want to weep and drove me wild. He wrapped his arms around me, holding me close.

'That's right, Vic, take what you need from me. That's it. Take it.'

I moved faster and faster. I was making love to Devlin. It was glorious. I exploded. There was no other way to describe that shattering of body and soul. I felt him gasp in his own release.

I fell on top of him, mindless and spent. For a time, we lay in silence, sticky with sweat and sex.

His hand was buried in my hair. I moved slightly to a more comfortable position, and already he was growing hard.

'Oh, for the love of god, Dev,' I said weakly into his shoulder. 'You can't possibly want more. You really do walk around with a constant erection, don't you?'

'I was just thinking of your mouth around me,' he chuckled, and rolled over me to kiss me.

I sighed and kissed him back. He rolled me over on my front, kissing my neck and back, while his fingers caressed the sensitive anus, then lower until he was touching my sex. He pulled me up on my knees and entered me again.

We spent the afternoon in bed. In between glasses of wine and snacks, we made love six more times, and I still wanted more. I could not get enough of him. He was insatiable. By the time darkness fell, we moved into my living room, sharing another bottle of some rare white wine. We were dressed by then, and simply talking about many nothings. I told him about Li and how she came to do what she did. He told me about Fran, and how proud he was of her good grades in school. She wanted to be a trader, just like him.

Devlin then reached into his coat pocket and pulled out an envelope.

My mood instantly soured when I saw that it contained a check.

He chuckled. 'Hold your daggers, Vic. It's not what you think. I've been trying to find you to give this to you.'

Disappointment washed over me. 'So you weren't trying to find me for a quick shag,' I joked lamely.

He looked at me seriously, but his eyes were dancing. 'No, not a quick one.' He gave me the cheque. 'You were right, about China, and about that storm. I kept your position open, as you told me too. This is your ten percent of the windfall.

I looked at the cheque and my eye grew wide. 'Fuck me,' I whispered. It was two years' worth of my wages at the firm.

He grinned. 'I know. I said the same thing the first time I saw my commission. Your reckless gamble paid off. You were lucky, Vic. Mr Ruttman nearly closed the position thrice. I talked him out of it. Told him to wait.'

I held the cheque out to him. 'Then it's yours. He said you underpinned my losses. I would have been bust if you had not put up the cash from your accounts. I was lucky, not smart.'

He huffed. 'It's pennies for me, my dear. Don't let pride rule your head. You'll never get ahead like that. It was your gamble and it paid off. You earned it. Take it and keep it. Next time you will be smarter. No one can claim a clean sheet in the trading game.'

'Not even you?' I asked sceptically.

He laughed. 'You give me far too much glory that I do not deserve. I lost my first seven trades, before I smartened up and began to make sound choices. I still lose now and then. Markets are like that. Takes everyone by surprise now and then.'

I put the cheque down. My head swimming with the numbers on it. I was sorted, at least for a time. I could rent my own place again, while I looked for another job.

Devlin was watching me, his face serious. 'You were right about us needing to talk...'

'Don't,' I warned him, my stomach lurching with anxiety. 'Don't ruin it.'

'Vic, I don't care what happened with you and Fred that night. I know you are not seeing him anymore.'

My anger was instantaneous and hot. 'Please stop,' I said quietly, trying to contain it.

'Just let me finish. I think we should start again. Maybe dinner, or a drink in a bar... just anything, Vic. I can make you forget Fred. I bet you weren't thinking of him this afternoon.'

I flinched. I could not take his doubts, his insinuations and accusations. Each one was a sharp stab. Perhaps I deserved it. Had I ever given him cause to trust me? Had I ever known anything but sordid trysts? No, I deserved his mistrust, his doubts. But I already thought so little of myself, I simply could not bear him confirming it for me every day. I could not stand him, of all people, looking at me in the same questioning, doubtful way that the rest of the world did. Especially not after what we had just done.

'Leave,' I said quietly, my heart breaking all over again. 'Just leave.'

Did he not see my feelings for him? I showed them to him again and again this afternoon.

'Vic, for god's sake. Just talk to me. Why are you angry now? I thought I was being reasonable.'

He would never trust me, never give me the chance to defend myself. He saw too much and not enough.

My lips curved cynically. 'Perhaps you were, if I was guilty of all you accused me of.'

He was still for a long moment. 'You mean... you and Fred. You didn't... He smiled as if sunshine had once again dispelled the darkness in his life, whilst the world dimmed and crashed around me. The universal balance. He gains, I lose. His fear and anxiety quashed, whilst my heart was bleeding and dying.

I stood up. 'Just leave, Dev. Don't come looking for me again.'

'Vic...' He put his hands on my shoulders. 'I am so relieved. You cannot possibly know...'

I spun and pushed him in the chest. He staggered a step back, probably from surprise. 'Get out, you fucking arsehole. I am so sick of you and your type. I don't need you running me down, Dev. I don't want your bloody high and mighty attitude lording over us lesser mortals. Just get out. You've told me what you think of me... how little you think of me. And fuck me, but you are probably right. At another time, I probably would have fucked Fred and any other man who asked. But that is not who I'm trying to be anymore. Did you even think to ask me what Fred was doing in my flat? I tried to tell you that day, but you saw what you expected to see and you ran away. And now you come back, looking for a fuck, and of course I give it to you, no questions asked. So why would I not give it to Fred, right? So take your forgiveness and choke on it, because I don't want it and don't need it.'

He was stunned speechless. But being Devlin, he recovered quickly. 'What was I supposed to think?'

'Exactly. What were you supposed to think? Definitely nothing better than what you thought. I don't want to see you again.'

I saw him wrestle with his own anger. 'This is not over between us, Vic,' he growled.

'It is. This was a mistake.' I choked out those words.

He flinched. Good. I hoped that he hurt as much as he'd hurt me.

I looked at the cheque he'd given me and saw it for the lie it was. It did not come from Mr Ruttman, or the firm, but from Devlin. I was sacked. There was no commission for me. I tore it into small shreds in front of his eyes. 'You can't buy everything, Dev.'

He turned and walked away.

I looked at the pieces of a fortune on the floor, and knew why fools like me were never going to be rich. I had too much pride, and probably too much stupidity to go with it too. But I did not need his saving graces and knightly rescues. I would get there myself. I would be better than a charity case or wastrel, or some shag-bag to be used and discarded. And I would start with Li's consort date. It was just a job, and I did not have to sleep with anyone. I could do worse.

Downstairs, the front door slammed shut.

14

The Consort Date

'Oh Vic.' Li patted me on the back. 'No need to cry.'

I took a swig from the wine bottle. 'I'm not crying.' I lay on my bed, unable to rise against the unshakable weight of the emptiness of my life. I felt sick. I wanted to cry. But what good would crying do?

'Sure you are, hon.' Li stroked my back. 'Just on the inside. He will come back, I'm certain.'

'I don't want him to come back,' I lied... sort of. 'I hate him.' That was less of a lie.

'Sure you do. I do, too. And if I see him, I will give him a piece of my mind.' In spite of her mild, soothing words, Li was angry, very angry. Her quiet anger made me feel better, if a little frightened. Once, she quietly stuck a needle in a bully-boy's back during a crowded school assembly. It was a pain point, Li explained to me later. The boy certainly screamed like he was being murdered. It was a thin needle, and there was hardly any blood. By the time he spun around, Li had melted into the crowd of kids. The boy limped for a week. Her revenge was like that, dark, subtle, and quiet. Truly, her anger was frightening.

'Please don't hurt him,' I said.

She was silent.

'I mean it, Li. I don't want his pain points prodded, or his remaining leg paralysed for a week. Or for his beautiful hair to fall out. Or for him to go blind for a month. I really don't hate him that much.'

'Oh, very well. If you agree to stop moping about him, and start getting ready for the date tonight. But I will still give him a piece of my mind when I see him next.'

I sighed and sat up. I took another deep, long swig of the wine. 'I'm not certain I am up for this *date* of yours today.'

'Sure you are, hon. It's the best thing for you right now. You can't lie here wallowing in self-pity for two weeks. Hell, even I was out of bed in a week when Pippy broke my heart.'

It had been two weeks since I last saw Devlin. He walked out and never returned. It could not be clearer that he was done with me. Good. I was glad to be rid of him. Then why did I want to curl up, and drink myself into oblivion?

'I'm too drunk to go,' I told her.

'Honey, it's eight in the morning. If you just put the bottle away, and don't drink another drop, you will be perfectly fine by six when our dates come to pick us up,' she said, speaking slowly and soothingly while stroking my hair.

I knew I was sulking like a child. He was gone. I did not need him. I never needed anyone but Victor and Victoria.

'You are right.' I tipped the bottle and drank the last of it, then handed the empty bottle to Li. 'I will go on this date. Get my money, get the best clothes money can buy, and get a job in the city. A proper job. Not one which promises riches. I will simply work my way to the top. I don't need anyone's bloody pity or charity.' I nodded drunkenly, the plan was solid.

'Well, I am glad to hear it, hon. Now come along, I will run you a bath.'

Li spent the rest of the day putting me to rights. She made me soak in the bath for two hours. Washed my hair, made me eat, and then eat some more, as I had apparently grown too skinny in my self-pity and all the time I'd spent wallowing in bed.

She spread out on my bed a beautiful silk suit in green and black, which could be worn by a man or a woman. I loved it instantly.

'It must have cost a fortune,' I said, brushing it with my fingers. 'Li... I don't have...'

'Oh, shut up, Vic. I know what you have and don't have, better than anyone.' She laughed, looking at my groin pointedly.

'Very funny,' I mumbled.

'Anyway, Mark treated me to another shopping trip. He is such a darling. He said I could buy anything that made me happy, so I bought you some things too. It made me happy.' She shrugged.

'You are rich,' I pointed out. 'Why do you need Mark to take you shopping.'

'Because shopping is boring by yourself. There is no one to tell me what looks good on me, or to help me carry my bags, or to complement my wonderful tastes. I like shopping with Mark. He likes to pay, and I like to have things bought for me. I guess I never outgrew that. Spending my own money is not as pleasant as spending somebody else's. I found that out when I had some.'

'Really?' I asked curiously. 'I'd love to spend my own money, if I had some.'

'No, you simply want to spend money. Your poor overused and confused pride tells you not to spend somebody else's. Once you have lots of money, you will notice that it is not pleasant to see it dwindle away. All your hard-earned cash suddenly becomes precious. It's even worse when the taxman demands his cut. It's like giving a beggar half my fortune. What did the taxman do to earn my money, anyway? Yet here he comes and says 'give me half of what you worked so hard to earn'. Ha! But I trick them. They can't tax me on jewellery and money gifts.'

'Ahem.' I cleared my throat, uncomfortably. 'Actually, they can.'

'Don't be silly, Vic. Who's ever heard of tax on gifts? Do you pay tax on birthday presents?' She laughed and shook her head, as if I just told her the moon was made of cheese. 'Go ahead and try this suit on.'

The silks felt wonderful against my skin. I thought of Devlin's kisses and nearly crumbled back on the bed in tears.

Stop it, Vic. You are acting like some simpering fool.

Li put a long dangling earring in one of my ears, and brushed back my hair with some gel. She then put me in front of the mirror. 'You look great.' She smiled. 'You know, you are quite stunning. Maybe not beautiful, but stunning. I could make you rich very easily.'

There was a knock on the door.

Li lit up like a sunrise. 'That will be my darling, Mark.'

'Since when is he your darling?' I asked.

'He has always been a darling.' She darted past me to answer the door.

I walked behind her.

A man in his middle years entered behind Mark. Mark scooped up Li, and they fluttered around each other like butterflies in love. The other man and I regarded each other. He was handsome, I guess, though not in the Devlin sort of way. His eyes were dark, and I suddenly discovered that I preferred the icy blue in men to any other colour.

He perused me and smiled. 'You look dashing, my dear. In truth, I can't tell. Li told me you were good. But I did not believe it. You can always tell, you know.' He licked his lips, as his eyes ran up and down my body, as if I was a giant present waiting to be unwrapped by him.

Yuk, you creepy bastard.

'Thank you, I guess,' I said dryly, feeling even more certain that this was a terrible mistake.

'Yes, you are a wonderful mystery, and worth every penny.'

His words made me feel dirty and cheap. How could Li love this?

I tried to tell myself this was no different to working in an office. Just another form of selling myself.

'Let's have some drinks before we go,' Li declared, and we went into one of her pretty guest rooms. She poured us each a glass of Italian red wine.

Mark finally managed to look away from Li long enough to notice us. 'Oh, yes, forgive my inexcusable rudeness. I forgot to introduce you. This is Vic Rash, Li's best friend, so be nice, Luke. And Vic, this is

Luke Forthflank, my business partner on the new Munroe and Forthflank shipping line venture.'

Luke smiled. 'Yes, I was just telling Vic, what a delight... Vic is. I must say, I don't know whether to call you a he or a she.'

'Just Vic,' I said.

We drank our wine. Li and Mark chatted away in the corner as if they had not seen each other in days, though Mark had spent almost every night here for the last two weeks, since Li refused to leave me alone to brood and drink myself into blissful oblivion.

Well, this was my new start. Time to move on. I tried to look at Luke and see all his good features. Except I found myself comparing him to Devlin, and each time I thought of Devlin, I wanted to curl up and weep. So I made a great effort to smile and tried to follow what Luke was saying to me.

'So, you've known Mark Munroe for a few years,' I said, trying to sound interested.

'My ex-wife introduced us. I did not realise that at the time they were sleeping together behind my back.'

I choked on the wine. 'I beg your pardon.'

He waved his hand. 'I am over it. In fact, it was their affair in the end that gave me the opportunity of a lifetime to work with Mr Munroe on this massive business venture. The man does nothing by halves. I think he may have felt a little guilty about shagging my wife while I was busy working day and night trying to earn her the lifestyle she wanted. When he offered me a partnership, I told him he was welcome to the faithless bitch. But he lost interest in her soon afterwards. Said he had another lady he was pursuing.

I assume that was your friend Li. He never stops talking about her.'

We both glanced at them speculatively. Neither Mark nor Li noticed. They were talking animatedly... and bloody hell, they were holding hands.

'Ahem. Mark tells me that you just broke up with a man,' he asked carefully.

'Erm.' My throat tightened. *I cannot do this. Sure you can.* 'We weren't truly together, so it's not so much a break-up as a 'let's never see each other again'.' Hell, it hurt more to say it aloud, if that was possible.

He smiled. 'Well, I hope I can distract you from whoever he is. I know what it's like to have your heart carved out of your chest and fed back to you in pieces. And let me tell you, a good fulfilling date can do wonders. And nothing beats sex as an antidote to a toxic breakup.'

I stiffened. 'I told Li to make sure that you understood I will not be having sex with you, Mr Forthflank.'

He waved his hand dismissively. 'Oh, I understood well enough. It is no secret that little Luke has been asleep on the job recently, so to speak. He's gone broody, if you know what I mean.' He chuckled. 'No, I will most certainly not be having sex with you. A real pity if I must be honest. But there are other entertainments one can indulge in, hey Vic?'

My warning sense bellowed an alarm. Since pa died, I had developed a keen sense of threat around me. It was rarely wrong. I had it the day I saw Lock in a bad mood, and in spite of telling myself to leave him alone, I taunted him and mocked him until he took it out on me. During the years of running with Lock's gang, I had learned to recognise men who were a threat to me. Mr Forthflank had that look to him. But it was too late to back out. I would just have to watch myself, and never be caught out by him alone.

Mark stood up and downed his wine. 'Right, everyone, time to go,' he said in his jolly way.

Li took his arm and led the way to the limousine. The driver held the door open as we got in.

The city at night was a different creature to its sober, industrious daytime twin. It was bright and daring, and at the same time full of shadows and mystery. People were dressed up for the evening's entertainment, looking for company, food, drink, music, and sex. We drove past brightly lit shops, busy food outlets and restaurants, and old theatres. Couples strolled by, holding hands. Laughing groups of youths were also out on the prowl. I felt my mood lifting. This was the city I loved, alive and vibrant. I allowed myself a smile. It did not matter who you were, or where you came from, cities accepted you in any guise.

You could disappear in a city. So many different people lived side by side here that, in the right places, I was not a freak but one of many androgynes. I had been to those bars where I felt comfortable in my own skin. But I did not go to them often. Perhaps it was an irony that I did not enjoy the company of other androgynes. The thought of bedding one never appealed to me. Li thought it strange. I did too. I guess I had always been attracted to the traditional masculine. Devlin was right. I could never threaten his masculinity, for I did not have enough of it myself. It was strange to suddenly realise that perhaps I was not so different from Lucy Valentine, after all. Devlin was the type of man who brought out the femininity in men and women. My lips lifted at the memory of Mr Ruttman crying on his shoulder.

Lucy was the opposite. She brought out masculinity in the same way. She triggered the protective urge. Again, I recalled with a pang of fresh hurt how Devlin had left me standing on the sidewalk when he took Lucy home. It did not occur to him that I needed protecting. I could not truly blame him. I, too, had felt that protective urge towards Lucy.

People like me incited neither protective instincts in others, nor were they sought out by those needing protection. We did not fit the traditional world, yet our type was as old as man. We have always existed. We have always lived side by side with traditional masculine and feminine. We were the third gender. The ancient Greek's might have thought of me as one of the male-female people who came from the moon. Perhaps my kind were the perfect state of balance, the harmony of masculine and feminine. Perhaps we were the mediators between the two extremes.

Whatever the reasons for me being this way, the truth was that I was happy to be this way. I did not want to be thought of as a man or a woman. I just wanted to be Vic, neither, or perhaps a little of both. And for all the society's bemusement at my kind, I would not have chosen to be born any other way.

Devlin accepted that. He accepted me as I was. He did not patronise me by pretending I needed his protection to get home. He saw me. He knew me, and still wanted me... and not for sordid sex, but for myself. Luke had said he could not tell, but Devlin saw.

Oh, hell. All my life I had wanted someone to want me as I was, as Vic. Not Victor or Victoria. And when one man finally did, I chased him away. I was a coward. I was afraid of losing him. I was afraid of rejection, so I never gave him a chance. Never gave *us* a chance. I ripped him up just like the cheque he brought me. Once again, I let my pride rule my head.

I looked back and realised that all my life I had been destructive, ever since the Universe destroyed my life by taking away both my parents. I hated those people who seemed to have everything. Yet it was not the Universe that sabotaged my happiness, but I. Devlin showed me that. Like me, he had been ground down into the mud as a child. He fought against it. He saw opportunities and grabbed them. He would not have ripped up that cheque. He would have given us a fresh start. He did not abandon me. He came back again and again. In spite of what he thought about me and Fred, he came back, determined to make us happen, determined to win me over. The Universe did not smile on him. He simply laughed at the Universe and his allocated lot, and took what he felt was his due.

Li nudged me. I was dimly aware of a conversation buzzing around me. I could not focus on it. My revelation was too great. I made perhaps the worst mistake of my life two weeks ago. It was not in bedding Devlin, but in pushing him away.

The car suddenly felt hot and confined. I needed to get out.

'Vic is prone to daydreaming.' Li laughed off my rudeness.

'And here we are,' Mark announced.

We arrived at the harbour of yachts and sail boats. The river was smooth and slick. The lights of the city reflected on its surface. It was the perfect night for sailing. I wished Devlin was here with me.

Luke gave me his arm. 'Shall we?'

I took his arm, feeling odd and uncomfortable. I glanced at Li, whose eyes shone at the sight of the yacht and the night ahead. Her smile was dazzling.

Mark's ship was four storeys high. At the top, in the wheelhouse, the crew was waiting to sail. Two of the crew stood guard at the base of the gangplank. They greeted Mr Munroe and wished him a good trip.

On the upper deck, I saw a pool and lounge chairs. On our level, there was a massive reception area, and it was already busy with guests. Waiters carried glasses of drinks and nibbles of food on trays through the gathered crowd.

Even before we had entered the room, I saw that I was not the only androgyne here. My face heated as I realised this was some kind of latest fashion in the billionaires' world, not too different to a handbag dog.

Luke leant in to whisper in my ear, 'You will be the best one here. There is a pool of money for the most convincing androgyne. There will be a display in a few hours, and I'm certain we will win. That's why I invested so heavily in you. Li assured me the winnings would be mine.'

I looked at Li with a sense of betrayal. How could she? She probably did not think twice about it. She would have loved being up on the stage. She would have laughed, and performed, and loved every moment of their attention. But she knew me better than that. She had known me all my life. She knew how much I'd hate such a display.

As soon as we entered the reception room, Mark was accosted by businessmen and women, many with an androgyne partner on their arm.

I was looked over, head to foot, and not subtly either, as if I was some fine breed of horseflesh Luke had acquired. Luke beamed and made some comments to the same effect.

Li was loving the attention she received, as she hung on Mark's arm. She snatched champagne glasses from a passing tray, offering him one, and popped nibbles of food in his mouth. I noticed other escorts were equally attentive to their clients.

Client. That was what Luke was. He was not a date, but a client. I had never wanted to be anywhere less. Li was wrong. I did not have the stomach for this world.

When Luke stopped to speak with one of his business associates, an androgyne man, the other man's consort, came to stand next to me.

He lent in and whispered, 'You are good. I'm jealous. I guess you can tell what I am.'

'It's not hard,' I said. 'Your apple is too obvious, and your makeup is too garish. You have a man's physique.'

He laughed. 'I think it would drive me mad if people could not tell, and always asked me whether I was a man or a woman.'

'They never ask,' I said dully.

'Really?' His eyes widened in interest. 'Strange I always thought...'

I shook my head. 'They'd rather chew and swallow their champagne glass than ask.'

He laughed. 'Vic, right? I like you. Maybe we can meet sometime?'

'Not going to happen,' I said, and returned to stand next to Luke.

He had finished speaking and was heading to the refreshment table. 'Smile, Vic. You look like you do not want to be here,' he said through a false smile of his own. 'Think of the ten grand coming your way at the end of the night.'

That made me only more miserable. I felt cheap and used. I tried to paste a smile on my lips.

'Devlin!' Luke said suddenly. 'Good to see you here. I wondered if you would make it. Never had a chance to thank you for that Midas tip. It came true, and I guess I owe you a small fortune.'

My heart lurched painfully, and my stomach felt like it would throw up at the same time. I turned and there was Devlin, alone, without a date. His eyes were hot and angry as he looked at me, and I could not breathe. I wanted at once to disappear and to throw myself at him explaining everything.

He smiled, dark and dangerous. The type of smile that warned men his next move would be to disembowel them. 'Glad to hear it, Luke.'

Luke put his arm around my waist. 'Meet Vic. My date for the night. And maybe many more nights to come, if I have my way.'

I felt sick. My tongue was numb.

Devlin's nasty smile widened, and he looked almost cruel. 'It seems money can buy you everything, after all. May I wish you all the best, Luke. If you will excuse me, I have someone I need to speak with.'

'Sure thing, Devlin. You still up for the game one of these weekends in my private box?'

'Maybe next weekend, if you like.'

And like everyone who was acknowledged by Devlin, Luke preened like a cock. 'Great. I will see you there, and maybe Vic too, hey?' And he patted my arse.

I had never been more humiliated and mortified in my life. For all my anger with Devlin over Fred, I suddenly realised how much worse this must look.

I could not meet his eyes as he walked past.

If I was not certain before, I knew that now I had lost Devlin forever. I had ruined any chance of the reconciliation I had secretly hoped for. With Fred I was innocent, but I could not claim such innocence with Luke. I came here as his date, knowing what was expected, and Devlin knew it too.

'You touch me again, and I will punch you in front of everyone,' I whispered to Luke and shook off his arm.

'I am paying you good money, dear,' he whispered back.

'Fuck your money. We do this my way, or no way.'

'Fine. But you'd better win the competition.'

'The competition was not part of the deal,' I said.

'Of course, it was. It's not like I can fuck you. Did you think you could just hang on my arm, drink champagne all night, and get paid outrageously? No one is that rich, honey.'

He was right. I knew this was a mistake from the start. Money never came easy.

'Oh, and by the way, I want a disrobing show for me and some of my acquaintances,' Luke continued. 'I want to know what you are by the end of the night. And I will pay you double if you let me watch you have sex with someone.'

I swung and hit him in the face. His nose crunched under my fist with that sickening sound. He screamed and grabbed his nose, blood pouring through his fingers.

I marched through the stunned party. Behind me, Luke was spitting invectives and insults. As I walked past a man with a tray of champagne flutes, Victor in me swiped his arm and knocked it out of his hands. The glasses shattered on the floor.

Once, breaking glass was my favourite sound of destruction. Today, it was the awakening I needed. There was no easy money. I would never again allow myself to be degraded, not for half the world's wealth. It was time I took charge of my own path. Mr Chen was right. In walking Li's path, I was getting trampled on it.

Outside, the gangplank was up and the crew were casting off. The boat was moving. The dock was too far to jump to. Damn it all, I could not be trapped in this hell.

I climbed on the railing, and jumped into the icy, cold water. For a moment, all went dark and silent, and strangely peaceful. I hovered in the dark abyss, feeling strangely free. How easy it would be to simply let go. And in that moment, I felt my past washed away, as if it was some mud clinging to my skin. In the black cold abyss, nothing existed but the future. One I could make myself. I kicked and surfaced, gasping from the cold. There were shouts of 'man overboard'. Crowds gathered by the railing, shouting and pointing. Someone threw a life ring at me. I ignored it and swam to shore, kicking as hard as I could as my body grew numb. I staggered out of the river onto the rocky beach, shivering violently and hugging myself. I walked onwards into the city, never once looking back. Time to begin again.

15
Another New Beginning

In a city, a man can disappear whilst walking in plain sight of those who know him best. After I jumped ship, so to speak, I went back to Li's house. I packed a bag with all that I'd bought with my own money, and left the rest behind. Then I sat down to write Li a note. It took me a long time, and many attempts to compose it.

I was angry with her. I wrote her an angry letter filled with thoughts of betrayal. I burnt it after I'd finished it. I was not angry with her, but with myself. This was her life. She was proud of it, happy in it. She wanted the same happiness for me. She thought I needed only to see the dazzle and sparkle to love it too. Besides, it's not like I had not undressed in front of others before. I had known plenty of orgies where others watched, and I watched in turn. I guess Li did not understand that I just did not want to be that person again. I wanted to be something that made my parents proud. I was the last piece of them they left behind in this world. I wanted it to matter, for in destroying myself, I was destroying the last memory of them. I guess I did not need to be rich, only happy. And one day I might even have what they once had together.

I wiped away the tears that suddenly swelled in my eyes, and wrote:

'Li,

I know you love me. And I love you. But I cannot walk your path. I have to find my own. I am leaving. I will return, but not soon. Do not wait up.

Vic

P.S. Just marry the bloody man. You two are clearly in love.'

I left her house, got on my bike and rode. I had no money to take me anywhere, and I could not go far on the fuel I had left. Three years ago, when I left the Wild Riders, I was where I am now: broke, homeless, with just a bag on my back that held all my worldly possessions. I had Li then. She took me in. This time, I would get by on my own.

I rode to a part of the city where no one knew me. After parking my bike, I spent the night walking the silent streets. I walked past bars and restaurants, looking into every window until I saw what I was looking for: a wanted notice for bar staff. I looked up at the sign above. *Failed Hopes and Dreams.* How fitting. I guess that was where adult life began, with the loss of childhood dreams.

Time to stop dreaming, Vic.

I found a sheltered spot in the basement entrance of one of the houses. It was below street-level and the low garden wall hid me from the eyes of the street. I sat down in the corner, with my back to the door, and slept.

A car horn woke me. In the street above, I heard heeled steps on the pavement. The city was waking up. I left my shelter before I was discovered and taken for a beggar or a thief.

I returned to the bar with the advert, and waited across the street for most of the morning until I saw a man with slouching shoulders unlock its front doors.

I approached. 'Sir?'

He was startled and spun around. He looked worn and beaten down by life's disappointments, though he could not have been older than his late thirties.

I pointed at the window with the notice. 'I've come to apply for a job. Do you want me to fill out a form?'

He looked me up and down, and scratched the day's stubble growth on his chin. 'Got bar experience?'

'Yes. And restaurant too. Used to work in the *Angry Dragon*.'

That got his attention. 'I hear it's a hard place to work. Why did you leave?'

I thought about lying. But the new me did not lie. 'I left for a flash job in the city. It did not work out. Made a mess of it. So here I am, trying to get back on my feet.'

His face relaxed. He pulled open the door. 'Come in then. You say you have bar experience? Know about setting up for the open?'

'Yes,' I said.

'Good, get to it. I pay minimum wage, but you keep any tips.'

I nodded and set to work. I swept and washed the floor. I knew it had been done last night, but Tony used to be fastidious about his bar, and he'd taught me to wash it in the morning also.

I took down the chairs off the tables and wiped the tables again. Then I set out the beer mats and went behind the bar to wipe down the cutlery from the dishwasher and place them in trays.

I worked silently, efficiently, and after a while, my new boss stopped watching me from the corner of his eye.

'Name's Mike, by the way,' he said after some time.

'Vic,' I said to his unasked question. 'Vic Rash.'

'Here is a form. Fill it in when you have a moment.'

'I'll do it now,' I said, and sat down at the bar. I looked at the first question and sighed. New life, new me. I was not going to lie any more. 'I'll let you know my address as soon as I know it myself.'

He stopped emptying the dishwasher to look at me. 'That bad, hey. Got a bank account, or must I pay you cash.'

'I have a bank account. I was staying with a friend until last night, and previously used her address when I needed to. Just thought it best if you know my circumstance.'

'Appreciate it,' he said.

I continued to fill in the form.

After a moment of silence, he spoke again. 'Got an empty flat upstairs. I've been using it as an office and storage for a few years, but recently I thought about renting it out. You can have it if you want. I can deduct the rent from your wages.'

I looked up at him and felt as if the Universe has finally smiled on me, and rearranged some dimmer stars. 'Thanks, Mike. I appreciate it.'

I worked long days. Mike was happy with that, since it meant he did not need to get more staff, and within a week, he'd begun to trust me to run the bar in his absence. He took a small rent from my pay. Too small for the size of the flat he gave me. I slept in my sleeping bag on the floor for the first few days, until Mike began to bring me his old furniture.

'Don't have the heart to throw stuff out,' he told me. 'This may be a better use for it than cluttering my garage.'

The sofa arrived first. I slept on it for a few days until the bed arrived.

I ate in the bar downstairs. Mike never deducted my meals from my wages. I suspected he felt bad about paying the minimum wage for what was quickly becoming a manager's role. Within weeks, the other staff began to defer to me in his absence. He put me in charge of ordering, and occasional book keeping. His absences became more frequent. I did not mind. I was happy with the arrangement. My rent was less than what Mr Gruleman charged me, and my new flat was three times the size of my old one. It was tidy too, with clean new carpets. I did not have to pay for food or bills. Slowly, my money built up. I bought some new clothes in the sales, and found out that Li was right, I did not enjoy spending my hard-earned coin. Thankfully, I did not have many needs. I did not go out. Mike allowed me a couple of pints after a long shift, and an occasional whisky at the end of the day.

I found peace, and maybe even some measure of happiness. It felt good to disappear. Here, in my new life, my past did not exist. After each day of hard work, I felt as if my soul was being cleansed. I still thought about Devlin every day, but on some days, it did not hurt as much. I buried myself in work and saved every penny. During the quieter hours, I took to fantasising about going on a road trip, and even travelling the world on my bike. Maybe when I saved some more, I told myself.

As is often the way, peace begets loneliness. It would strike me unawares, and I would think of Li, and Fred, and even the conniving coffee machine. It was worse on days when Mike left me alone behind the quiet bar, watching the silhouettes of people walking past the closed doors of my silent world.

One day, after a long shift behind the bar, which lasted well past midnight, Mike and I sat in the empty, dark pub with two pints of beer in front of us.

He rarely asked me questions about myself. I liked that about him. This night, I guess, his curiosity got the better of him. 'So, what are you saving up for?'

I shrugged. 'A better life.'

'Figured out that much myself,' he grumbled. 'What did you do in the city, then?'

'Wheat trading,' I said. 'I imagined making myself a millionaire by trading stocks and futures. You hear about those high-flying jobs people have, with bonuses the size of annual wages. Thought I'd get me one of those.'

He snorted. 'For every winner, there are a thousand losers like you and me.'

'You are hardly a loser, Mike. You have your own bar.' I waved a hand at the surroundings.

'Not what I wanted,' he said. 'I came to the city from a farm. Same dreams as you. Never worked out for me either. I could not break into the golden circle of high-flyers. So I had to find a job to get by, while I waited for my one opportunity. Got hired in the bar, and just stayed there. I sort of gave up trying after a while. I've regretted it ever since. I reckon if I'd just kept going and trying, I might have made it. Gave up too easy. It's like that Knightsbridge bloke on TV says. Those who give up, always lose.'

'What?' I hated the way my heart leapt at the mere mention of his name.

'You know, that Midas bloke on TV... oh yes, I forgot. You don't have a TV. I could probably sort you out with a small one...'

'You were saying about the bloke on TV,' I urged, hungry for the smallest morsel of Devlin.

'Oh yes, the Knightsbridge bloke, from the *Spot Market Analyst*. Since he's become the weekend presenter beside Sarah Bern, he's been giving people advice on how to get ahead and get what they want.'

'Arrogant arse, as always,' I muttered into my pint.

'No, no, he's not like that. I like him. Real nice type of bloke. You know, a solid man's man type. He's honest about his failures, and came right out with it. When Sarah asked if he had ever known loss and defeat... well, his face sort of changed. The bloke knows loss.'

'What did he say?' I asked under my breath.

'He said the greatest loss is not financial, but the loss of dreams. He said he'd lost plenty of those. One recently, the dream of his heart. He said that was the hardest to lose of all. Said he did not fight hard enough for his dream. Thought he had plenty of time to right the wrongs and misunderstandings. Then the dream fled out of his reach, and now he could not find it again.'

Compose yourself, Vic. He is not referring to you.

'Anyhow,' Mike continued. 'I like you, Vic. You work hard, and you are honest. But I know your heart is elsewhere. Your eyes have that lost look to them. I don't think you should give up on the dream that took you into the city. Mr Knightsbridge inspired me to go back and try once again to pursue my own dreams. I was thinking of selling this bar and moving on. I can sell it to you if you want, and you can pay me back in profits over time. It could be yours in less than a year. Or maybe you should just go and see about getting that trading job you were after. Just because one did not work out, does not mean you should give up.'

'What do you plan to do if you sell?' I asked.

He drank his beer before answering. 'Always wanted to sail the Caribbean.'

'You can sail?'

'Nope.'

'I see,' I said, and for once, I did. You had to work for dreams, perhaps harder than you worked for anything else.

'Yep.'

I could not sleep that night. Mike offered me a rare, once in a lifetime opportunity. I could own my own bar and flat above. I could have something that was entirely my own. I was a failure at the trading game. I struck lucky, as Devlin had told me, but I could not make a living on luck alone. Devlin would also tell me to grab a good opportunity when it was offered. I would not be on minimum wage, I would be the owner. I would have people working for me. And yes, I was afraid, terrified even, of failure, of doing everything wrong, of letting Mike and myself down. But this time, I would not run away from the chance I had been offered.

My head suddenly filled with all kinds of ideas for my own bar. I could make it successful, much more than it was. I knew the bar scene. I knew good coffee by day, and good drink by night. My imagination fired up. I suddenly knew I wanted this above everything else. This was my chance to prove I could be more, one chance to make my parents proud.

Next day, I opened the bar alone, as I had done every day for four weeks. It was a sunny, summer day outside, yet I was eager to go inside. I walked in and felt a calm sense of being home, tinged with the excitement of seeing many possibilities before me. Already, this bar felt mine. I polished the tables and the counter. I wiped the shelves and rearranged the bottles. I washed the floors twice and cleaned out forgotten corners.

When Mike came in, he looked around and grinned. 'You've been busy.'

'I've decided to accept your offer,' I blurted out, unable to hold it back any longer.

He closed his eyes in relief. 'Sweet mercy, it feels good to be done with this place. I'll get the solicitors to draw up the contracts. You'd better start looking for my replacement, if you need one.' He turned on the heel and left again. And did not come back.

Five days later, as I was setting up for the open, a knock sounded on the door of the bar.

'We are closed,' I called out.

The man outside ignored me. He pushed on the door and came in, looking around until his eyes found me. 'Vic Rash?'

He was suited and serious-looking, and carried a very imposing dark leather case.

'That's me,' I said uncertainly. 'Who's asking?'

'I am Michael Thompson's solicitor.'

'Never heard of him,' I said, feeling suddenly nervous. What would this Mr Thompson and his solicitor want with me?

He just looked at me. 'Mr Thompson owns this place. Are you saying you've never met him?'

'Oh, you mean Mike. I haven't seen him in five days.'

'Yes, well, last time we spoke he was in the Caribbean.' The solicitor pulled out some documents from his case. 'These are the ownership exchange documents, and some contracts for you to sign. The bar is now yours. Congratulations.' He did not sound congratulatory. 'You are to pay the purchase price over the twelve-month period. The account details are in the document.' He pulled out a pen from his suit pocket. 'Sign where you see the little 'sign me here' stickers.'

My hands shook as I looked over the papers and signed them. This was really happening. For the last five days, a cynical part of me believed that Mike was playing some joke on me, and would soon return laughing. Even now I wondered if this was some extravagant hoax. Yet as I read the contracts, it dawned on me that this was no joke. The bar was mine.

The solicitor waited patiently, looking bored, and maybe a little suicidal, while I scribbled with trembling hands what might pass for a signature. Then, very officially, he pushed a copy of the document to me, and put away the rest back into his case. 'Congratulations again, and all the best,' he said gloomily. And with that, he left me alone in my own bar.

After a stunned moment of staring at the door, I laughed aloud. It was an ugly, barking laugh, and I was glad no one was near to hear it. I've done it. I had my own place, my own bar. Every penny that it earned was mine. I looked around and saw how rundown it was.

For the last five days, I had kept on top of the account books for Mike. The profit was not large, but there was enough left over at the end of the week for repairs and minor renovations. The tables had to be sanded down and revarnished. The sign had to be modernised. I decided to change the name from *Failed Hopes and Dreams* to just *Hopes and Dreams*.

I picked up the phone, and before the first customer walked in, I had a sign designer and fitter booked in for the next day.

I put my ownership papers under the bar where I could see them and remind myself that the bar was truly mine. That day was the happiest day of my life. I was finally home. I was a somebody. I owned my own business. I told Jenny and Simon, my bar staff, that I was the new owner, and Mike was not coming back. They asked if I was keeping them on. When I said yes, they nodded and got to work. Jenny and

Simon had worked in this bar for years. They were part of my family now.

Over the coming weeks, I revamped the bar. I made it chic and trendy. I added more lights and introduced a new menu, which became an instant success. Some of the ideas for the menu came from Mr Chen's *The Angry Dragon*. I knew he would be happy that I'd used his most popular dishes for inspiration in my own bar. I bought in the best coffee and changed the cheap wine for fine. Eventually, I bought in a large collection of rare whiskies, which attracted the wealthier clientele from the city. 'Suits' began to stroll in for lunch and evening drinks. Money flowed. I hired two more staff.

One day, I went shopping and bought myself a whole new wardrobe of suits in bright colours and classic cuts. I styled myself as the stylish owner of my bar. I changed the uniforms of my staff to match my own. At first, they resented the bright colours, but when the atmosphere of the bar began to change, they thought them cheerful and trendy.

We quickly became one of the most popular bars in the city. I worked behind the bar, and took the occasional turn on the floor to fraternise with my regulars. Every penny that I had not spent on expensive stock or improvements I paid to Mike. I was determined to pay him as early as I could, and add a little extra as interest. With the pickup in trade, I expected to pay him off in six months. I'd heard nothing from him since he had walked out that day. I hoped that he was happily sailing the warm seas and not thinking of us.

I was happy in my new life. I could not complain. I found all that I had ever wanted... but one thing. Alone in my bed at night, I missed Devlin with an ache that never seemed to dim. During the day, the pain was buried beneath the activities of my busy bar. But at night, the pain was there, a deep, eternal stone of regret.

Some weeks ago, I bought myself a large TV, and morbidly tuned into the business channel, just to torture myself. And there was Devlin, looking as dashing as always, smiling charmingly at Sarah Bern. Jealousy and anger, and then hurt, pulsed through me. I was suddenly jealous of everyone who saw him each and every day. Did he still flirt and wink as he strode through the office? He was most certainly flirting with Sarah Bern. I turned off the TV and have not turned it on since.

But Devlin's shadow would not go away. At night, it haunted me.

16
The Question of Love

The bar was busy again. Many of the customers were regulars whom I knew by name, and who greeted me by name. I had owned the bar for seven weeks. In that time, I had changed it as much as it had changed me. Both of us received a much-needed lift and a breath of new life.

I thought back on who I had been two months ago, and did not recognise that person. I often thought back on my last argument with Devlin. My lips curled up with a touch of sad amusement. His accusations would not have hurt me now as they had then. I had learned in the last weeks that confidence was armour. Anger used to be my armour. Anger pushed aside the hurt. Now it was my self-worth. I owned all this. I made it successful. I hired people.

Dave, from the offices across the street, sat down at the bar with a heavy sigh of misery. I put a shot of whisky in front of him. 'Hard day at the office?'

He sipped his glass. 'Not office, but my Betsy.'

I cast a glance at Jenny and Simon. They were managing the bar well enough without me. This often left me free to speak with the regulars.

'What did the dear old lady do now?' I asked.

'Betsy told me she was going to kill our cat, unless I confessed to cheating on her,' Dave said into his drink. 'Now what is a man to do about a threat like that.'

Dave was one of many who seemed to want my advice on the opposite sex. I did not know what it was about me, but it was baffling to be asked advice on relationships, considering that I had never actually had one. And my one chance at one was a resounding failure.

I folded my arms and leant on the bar. '*Did* you cheat on her?'

'Of course not. Where would I find the time between the work and my time here at the bar before I go home?'

Save me from the bloody fools... save me from myself then.

'Erm. Have you considered simply inviting her to the bar with you after work?'

'Oh, Betsy would never drink alcohol.'

I waved a hand at our shining coffee maker in the corner. 'She can drink tea. Or coffee. And we serve juice and cocktails.'

'Cocktails are alcohol,' he pointed out.

I waved a hand at him. 'Cocktails are bright candies. Very popular with the old ladies.'

'Really? Fancy that.' He thought about it. 'I'll tell her you said so. I've told her all about you, Vic.'

Oh hell, the man's an idiot. 'Um, Dave. You don't by any chance go home and tell your little old wife how you spend all your evenings with Vic at the bar?'

He blinked. 'I am always honest with my Betsy.'

'You don't suppose she thinks you are cheating on her with me, by any chance?'

'Now why the hell would she think that? I like you, Vic, you are a nice young lad, but I'm... ahem, I am a little old fashioned for that sort of... ahem.'

Ah, so Dave thought me a lad. I had wondered. I guessed he would be too old fashioned to confide in a woman about his marital problems.

'How about you bring her out for coffee and cake on a Sunday and set the poor woman's mind at ease.'

'I might do that. Oh, and I love the changes you made to this old place. Never liked coming here before. But this is good.'

The door opened, and the warm evening air blew in. I never believed in eerie things like a sixth sense, until that moment. I just knew without looking up who had come in. It was like the air charged and heated, and I suddenly could not breathe. All my nerves tingled, alarmed and cried out, and goose bumps ran up and down my spine. I was both afraid and elated at the same time. I was afraid to look up, in case I was wrong, and in case I was right.

I took a breath and met his ice-blue eyes. Except his gaze was not cold.

Bloody hell, the man is a walking inferno.

Then someone stepped between us, severing some hypnotic thread, and I could suddenly breathe.

'Vic? You alright there? You look a bit overset,' Dave said, and looked behind him at Devlin.

Devlin approached the bar and sat down next to Dave. 'Hello, Vic.'

'Let me guess, it is not an accident that in all the bars in the city you walk into mine. Or is it?'

His lips quirked. 'No.'

'You want a drink then? I have a good whisky collection.' I nodded at the shelves of golden liquor behind me.

'I want you,' he said.

I heated.

Dave next to him choked on his whisky. I quickly gave him a glass of water and patted his back.

'Hell, Dev, why are you here? What do you want? Wait, how did you even know where to find me? Not even Li knows.'

He smiled, but his gaze looked pained. 'I know. Li showed me your note after I forced my way into her house to search for you. I thought she was lying when she said she did not know where you were. Showed me your note, and gave me a right earful of all the ways I've been an idiot. It appears there are many ways one can be an idiot.'

'You forced your way into her house? Bloody hell, Dev. Li is dangerous. She didn't... she didn't by any chance stick you with a needle?'

'What? No! Why would she?'

I sighed with relief. 'Just try not to annoy her in the future.'

'You simply disappeared, Vic. I was worried. Li said you did not have family, and she was afraid that you'd gone back to your old gang.'

I looked away. Strange that it could still hurt, such beliefs from people who knew me best.

'I told her you would never do that,' he said softly.

I looked at him then. 'You told her that?'

He nodded. 'I know you, Vic. I know what you want. I was there once myself, many years ago. My success was not overnight, you know. I'm in my thirties. While you are what, twenty?'

'Twenty-three, I said.

He looked around. 'You are doing well for yourself here. Much better than I was at twenty-three. And you made it all by yourself. It's what you always wanted, isn't it? Imagine owning this now. I guess you don't want to return to the office, then?'

'How do you know I own it?' I demanded.

He laughed. 'Hell, Vic. I told you before, money buys information, and I'm not above bribing, threatening, or stealing to get it. I had men looking throughout the city for you. I used to live in one of the roughest part of town, and ran with some rather unpleasant characters. Some owe me. So I got a tip about this bar a few days ago. I broke into the solicitor's offices, since they refused to disclose the information, to see what the deal was with it. I found the contracts.' He shrugged. 'Like I said, you've done well. Michael Thompson gave you a real gem of a real-estate, in case you have not realised it yet.'

'I realised.'

'Oh, and by the way, you should really change your address with your bank. They are still sending your statement's to Li's.'

'How the hell do you know about my bank details?'

'Oh, come on, Vic. Half of my clients are bankers. I simply asked one of them for the registered address on your account.'

'Just my address?' I asked suspiciously.

He shrugged. 'I must admit a little of my curiosity was aroused. I figured I might be able to track you from where you shopped, and when I saw the sums coming into your account... well, I did wonder what you were up to.'

I crossed my arms. 'So you hired thugs to find me, broke into legal offices, threatened my best friend, spied on my personal accounts, income and spending...'

'All just to find you,' he interrupted quickly. 'We need to talk, Vic.'

'You found me to dump me?'

He laughed again. 'Do you have somewhere more private we can talk?' He jerked his head pointedly at Dave who was raptly watching our conversation.

'Oh, don't mind me,' he said. 'Vic and I have no secrets. Or at least I don't. I won't get in the way of whatever you've got to say.'

I sighed. 'I live upstairs. Hell, but you probably know that anyway, hey Dev.'

Devlin followed me out back and up the stairs. I suddenly felt embarrassed by my apartment. It was clean and better than what I had before. But it was sparse, the furniture the same old pieces Mike gave me. I had not had time to furnish it to my taste... whatever taste that may be. Besides, I was not certain whether Mike wanted his pieces back. He may yet come back for them after his tropical adventures.

Devlin came in behind me and closed the door. We were alone, and I was heating at the thought of what might happen. I quickly walked into the living room, and straight to the bar where I poured two glasses of my best whisky. I gave one to him. 'It's not equal to your collection, but I like it,' I said, feeling oddly shy and apologetic.

'Classics are often the best,' he said, and sipped. He sat back on my small sofa, taking up most of the room with his size. He put his arms on the back, looking every bit the lounging lion in his den. He looked around. There was not much to look at.

'I guess you want to know about Luke,' I said, suddenly uncomfortable with the silence. I wanted to explain everything. I felt I owed him that much.

'No,' he said. 'I saw enough, and what I did not see I deduced.' He smiled. 'You have a good right hook on you.'

I looked down at the floor. 'Once again, I was looking for a quick way to riches.'

'Does not happen,' he said quietly. 'You have to sacrifice a piece of yourself to get there. I'm not proud of how I got to the top. I cheated, lied, used, stole, blackmailed. I am only proud that I got there from nothing. You've done well for yourself, Vic, and you've done it better than me.'

'You live in a palace,' I said.

He shrugged. 'Feels like a giant bloody mausoleum.' Then his face became serious. 'Always had until that one night you were there. It felt like home then.'

His words were a dream come true, one I feared more than anything. I looked away. I could not do this. It would destroy me if he discarded me one day. 'Dev...'

'I love you, Vic,' he interjected. 'You are either a blind fool, or too afraid to face it. Which is it?' He voice was harsh.

Oh god. I did not know what to think. I was terrified, I was overjoyed. I wanted to run away, and have him drag me to bed.

'I...' My tongue just could not make out the words. I did not know what to say. I loved him. I was afraid.

'I know you love me too, Vic. Li gave me a good earful of how I had hurt you.'

I became indignant on his behalf. Devlin did not deserve her wrath. 'Li is just a loyal friend. It was not your fault, but mine. I pushed you away, because I was too afraid to lose you.'

His lips twitched as he fought a smile. 'That makes no sense. You know that, right Vic?'

I shrugged. 'It sort of makes sense to me.'

'Come here,' he said softly.

I did not move. His eyes were hot, wanting. My whole body came to life. I began to ache in places I had not ached since the last time I lay awake thinking of him.

'Come here, Vic,' he repeated, equally softly.

I could not resist. I moved forward, sipping my whisky. The ache intensified under his hot gaze. Hell, the man was sex. He was leather, and whisky, and my bike bound together in solid warm flesh.

When I stood before him, he moved forward. He put his arms on my hips and slowly turned me around, then lowered me onto his lap, his erection pressing against me. I shifted and rubbed against its desperate hardness.

His breath caught, and he bit my neck gently. 'Tease.' He chuckled. 'You are mine, Vic. You cannot run from me, from this.' His hands slowly moved down my body, touching, caressing. One hand slid into my trousers, and I buckled against him. My breathing grew heavy.

He unfastened my trousers and pulled them off in one tug. He widened my bare legs, and stroked me with his hand, as his other undid his own trousers. He moved me up and entered slowly, his hand still on me.

My head fell back on his shoulder. I groaned. He moved slowly, gently, the urgent swell of his cock stretching me. His breathing was strained. 'I want you. I lie in bed thinking of you and touch myself. Do you think of me, and do the same.'

'Yes,' I breathed.

He moved harder, firmer. 'This is not fucking, Vic,' he whispered in my ear. 'Each time I am inside you, I am making love to you. This is divine.' He kissed my neck. 'Now tell me what I want to hear, tell me what you want.'

I strained against him, against his hand. I was close to bursting. 'You. I want you, Dev. I want this!'

I came hard and cried out. I felt him gasp, and pulse inside me.

I fell back and we just sat there while he caressed the inside of my legs, my chest, my stomach. He slipped out of me but did not let go. His arms tightened around my waist, as he raised his head to say into my ear. 'No more running, Vic. This time you stay.'

'Yes,' I whispered.

He spent the night. We drank, and spoke, and made love into the early hours of the morning. He was gentle one time, and wild the other. And he was insatiable. When I was half-asleep, he crawled over me to make love to me again, as eager as the first time. I chuckled. The man was impossible.

Then he held me as we spoke into the dark.

'There is a job for you back in the office if you want it,' he said.

'Let me guess, you convinced Mr Ruttman to hire me again, seeing how my lucky predictions came true.'

'Mr Ruttman is gone. Retired due to health issues. Seems his heart is no longer cut out for the stresses of work, and modern-day coffee machines.'

'What's his problem with *her*?' I asked sulkily, remembering how she set the mob on me.

Devlin chuckled. 'It appears he is not just traditionalist with regards to the sexes, but also technology. Thinks machines should know their place, and not argue with men who built them. Anyhow, I am in charge now. Mr Ruttman is happy with me running the firm, while he spends more time in the garden, as per his doctor's instructions.'

I sighed. I missed the office. I missed being a 'suit'.

'I don't know if I can, Dev. I have the bar. And I was never really popular in the office. Lucy is probably still pissed with me, and the coffee machine hates my guts.'

His hand tangled in my hair as he gave me a soothing scalp massage. 'Since when do you arrange your life around what the coffee machine likes? And Lucy is just Lucy. I think she is angling after Fred now, to keep her weird boredom at bay. And before you ask, Fred misses you too. Told me the day you left that he thought you should be hired back. And no, I'm not jealous of Fred. You clearly can't get enough of me. The poor guy has no chance.'

I smiled. 'Is that so? Seems the last time I tried to sleep, it was you who could not get enough of me.'

Devlin's eyes glittered with devilish amusement. 'Keep talking like that, and soon I will be 'not getting enough of you' again,' he growled. 'Now stop distracting me, I have not finished convincing you to come back. What was your other objection? Oh yes, the bar. You are turning over enough to hire a full-time manager.'

My head shot up. 'How the hell do you know that?'

He looked oddly at me. 'Your accountants, of course. How else? Oh, don't look so mad. I was not going to come here unarmed against you.'

'Let me guess, you broke into their offices?'

'Of course not. I'm not that good with encrypted computers. But I know this bloke who is a great hacker. Actually, more of a kid. One of Fran's classmates. Told me he did not even need to go to the accountant's office to get me the files I needed for this place. Charges a fair penny, too, but worth it.'

Devlin looked far too relaxed in his criminal endeavours.

'You have not murdered anyone by any chance, in your attempts to find me, or spy on me?' I asked dryly.

'No, but I did knock one of Luke's teeth out after you threw yourself overboard.'

'You did that.' I barked a laugh, forgetting myself. Then turned pink. 'Sorry. I try not to laugh in front of other people.'

He burst out laughing. When he got himself under control, he rolled me on my back, and lay on top of me. 'So, will you come back to the office?'

'I'm not a good trader, Dev.' I moved my hips against his arousal. 'Oh for god's sake, move.' I strained against him.

He did not move. His face remained serious, as if we were at a job interview. 'I can teach you to be good at it. Not my dodgy tactics, mind you. Just the legal, yet profitable trading strategies. It won't earn you a palace, so you'll just have to move into mine.' He kissed me slowly. Everyone misses you. Even Sally. They think Mr Ruttman was hard on you. I guess it was my fault. I made my interest in you rather blatant from your first day on the job.'

'You did?' I asked, staring at him. 'You could have fooled me.'

'Hell, Vic. You are the only one who did not notice. Everyone was whispering about my fancying you behind my back... and yours too, I guess.'

'I thought you fancied Lucy.'

He moved then and kissed me deeply. 'No, only you, Vic. Just you.'

Epilogue

I strode into the office at nine. Sally did not look up. 'Morning, Vic. Good to see you managed to come in on time.'

'Morning Sally,' I greeted her cheerfully.

She gave me a sour look.

I chuckled. My first day back after months of absence, and Sally acts as if I had never left. It was warming and welcoming.

No one looked up as I walked past. No one thought it out of the ordinary that I should just stroll in this morning. Fred was already at his desk.

'Devlin hit me,' he said as soon as I put my helmet on my desk.

I patted him on the shoulder. 'I know, buddy. I told him not to do it again.'

'After he interrogated me about where you were living, he hit me and told me to never to touch what was his again.' Fred pouted adorably. 'I don't know how he knew I touched his car. I only wanted to know if it was really gold-plated.'

I tried not to smile, or glow, or look pleased in any way by Devlin's wild possessiveness. 'Don't let him bully you. He is a sweetheart really.'

'How was your time off?'

'It wasn't time off, Fred. I was sacked, remember? Then you came into my flat, and pretended there was something between us.'

'Anytime, Vic, glad I could help. Oh, and Mr Ruttman has retired. Sorry you missed his going away party. He cried a lot on Devlin's shoulder.'

The atmosphere suddenly changed in the office, and the calls of the wild could be heard. I looked up. And there he was, striding through the door, fifteen minutes after nine.

'Morning, my fair Sally.' He winked at her. 'Now that I am the boss here, you sure you won't ditch your old man for the life of riches?'

'I'll think about it, Mr Knightsbridge.' She chuckled. 'I left your schedule for the week on your desk.'

'What would I do without you?' He smiled, and dimples appeared in his cheeks.

Oh hell. I was staring. *Look away, look away, before everyone realises what you and Dev did last night.* And the night before last... and after breakfast, and before lunch, then during dinner — after his snotty little niece, who hated me, ran off in tears following Devlin's announcement that I had moved in and was there to stay with them forever. When Francesca abandoned her half-finished meal and ran off, Devlin gave me a hot look, then grabbed me, kissed me, pushed me on the table, ripped off my pants and made love to me, before calmly resuming his dinner.

He saw me staring now and winked. I quickly turned back to my computer screen. The man was impossible. I was certain he was planning to drag me into the bathroom at lunchtime.

As always, he strode past my desk, which was not even on the way to his office.

'Hey, Victor-Victoria.' He winked and I turned red. Recently, he liked me to play both of them in bed for him. Asking how did randy Victor like it, and how did naughty Victoria want it.

'It's just Vic,' I mumbled, and he smiled knowingly.

'Settling in alright?'

'It's been fifteen minutes since I came in. I'm settled.'

'Oh good. Did you enjoy the game yesterday?'

I grew hotter, redder. 'Erm, I did not see much of it.'

His smile was the devil's own. 'Perhaps next time you should face the screen, hey Vic?' He winked again and strode off.

Arse. I smiled, holding back my ugly laugh.

'I need a coffee,' I said after he left. 'Did not get a chance to grab one this morning.' *Thanks to Devlin's insatiable appetites.* 'Want one, Fred?'

'Sure, why not.' Fred got up and followed me into the kitchen.

'Hello, Vic,' the coffee machine said in her usual cheerful voice. 'Would you like your usual, black with one sugar?'

'So, you decided to speak to me again.'

'Please use the following commands, 'yes' or 'no'.'

I sighed. 'Yes.' And placed my cup in station four.

'Please place your cup in station three.'

'What?' I asked in surprise.

'Please place your cup in station three, or say 'cancel my order."

'Oh, for the love of...'

'Just do what she says,' Fred whispered from the corner of his mouth. 'I think you've been promoted to station three.'

'Are you saying that I have just been promoted to 'dislike'?' I asked mulishly.

'Yes, and it's only one station away from the 'like' station,' he said.

'Oh, very well.' I slammed my cup down into station three. 'Happy now, machine?'

She poured me a delicious steaming cup of syrupy black coffee. I would have forgiven her murder then.

'Have a good day, Vic. Hello, Fred. Now that Vic is back, I suppose you want black with one sugar, too?'

'You know it's my favourite coffee, Machine,' he said, glancing at me.

'Sure it is. Oh alright, station two, go on. You know what to do.'

'Do you think there is a way to disable her voice commands?' I asked Fred.

He looked at me aghast while his coffee was being poured. 'Why on earth would you want to do that? Now don't you go thinking appliance-murdering thoughts again. Just be nice.'

'Why should I be nice to her, when she is never nice to me?'

'Because you are never nice to her, so she is never nice to you,' he explained patiently.

'Have a good day, Fred,' the machine piped cheerfully.

Fred and I sipped our coffee in silence for a time.

'I hear you've been given the coffee portfolio,' he said.

'So Devlin tells me. Know who's got the wheat portfolio now?'

He shrugged. 'Some spotty know-it-all school kid, fresh out of Uni. Starts tomorrow. Wants to get rich quickly, like the rest of them.'

I chuckled over my cup. 'He is in for a shock, hey Fred?'

He shook his head. 'I remember when I started out on wheat. I could not afford to pay for a pint out of my weekly commission.'

'Yeah, I know what you mean. Let's get back and see what the markets are doing, hey buddy.'

As we went back to our grey cubicle, I looked up at the fluorescent lights, and hoped that mother and father were somewhere they could see me, and be happy for me.

THE END

Author's Note

Thank you for reading *The Androgynous Love Tale*. If you enjoyed this book, please subscribe to my readers club at https://judeavery.com, or click on the link below, to be the first to know about the upcoming sequel to this story, *The Courtesan and the Spy*, and other new launches.

If you can spare a few words and your time, please leave a review. I read them all, and ultimately your feedback will help me as a writer.

Is Vic Victor or Victoria?

This book was, in part, inspired by my favourite tales of disguise and gender confusion, more commonly girl-posing-as-boy stories. In some ways this is a modern-day version of those tales.

From the start, I had hoped to write a truly gender neutral character, uninfluenced by my own gender identity or a natural inclination to categorise Vic as male or female. It was a struggle not to allow my own preconceptions of wishes for Vic's gender from firming in my mind. As such, I have never in truth assigned Vic a birth gender. Though they do have one.

Did I succeed in writing a gender neutral character, or did my own gender identity get in the way? I would love to know what you all think. *Is Vic Victor or Victoria?* I would like to invite the readers to take a poll at:

https://judeavery.com/victor-victoria-poll/

About the Author

Jude Avery lives in Brisbane, Australia. She comes from a scientific background, but writing is her true passion. For more information about the author and links to her social media pages, please visit Jude Avery's website at www.judeavery.com.

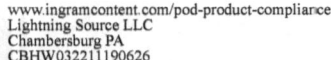